Past Perfect Life

Past

Perfect

Life

Elizabeth Eulberg

BLOOMSBURY

NEW YORK   LONDON   OXFORD   NEW DELHI   SYDNEY

BLOOMSBURY YA
Bloomsbury Publishing Inc., part of Bloomsbury Publishing Plc
1385 Broadway, New York, NY 10018

BLOOMSBURY and the Diana logo
are trademarks of Bloomsbury Publishing Plc

First published in the United States of America in July 2019
by Bloomsbury YA

Bloomsbury books may be purchased for business or promotional use. For information on
bulk purchases please contact Macmillan Corporate and Premium Sales Department at
specialmarkets@macmillan.com

Library of Congress Cataloging-in-Publication Data
Names: Eulberg, Elizabeth, author.
Title: Past perfect life / by Elizabeth Eulberg.
Description: New York : Bloomsbury, 2019.
Summary: Seventeen-year-old Ally is focused on college scholarship applications,
spending time with her widowed father, friends, and possible boyfriend, when she learns
that everything she knows about herself is a lie.
Identifiers: LCCN 2018045380 (print) | LCCN 2018051377 (e-book)
ISBN 978-1-5476-0092-2 (hardcover) • ISBN 978-1-5476-0093-9 (e-book)
Subjects: | CYAC: Secrets—Fiction. | Identity—Fiction. | Fathers and daughters—Fiction. |
Single-parent families—Fiction. | High schools—Fiction. | Schools—Fiction.
Classification: LCC PZ7.E8685 Pas 2019 (print) | LCC PZ7.E8685 (e-book) |
DDC [Fic]—dc23
LC record available at https://lccn.loc.gov/2018045380

Book design by Danielle Ceccolini
Typeset by Westchester Publishing Services
Printed and bound in the U.S.A. by Berryville Graphics Inc., Berryville, Virginia
2 4 6 8 10 9 7 5 3 1

All papers used by Bloomsbury Publishing Plc are natural, recyclable products made from wood
grown in well-managed forests. The manufacturing processes conform to the environmental
regulations of the country of origin.

To find out more about our authors and books visit www.bloomsbury.com and
sign up for our newsletters.

For my very own crew of

boisterous cousins, who prove that—

when it comes to families—bigger can

be better. The Gleasons have

nothing on you all.

—

I don't . . .

I can't . . .

This can't be happening.

This has to be a horrible joke. Some sick prank.

While I have the capacity to comprehend the meaning of every word coming out of Sheriff Gleason's mouth—I can break down what he's saying into nouns, verbs, and adverbs—none of it makes sense. It's as if he's talking about somebody else. The names and locations he's including are foreign to me. Yet I am the subject.

How can that be possible?

Numbness overtakes me as he continues to list names I've never heard before. Places he says I've been. He seems convinced he's speaking sense, but there's no way this is real.

I finally glance at Dad, who looks like his entire world has been shattered: his posture is crumpled, tears stream down his face, his eyes gaze blankly at the floor.

No. This is simply a nightmare.

Because if what the sheriff is saying is true, my entire life has been a lie.

Chapter
ONE

Describe a significant event in your life and how it has influenced you.

Seriously? I can't believe that years of hard work, studying, and planning has come down to having to answer these kinds of questions.

Okay. I can do this. I've written fifteen hundred words on how prehistoric drawings influenced how we communicate today. I can certainly wrangle up something about myself to persuade a scholarship committee to give me money.

No pressure or anything.

What do they even mean by "significant"? I'm seventeen. Getting a huge pimple right before class photos is a major life event. Being called on in class when you don't know the answer is a big deal. Let's be real: when our small town got a second screen added to the movie theater, it was front-page news for weeks. So my idea of significant might be a tad underwhelming to anyone else.

I get they probably mean something truly momentous. That right there is the problem. I have a pretty quiet life. I do really well in school and stay out of trouble. My life is the opposite of significant. It's . . . my life.

I live in the tiny town of Valley Falls, Wisconsin. Nothing here really changes, and I like that. Dad and I had lived in five different cities before we finally settled here eight years ago. It's a great life, but that doesn't help me answer this essay question.

Has my existence truly been unremarkable?

Seventeen years and nothing to show for it.

"Well, Baxter, I give up," I say to my brown Boston terrier sitting on my twin bed. I stand from my desk and collapse next to him. Baxter replies by licking my cheek.

At least Baxter sees me as a significant person. He does rely on me for food and walks, so probably not the most unbiased source. If only scholarship committees could be as loving and dependable as a dog.

Baxter jumps off the bed and twirls around in a circle. He barks twice at me and then runs into the hallway. Which means one thing: Dad's home.

The front door opens as I take a step out of my bedroom and into our living room. "Hey."

"Ally! How was school?" Dad asks as he takes off his work boots and hangs his tool belt on one of the hooks near the door.

"School was good." I try to give him a convincing smile, although I know he'll see right through it.

"Uh-oh." Dad tilts his head at me. "What's wrong?"

"Oh, it's nothing, really." I plop down on our worn dark gray couch. "Did you know that I've not had one single significant event in my life?"

Dad pauses for a moment, then holds up a grocery bag. "I would disagree. It's Taco Tuesday."

"Ah, yes. That does take a little of the sting out," I say. "I hate to be the one to tell you this, but it looks like Taco Tuesday is now Scholarship-Planning Tuesday. In fact, all fun events have been canceled until I've successfully applied to every scholarship available in the state of Wisconsin."

Dad walks over to stand in front of me. "Don't be too hard on yourself, Ally Bean. Plus, I got hard and soft shells, so win-win!"

"Did you also pick up answers to these impossible essay questions?" I ask, to which he looks around in his bag like he might pull out a completed essay. "They're all about accomplishments and life goals. It's making me feel a little . . . unaccomplished."

"Unaccomplished? My daughter? My *pride and joy*?" He sits down and puts his arm around me. "I need names. I need contact information. How dare they make my brilliant daughter feel *less than*. They will not get away with this injustice." He nudges me and continues until I crack a smile.

"It's a lot," I admit. I made myself a list of all the scholarships

I'm eligible for. If I do four a week, it'll take a month to apply to them all.

"Maybe you should only apply to the ones that ask you about the person who has had the biggest influence in your life. That one will practically write itself." Dad clears his throat loudly and points both thumbs at his chest.

I groan, even though he's speaking the truth. I know it's cheesy when someone says their parent is their best friend, but that's who my dad is. It's just been the two of us for as long as I can remember. He's the one I can tell anything to, the one who knows how to put a smile on my face when I'm feeling down or under a lot of pressure.

Especially when I'm being overly dramatic about one silly scholarship essay.

"You're right," I admit.

Dad puts his hand up to his ear. "I'm sorry, what was that? I need it repeated. Loudly. Actually, wait. Let me get this on video." He reaches into his back jeans pocket and removes his outdated flip phone. "This is the only time I wish I had one of those new-fangled gadgets you kids can't get enough of."

A laugh escapes my throat.

"There's my girl."

I lean into him. I know what comes next: one of Jason Smith's patented pep talks.

He rubs his light brown stubble thoughtfully. "You know that any college would be lucky to have you."

I don't know about lucky, but I've got the grades and ACT scores to get into any state school.

"And you're going to get that Academic Excellence Scholarship," he states confidently.

"That's not guaranteed."

The state of Wisconsin gives a scholarship to the top student of each graduating class for tuition at most state schools. My plan is to attend the University of Wisconsin–Green Bay, and major in education. The scholarship would make a nice dent in the tuition. I'm currently in the lead, but Dana Harris is only one-tenth of a GPA point away from tying.

I don't excel in sports, I'm not particularly artistic. All I have is my brain and its ability to comprehend whatever my teachers throw at me.

So getting accepted may not be a problem, but the money to pay for it will. I need as much scholarship money as I can get. Dad works in construction, and there are sometimes weeks when he isn't working. I babysit whenever I can and save every cent. We live modestly in this small, slightly dated one-story, two-bedroom house that Dad rents from our next-door neighbor. Our rent is reduced because Dad does odd jobs for our landlord.

We get by.

Wait, that's not entirely true. We more than get by. Sure, looking at our house, it isn't much. Some of the furniture is old and shabby. The kitchen hasn't been updated in decades. It's cold in the winter and hot in the summer, but it's ours. Every trinket is a memory. Every rip in the upholstery and stain on the rug is a story.

Over eight years, Dad and I have accumulated a life here out of practically nothing. We knew no one. We had very little. But here we are now.

And I wouldn't trade it for anything.

"I know that look." Dad smiles at me, and the corners of his brown eyes crinkle. "You're thinking of something."

"Perhaps it's possible my life hasn't been that tragically boring and uneventful," I reply.

"Well, thank God for that." He stands up and wipes his calloused hands on his flannel shirt. "I'm hungry. Let's get dinner ready."

We walk into the kitchen, which overlooks the living room. Dad starts handing me items from the shopping bag to prepare. He takes out a frying pan and turns on the gas stove, while I put my collarbone-length wavy brown hair up in a ponytail. One time, and I mean *one time*, there was a piece of my hair in our food and he's never let me forget it.

"Smart move"—he gestures at my hair—"I wasn't in the mood for a side of hairball with our tacos. Now, cue up some music, please. And I must specify, *proper* music."

"You mean old people's music," I fire back as I turn on his favorite classic rock station.

As Dad starts browning the ground turkey, I prepare all the fixings for Taco Tuesday. "Wait a second, I thought we didn't count iceberg as a green?" I start cutting up the lettuce. Dad and I have an agreement that we have to have a fruit or vegetable with every meal, and one green thing with dinner. You know, healthy living and all that.

"Listen, we've got onions and salsa—which is made up of tomatoes and other vegetables. We're more than doing our due diligence."

"We're the epitome of good health."

"We should write a cookbook or go on one of those cooking competition shows. We'd dominate, as long as the challenge involves making tacos or heating up a pizza. Oh, don't forget all the calcium we'll be consuming." He hands me a bag of shredded cheddar cheese.

"Yes, I'm a growing girl." I get a bowl out for the cheese but can't help but put a few pieces in my mouth. Maybe more than a few. "I can verify that the cheese is at its top cheesiest."

"I should probably also check, to be safe. I need to be a good parent." He opens his mouth, and I put a few shreds in. "Oh, you're right."

"I'm sorry, can you say that again? I need to get this on video." Then I pull out my own outdated phone. While mine is not of the flip variety, it's not a smartphone. It's actually pretty dumb, but it texts, so that's all I need.

"Since I'm being a model father, I should probably make sure you've finished all your homework." He backs up from the stove and starts playing air guitar to whatever song is on the radio. *Such the model father.*

"It's all done. I even read ahead in English since I have to go to the Dorns' tomorrow after school to babysit."

Dad pauses his solo. "Really? How late are you going to be? Will you just be missing the pizza portion of pizza-and-bad-movie night or the whole thing?"

"I'm not sure. I'll find out." I get out the plates and silverware. "We can always watch the movie on Saturday before Lee's birthday party."

"Sounds like a perfect way to prepare yourself for the royal family. Let them eat cake!" Dad says with a flick of the spatula.

"That's Marie Antoinette."

"Well, then . . . Off with their heads!"

"That's from *Alice in Wonderland*," I say with a shake of my head.

Dad lifts his eyebrow. "Shakespeare did it first."

"Of course he did."

"See, your pops can still teach you a few things! Now, on to more pressing issues to discuss." He takes the shells out of the microwave. "What's your prediction: Is Josefina going to run off with the priest? Or is she going to save her family's farm by marrying el jeffy?"

"It's jefe," I correct him. "You forgot that Josefina's sister has blackmail material that might get them out of it."

"But will she get there in time?" He grabs me by the shoulders. "Will she? I need to know!" He then sucks in his breath as he puts his hand to his heart. "Dios mío!"

My hand flies up dramatically to my forehead. "Mi corazón!"

Dad stops the overacting. "My head?"

"My heart. Head is cabeza."

"Ah, see, I'm learning. Before you know it, I'll be muy fluent." He bobs his head to the new song playing.

"Aha! But who relentlessly teased me when I started watching telenovelas?"

"Now, now, I was just being the thoughtful and concerned parent that I am. Add selfless to that. And excellent browner of meat." He takes the skillet off the stove and begins filling our taco shells.

"You truly are so selfless," I tease, although I like that we started watching these shows together.

Last year for extra credit in Spanish class, we had to watch Spanish-language programs without subtitles. While scrolling through streaming options, I decided to watch a program called *Mi Amor, Mi Vida* (*My Love, My Life*), about a couple torn apart by a family rivalry. Dad would occasionally walk by and comment on the overacting, but then he'd start asking questions about what was going on. I'd tell him of the crazy plot twists and how everybody was connected. One week he sat down to watch with me.

It's been one of our traditions ever since. Along with stuffing our faces full of delicious tacos.

We both settle on the couch with our plates as we start to watch our current telenovela obsession, which we decided is a female version of *The Count of Monte Cristo*, but with the Mexican drug cartel. At least that's what we think it is. Sometimes Dad and I start making up our own backstories for the characters, so we get a little sidetracked.

Dad sinks back in his seat, a wistful expression on his face. "This is how I like my Tuesdays: good food and good company."

"I think you mean the best company," I correct him.

"Obviously. And now for the only way I like my drama: in television form."

"Hear, hear!" I clink my glass with his.

Chapter
TWO

"Let me guess," Marian says as she arrives at my locker the next day. She places my lunch bag to her forehead. "Leftover taco mix and chips."

I grab my bag from her. "I didn't realize you're clairvoyant."

Hmm, what if I changed up all my habits? Maybe that would make a good essay topic. Imagine it: Ham sandwiches on Wednesdays! Watching telenovelas on Mondays! The scholarship committees would need an armored truck to bring me all my money.

Or not.

"I hope you brought me extra chips." Marian pulls her thick, curly black hair back in a clip.

"I think that is up there on the rules of being your best friend: Thou shalt share food."

"Yes!" Marian grabs my elbow. "Speaking of food, do you

want to go for a drive after school for some McDonald's french fries and girl talk?"

"Is Rob actually letting you drive his car?"

"Of course not." Rob's the only one in our group with his own car, and he's more protective about it than any human should be with an inanimate object. "But we'll obviously ignore him."

"Obviously." Sometimes I wonder if Marian only dates Rob because of his car. "As tempting as that is, I can't. I'm babysitting for the Dorns."

Marian groans. "Can it be this weekend already? I can't wait for Lee's party. There's going to be so much cake."

I accidentally let out a snort, but in the most ladylike way.

"What?" Marian asks.

"It's just something with my dad last night. You know he likes to refer to you guys as the royal family."

Marian looks thoughtful for a moment. "Yes, and I'm obviously Kate."

"Obviously."

"Do they even have enough members of the royal family for all my family to have doppelgängers?"

Good point. There are a lot of Gleasons.

"Neil would be Harry; that one's easy." Marian gives me a little nudge.

We walk into the buzzing cafeteria and go to our usual table, which is already thick in discussion. It's par for the course when you get enough Gleasons together. There's always plenty of talking and teasing.

"Anybody else almost smash their computer against the wall filling out college applications?" Julia asks.

The replies range from groans to throwing a napkin at Julia's face. Glad it's not only me.

Jan steals a potato chip from her sister. "Like you have anything to worry about, Miss Head of Every Committee."

"Oh, okay, Miss Guaranteed to Get an Athletic Scholarship. And stop stealing my food. You could've packed chips yourself." Julia pulls her bag of chips protectively to her chest.

"And I'll tell Mom you're not sharing," Jan threatens.

Julia grimaces as she holds out her bag.

While they act like twins, and look similar with that thick, curly Gleason hair, Julia and Jan are thirteen months apart. Their parents decided to have them be in the same grade, since they were allegedly inseparable as kids. While still extremely close, they couldn't be more different. Julia's president of Student Council, Key Club, and Future Farmers of America, and vice president of the senior class. She's perpetually outfitted in a cardigan and ballet flats, even in the dead of winter. Jan, on the other hand, is one of the best athletes in school and only wears yoga pants and fleeces and puts her hair in a tight ponytail with numerous bobby pins to tame it. They are two of the four Gleason cousins Marian has in our grade.

Neil (aka the Harry), the "red sheep" of the family with his dad's ginger hair, also sits with us. Lee hangs out with her own friends, as she has fought against being defined by her family her entire life.

Dad isn't really kidding when he refers to the Gleasons as the royal family. As one enters Valley Falls, they're greeted by Gleason's Garage, which is owned by Marian's dad, who also happens to be the town mayor. Five blocks down Main Street is Gleason's Grocer (run by Marian's uncle Peter and her grandfather), which is the heart of the small downtown district.

"We need to get on this family's good side," Dad had joked as we first entered town all those years ago. And that was before we realized that Marian's mom is the elementary school principal, her uncle Brian is the sheriff, her aunt Karen is the city comptroller, and her grandmother is editor in chief of the community newspaper.

You can't walk more than a block without running into a Gleason. Marian took me under her wing on my first day of fifth grade. She guided me gently by the elbow and started introducing me to everybody.

I've been by her side ever since.

The entire Gleason clan has, in a way, adopted Dad and me. We go over to one of their houses—all within two blocks of one another—for holidays. I might still be full from Thanksgiving last week. We're invited to any family event. And man, do the Gleasons always look for an excuse to get together and celebrate. They're a friendly, funny bunch, and also extremely loud. I guess if you're one of ten cousins within eight years of one another, you have to shout to be heard.

"SHUT UP!" Jan yells at Neil now. "Let's go outside, and I will wipe the floor with you. Girls can be just as fast as guys."

"Especially if the guy in question is Neil," Julia replies with a snort.

"Hey," Neil protests, and then tries to flex his skinny arms.

"What's going on?" Rob asks as he sits down next to Marian. "Did I miss everybody picking on Neil? Because if so, let's start from the beginning."

Neil shakes his head as he takes a bite of his sandwich, his cheeks matching his ruddy hair.

"We're talking about college applications," Marian says, always the peacekeeper of the family.

"Can we talk about Neil instead?" Rob winks at Marian before pulling her in for a kiss.

The Gleason clan reacts by gagging.

Neil wisely ignores Rob and turns to me. "So, Ally, how are applications going? Not like you have to worry about getting into schools."

"Yeah, Miss Valedictorian," Jan says with an overexaggerated bow of her head.

Marian groans. "Did I miss the memo that we now refer to everybody as Miss Something or Other?"

"Miss Bossy," Jan and Julia reply in unison.

"I'm struggling with the essay questions for scholarships," I admit.

"Right? Who are the sadists who come up with this stuff?" Rob asks as he pushes back his long black bangs that are always in his eyes. "Where do I see myself in ten years? I don't even know where I see myself this weekend."

"Which is why I'm in charge of our social calendar. And we have Lee's party on Saturday," Marian reminds him.

"Right, right . . ." Rob's dark brown eyes stare at my plastic container of taco mix. "Are you going to finish that?"

I push my remaining lunch at him. Rob eats more food than should be humanly possible. Even though he has the tall and sturdy build of a football player, the only exercise Rob gets is by working his mouth overtime.

"Rob, for the love of God, let Ally eat her lunch," Marian says with a shake of her head.

"It's okay," I reply. I was finished. Plus, I'm not afraid to use my fork on Rob when he forgets to ask. Which is often.

"So, Ally," Rob begins as he inhales a tortilla chip full of my leftovers. "What questions are you stuck on?"

"Apparently, I haven't had any *significant* events in my life."

Neil places his hand on my forearm, and I feel a jolt. "Same. All I could think of was that one time I forgot my phone on our way to Green Bay. I had to go an entire day without it. I'm still scarred."

"I'm so glad you brought up phones," Rob says with that cocky smile he has, and I already know what he's going to say before it comes out of his mouth. "I found some string the other day and have a metal can, so I was wondering if you want it, Ally. It would probably get better reception than that antique brick you call a cell phone."

"My phone works just fine," I say, but then I can't resist it.

"I like that I can't access social media twenty-four-seven. Less opportunity to see your face, the better."

"Burn!" Neil says as he holds up his hand for me to high-five. I happily oblige. Then I give Rob a taste of his own medicine and steal a cookie that he has left on the table. He should know better with this company.

"Just ignore him," Marian tells me with her lips curved ever so slightly. She'll tease Rob with the rest of us (because it's so easy to do), but he makes her happy. I guess every group needs to have a well-intentioned-yet-oftentimes-annoying goofball. Plus, I mentioned he has his own car, right?

Rob puts his arm around her. "As if you could ignore me."

Marian raises her eyebrow at him. "Is that a dare?"

Rob pulls his arm away and holds his hands up in surrender.

Here's one thing everybody knows about a Gleason: you never dare them. Ever. I've witnessed the grossest things being eaten or drunk all in the name of pride. Jan and her older brother, Don, once did a push-up contest that got so competitive neither of them could move their arms the next day. For the record, Jan won—never letting a boy beat her at anything.

"Let's get back to something more pleasant," Jan offers. "Getting out of town."

The table starts talking about colleges in Madison or Milwaukee.

Unlike most of my classmates, I'm not that eager to escape. I don't want to be too far from Dad. Green Bay is less than an hour away. I could technically still live at home, even though that would require a car, but Dad keeps telling me that isn't "part of the college experience." Not like he knows. I'll be the first person in my family to go to college.

Which is why it's so important for me to get into a good school (and be able to pay for said school). Dad has always stressed how important education is, and he wants a better future for me. Even though I like my present. But I get it. I see the toll his construction job takes on him: the ache in his back from carrying heavy loads, the limp he has when he gets up from the couch, along with the stress from the uncertainty of where the next paycheck will come from when he finishes up a job.

So I have to nail these scholarship essays. Not just for me, but for Dad, too.

As if she could tell what I was stressing about, Dana Harris approaches our table. She is the only one who can take away the Academic Excellence Scholarship from me. Dana always walks with an extra bounce in her step, causing her impossibly long, waist-length blond hair to bobble behind her. "Hey, Neil," she says with a bat of her eyelashes.

Oh, and she also continually throws herself at Neil. *Not cool, Dana. Not cool.*

"Hey, Neil," Rob and Jan mimic. Rob even puts his chin in his hands and stares across the table at Neil with a lovesick expression.

"What's up?" Neil replies without looking at her.

"Are you done? I thought we could walk to Physics together."

"And, you know, have our own physical relationship," Rob says, not even attempting to be quiet.

Neil gets up, probably in an attempt to avoid Rob embarrassing him even more. "See you later." Neil looks at me to save him, but all I can think to do is shrug.

"*Love, exciting and new,*" Rob sings in a cheesy lounge-singer voice he's imitating from this old TV show Dad and I sometimes watch if he wants to get "nostalgic." (In case this wasn't already obvious, Dad and I watch a lot of TV.)

Marian waits until Neil and Dana exit the cafeteria before she hits Rob on the arm. "Leave Neil alone. You know he doesn't like Dana."

"Yeah, but Miss Clueless has no idea he likes her," Rob fires back.

"Can we stop with the Miss stuff?" Marian gets up from the table.

"Who's Miss Clueless?" I ask. Neil and I talk every day on the way to school, and he hasn't mentioned anything to me. Oh God, maybe it's because he knows that I kind of, I don't know, maybe . . . I don't know. Clearly.

"Let's go, Ally." Marian balls up her lunch bag as I get up and follow. When we arrive in the hallway with the senior lockers, Marian looks around suspiciously.

"What's going on?" I ask. Marian usually isn't concerned about who can hear her. It's pretty hard to keep a secret in a town of two thousand people, especially if you're a Gleason.

"Nothing, it's just that I know what your topic can be for your essay."

"Ah, thank you!" I reply. Somehow I knew Marian would have the answer for me.

"Maybe you should write about your mom," she says softly.

Oh.

"I know you don't like talking about it, but losing—"

"There's nothing to say." I cut her off.

I have a hole in my head and heart when it comes to my mother. She died when I was three. I only have one photo of us: her holding me right after I was born. Whenever I look at it, there's absolutely no recognition of her. None.

As heartless as this may sound, I'm almost grateful for it. I see what her absence has done to Dad, not like he ever talks about her. It's still too painful for him. Both his parents had already died, and then he lost a wife and had to raise a daughter by himself. I've only ever known life as the two of us.

He's the one who lost something.

Marian holds up her hands. "Just hear me out. All I'm saying is that you're looking for a significant event, and losing your mom must've had some kind of impact on your life. It's pretty much the definition of 'significant'."

I shrug as I fight the sting behind my eyes. "I've got to get to class."

I turn before I completely lose it.

Yes, there were times it was really tough not having a mom around for certain moments, but I don't think about it a lot because it's something that I had absolutely zero control over. Writing about her for an essay isn't going to bring her back.

What does Marian expect me to do? Write about how my dad isn't enough? Because he is. He has to be. We're all we've got.

Besides, it's hard to miss someone you don't remember.

Chapter

THREE

A rare moment of quiet has descended upon the Dorn house.

All three kids are in bed with their teeth brushed, faces washed, and pajamas on. Two bedtime stories successfully read. The dishes from our dinner are in the dishwasher. The granite countertops and kitchen table are clean.

Now the only thing left to do while I await Mr. and Mrs. Dorn's arrival is to try to finish one more scholarship application.

Discuss a special attribute or accomplishment that sets you apart.

I can't believe I'm about to say this, but Rob is right. Just thinking that leaves a bad taste in my mouth. But he has a point: Who *are* the sadists who come up with these questions?

Every person has to be unique in her own way, right? So all I need to do is think about something special about me. Besides the fact that I let these scholarship questions destroy my self-esteem.

There's a quiet knock on the front door. Even though Dad and I are obsessed with horror movies, I don't get worried about this classic B-movie horror setup: babysitter in a big house when it's dark outside.

In Valley Falls, nobody can really do anything without setting off alarm bells. The Dorns' neighbors would have already dialed 9-1-1 if they had seen somebody on the street they didn't recognize.

When Dad and I first moved here, it took only two days before practically the entire town had come to introduce themselves, our refrigerator overflowed with casseroles, and our calendar was packed with playdates and town meetings. Now we're part of the welcome wagon when someone new comes to town, rare occurrence as it is.

So I don't even bother to check if it's safe before I open the door.

"We've got a noise complaint," Sheriff Gleason greets me with a crooked smile. He's in full uniform, his cop car parked in the driveway. He looks past me into the quiet house. "I see you've hidden the keg."

"So, I guess I should tell the meth dealer not to come," I reply with a straight face.

Sheriff Gleason laughs, which he probably shouldn't when anybody jokes about drugs. But it's me. So it's funny. Straitlaced, predicable Ally Smith.

"What can I do for you?" I step aside so he can come in.

"Just dropping off this pan Nina left the other day." He hands me a glass pan. "Don't want to interrupt your kegger."

I sigh. "Yes, these essay questions aren't going to rage on by themselves."

Sheriff Gleason takes off his hat, and his thick curls stand up in all directions. "How are the applications going? Jan and Julia are at a boiling point with them."

"Pretty much the same."

He gives me a warm smile. "You're a smart girl, Ally, and responsible. Any school would be lucky to have you."

So I've been informed.

"Is Mom back?" Five-year-old Annie pads into the kitchen with her bare feet, rubbing her eyes.

"Sorry, sweetheart," Sheriff Gleason says in a soft voice. "I didn't mean to wake you."

"They'll be home soon." I brush my hand against her pillow-creased face. "But you need to go back to bed. You have school in the morning, and your mom will be disappointed to see you awake this late. Plus, we don't want Sheriff Gleason to arrest you for staying up past your bedtime."

"That's right," he replies as he pulls up his belt. "I think what we have here is a five-sixty-eight: minor ignoring bedtime."

Annie's eyes get wide as she starts to head back to her bedroom.

"It's okay," I reassure her. "I'll check on you in a few minutes."

Sheriff Gleason puts his cap back on. "Well, I see my job here is done. Pan delivered so the wife will be happy, and Annie back to sleep so the babysitter can get some peace and quiet. Not a bad day's work."

"Thanks." If I get the essay done before the Dorns arrive, I'll have just enough time to watch a so-bad-it's-good ninety-minute movie with Dad before he turns in early due to his seven a.m. start at the site.

"I'll leave you to it. Good luck with those essays." He turns to go down the porch stairs, but pauses. "Or not. Looks like you have another visitor."

I look out to the sidewalk and see Neil approaching the house. "Hey, Uncle Brian," Neil replies with a sheepish grin.

"Don't stay out too late," Sheriff Gleason orders his nephew. He tousles Neil's hair as if Neil were a toddler instead of a nearly six-foot-tall eighteen-year-old.

"I'm just bringing Ally something," Neil replies as he gives me a shy look.

"Come on in," I say to Neil as we both wave goodbye to the sheriff. I lower my voice. "But we need to be quiet. Annie has already come out here once."

"Okay," Neil whispers as he wipes his green-and-white Vans on the doormat. "Marian told me you were here. My mom made brownies tonight, and I thought I'd drop off a couple for you. I remember how much you like them." He hands me a plastic bag, which contains two giant chocolate brownies.

I open the bag. "Thanks and *yum*."

"Yeah, I think we all lost count of how many you had at Thanksgiving." He looks down at the kitchen floor.

"Hey!" I say a little too loudly, and cover my mouth.

"The children," Neil whispers as he shakes his head. "Think of the poor sleeping children."

"Yeah, because I'm so not sharing with anybody."

"Hey, be nice. I stopped playing a video game to walk the entire block and a half here to give you that."

"Okay, you can have half a bite," I relent as I break off the smallest piece for him.

Neil tugs at the sleeve of his navy blue down jacket before taking a step toward me so we're only inches apart. I mean, we have to keep our voices down and everything, but I'm rarely so close that I can count the freckles on his nose.

I look away.

"So, ah, what are you working on?" Neil gestures at my outdated laptop on the kitchen table.

I sit down and look at the one whole sentence I've written. "Another scholarship."

"Need any help?" He pulls a chair over to sit next to me.

"Since you offered, do you know what special attributes I have that set me apart from others?"

Neil looks thoughtful for a moment. "How many do you want?"

"Ha ha," I say. It was stupid for me to even bring it up.

But Neil starts listing off items on his fingers. "You're really smart, a good listener, you're really funny, and since you're sometimes quiet—which I know how hard it is to get a word in around my family—it makes it extra funny when you say something hilarious. Um"—he gestures around the Dorns' house—"you do a lot of things for others."

"I'm getting paid to be here," I remind him.

"Yeah, but you do extra things like clean the kitchen. Nina always tells my mom how horrified she is that the house is cleaner when they come home. So that makes you a really hard worker as well. Is that helpful? Because I can continue."

I feel my cheeks reddening. While it's sweet for Neil to say all those things, it's sort of embarrassing.

But I did ask him.

And I like hearing those things from him.

"It's nice of you to say."

"Well, it's the truth." He's looking at me expectantly.

I drop my gaze. "Yeah, I, ah . . ." I pause, trying to refocus my thoughts on the topic at hand. "I have no idea what they're looking for. Most people applying for this scholarship will be smart. That doesn't make me stand out." I feel my shoulders tense from the stress. I take a deep breath and close my eyes. I try to tell myself that it will be fine and it will all work out. What if it doesn't?

"Is everything okay?" Neil asks.

"Yeah." I want to change the subject and not think about scholarships or essays.

There's something that's been in the back of my mind since lunch. Okay, I may have spent a lot of this afternoon thinking about it. And, well, he's here in front of me, so might as well give it a shot.

"You know who else is really smart?" I wiggle my eyebrows at him. "Dana."

Neil leans back in the chair. "Yes, she is."

"So what's going on with you two?" I put my index fingers together in a kissy motion.

Neil gives me a look to show me that he's not remotely amused by my childish antics. "No. We're just friends."

"That's not what I heard," I tease. Although I'll admit I absolutely don't want there to be anything going on between them.

"Well, I'm telling you there's nothing." He clenches his jaw.

"Sorry," I reply. I hate seeing him like this. "See, I'm not *that* funny."

He sighs. "It's okay, I'm just . . . I'm a little stressed about college. I'm a Gleason, even though I don't have that name or—" He gestures at his bright red hair that he gets from his dad's side of the family. "I want to go to a school where I can simply be Neil van Horne and not Kyle's younger brother, or the comptroller's son or the sheriff's nephew. Where I'm allowed to screw up every once in a while. We're always told to learn from our mistakes, but Gleasons aren't allowed to make mistakes. Or if we do, it's a town scandal."

Of course my first thought is how that would make an amazing essay topic.

Although I don't know what to say, since I can't possibly understand what it's like to be under that kind of pressure. I guess I never really thought about what it means to be a Gleason. I only looked at the good side: a big family support unit, fun parties, and huge holiday gatherings.

I'm not totally naive—I know how careful they have to be to

avoid gossip. All the cousins use fake names for social media, so they can post pictures without the prying eyes of the town. At first, I was into it. We got to have aliases! I played along not only to protect them, but to get Dad off my back, too. He was always harping about being careful about posting personal things online. He loves to get on his little soapbox about privacy, catfishing, and online predators, in particular whenever there's a case on one of our true crime shows.

To me, it was all a fun game. I got to be "Erin Rodgers" (because I'm a Green Bay Packers fan *and* a dork). I didn't really think about how much Neil and his cousins have to guard themselves.

Neil continues, "But then I think about being alone. Not having family to rely on, and I wonder if I can even do it. Maybe I can't stand on my own."

"I get it. I think the same thing about me and my dad," I admit. How will I get by without him? How will he do without me? I put my hand on Neil's back and he tenses up so I pull it away. I think about what Dad tells me when I get freaked out about the future. "All of this is part of growing up."

"Growing up sucks."

"No kidding."

We both laugh a little. I always thought senior year would be a relaxing one. I'd spent the past three years ensuring I'd have good grades and enough committees and volunteer experience for my college applications. But it's been nothing but anxiety. How is anybody supposed to know what she wants to do for the rest of her life at seventeen? Oh, and the whole what-school-do-I-go-to question? What school I pick will decide who will be my new friends. When I think about the major life shift that's going to happen in nine months, it freaks me out.

Right now the plan is to graduate from college, get my teaching license, and then find a job at an elementary school nearby. It may not seem like a big dream to some, but I like living in a small town. I like school. (As I was saying before: *dork*.)

So that's the plan. For now.

Last year, I was thinking of becoming a veterinarian. There's always the chance that college will shape me in a way that I'll want to do something else. So despite the popular essay question, I have absolutely no idea what I'll be doing in five years. I should be excited about all the different possibilities ahead of me, but sometimes it gets to be too much.

"I'm sorry," Neil says as he looks down at his hands. "I came here to give you sugar, not for you to be my therapist."

"It's okay. I'm stressed out, too," I confess. Although I don't think I've been as good as Neil at hiding it. He's always so sturdy and reliable, the relatively quiet center of the Gleason storm. I say *relatively* quiet because the quietest Gleason is still hella loud.

There's an awkward pause. I'm not sure what else there is to say. A car honks down the street. I look at the clock on the microwave. The Dorns will be home any minute now.

"Should I go?" Neil asks after seeing me glance at the clock. He hesitantly gets up from the table.

"Probably. I don't think they'd mind you being here, especially in the name of baked goods, but who knows what will be spread around town." This past summer, my dad ran into a married woman at Gleason's Grocer. They started chatting about the timeline on the house he was working on. So, of course, that fifteen-minute conversation caused the whole town to think they were having an affair.

You can never be too careful. And as much as Dad and I are members of the community, we weren't born here and will always be considered outsiders.

"Would that be so bad?" Neil asks, so quietly I'm not sure if I heard him correctly.

Did he mean a rumor about a boy and me? Or about him and me?

Oh my God. Am I Miss Clueless?

And the fact that I need to even ask that question confirms that I am, indeed, clueless.

So here's the thing: I like Neil. A lot. He's one of my closest friends. And a few weeks ago, I thought something was starting to happen. We'd spent practically all of Homecoming together on the dance floor. We always made sure to sit next to each other. Every time we were together, I felt a simmering between us. It wasn't like I could ask Marian for intel. He's her cousin and I don't want things to be weird. But since I'd been waiting for him to make a move . . . nothing. Maybe I was imagining it, but I thought he felt the spark, too.

Wouldn't be the first thing I'd been wrong about.

Then Neil takes a step closer to me, and I feel my breath catch. The way my heart is racing I know I want it all to be true.

We are only inches apart. I can't breathe.

And then my stupid cell phone rings.

Neil takes a step back as I curse technology for ruining a real-life moment. (Oh God, that is such a thing my dad would think.)

It's Mrs. Dorn telling me they'll be home in twenty. She couldn't text me that? Or, you know, just show up whenever. Although I wouldn't want her and Mr. Dorn to walk in on Neil and me in a full make-out session.

Not like that was going to happen. Or just whatever.

By the time I hang up, Neil is already at the door. "I guess I should go."

"Yeah, I guess. See you tomorrow, same time, same sidewalk." I shudder inside with how much I am blowing this.

Neil gives me a small smile as he opens the front door. He pauses for a moment before turning around. "It's all going to be okay, Ally."

I don't know what he's talking about. College? Scholarships? Us?

Whatever it is, I hope he's right.

Chapter

FOUR

"I'm about to burst," Marian says as she rubs her stomach Saturday evening after Lee's birthday party.

Once again, the Gleasons overdid it on food. So now we're both lying on the floor in her bedroom, our legs up on her bed, staring at the fairy lights she has strung alongside her ceiling. Her black cat, Gizmo, keeps circling us. Baxter is going to lose his mind when I come home tomorrow smelling like cat. He always gives me a look like I've betrayed him somehow.

"We do this every time," I remind her.

"We sure do." She pauses. "But we're totally going to have leftovers in a few hours, right?"

"Duh," I say with a laugh, even though it hurts to move my stomach. All during the party, as I observed the Gleason clan, I thought about what Neil had said about being part of their family. "Hey, Marian, do you ever feel pressure being a Gleason?"

"You mean the constant struggle to be the loudest person in the room? Ha!" But then she adds quietly, "Sometimes. It would be nice to be able to have some privacy every once in a while. God, the first time Rob tried to kiss me, we practically had to drive to Door County so nobody would know about it."

"I could see how you would want to keep that a secret," I tease.

"Totally. But while I'm going to miss my family and this"— she grabs my hand—"I'm also excited for the next chapter. College. Susan loves being away at Stout so much. I think being part of a big family has helped prepare her for not having much privacy in the dorms. Although I'm also positive that living in a coed dorm doesn't hurt her enthusiasm."

"Dad told me that if I even *apply* to live in a coed dorm, he's sending me to a nunnery."

"Hey." Marian gives my hand a squeeze. "Sorry if I upset you the other day bringing up your mom."

"It's okay." I squeeze back.

"You're just so open about everything. And like, the most sure-of-yourself person I know."

I let out a snort. "You've got to be joking."

"No, for real. You knew before any of us where you wanted to go to school. Like freshman year, you had this plan in place. You needed to get X, Y, and Z done to be accepted into Green Bay and have most of your school funded. Hell, I still don't know where I want to go next year."

"But I'm not this overly confident person." Images of Dana flaunting her GPA and accomplishments flash in my head.

"You know what you want with school and your future. I mean, you could use some of that planning when it comes to other things." Marian forces a cough while saying, "Boys."

So, yeah. I haven't really dated. Okay, not at all. But I'm not the only one. Jan and Julia haven't, either. We have a small class. The options are fairly limited, and then there's the whole weirdness that happens when a couple breaks up and people have to pick sides. Don't think that hasn't been one of the deterrents for coming clean about Neil.

I quickly veer us off the boy detour. "Well, I am happy to give you the many benefits of attending the fine university in Green Bay, including one of its incoming freshman."

"You know that's a huge bonus."

"The biggest, obviously."

"Obviously."

We both sit in silence for a few beats. I'm sure Marian is thinking through her options, while I'm busy regarding what she's said. I guess I have always been focused about school. I like having tangible goals. Figuring out how to go from point A to point B and making up a to-do list to get there. Nothing feels as good as crossing something off.

Probably one of the reasons I've turned into the kind of student I am is because of the star system Dad came up with. When I started middle school, we had a calendar posted on the refrigerator that listed all my school assignments. For every day that I completed all my tasks, I got a star. Every ten stars meant we'd go out for frozen custard.

Some may call that bribery; I call it motivation.

"Oh!" Marian turns on her side. "I know what we should do: play two truths and a lie."

I turn to face her. "Yes!"

When I first started sleeping over at Marian's—usually with Jan and Julia along—we'd play two truths and a lie. Someone comes up with a topic, and then you have to tell two truths and one lie about yourself while the rest have to try to figure out the lie. Of course, it usually devolved into discussing crushes.

On second thought, this might be a bad idea.

"You pick a topic first," Marian suggests.

"Okay!" I pretty much know everything about Marian at this point. During one late night, we found out that she loves all things gummy, except gummy worms make her gag. So, of course, Jan and Julia got her a bulk bag of gummy worms for Christmas that year. I don't want to go with anything college related since nobody needs that stressful topic. "Things you want to do before the end of senior year."

"Oh, I like it." She closes her eyes for a moment. "Cut class, ace Calc, and wear something so sexy to prom that Rob will be in agonizing pain."

"Ew! Won't someone from your family be chaperoning?"

"Which will just make his torture even more delicious."

"You're evil," I say with a nod of respect because that is going to be hilarious to witness. "So that's a truth. You just aced your last Calc test, so I call cutting class as the lie. No way you'd ever get away with it."

"Not in this town. Now you."

"I guess it would be to get enough scholarship money, um . . ." Sometimes I'm really bad at this, even when I pick the topic. "Dance so much at prom that I'll have to walk barefoot for a week, and get an A plus in AP Chemistry."

"Chemistry," she replies right away. "You're extremely smart, but no way can anybody ace Ms. Fiehl's class."

"Do you think she was a nicer teacher before she married Mr. Fiehl? Like, she was reasonable and then once she married a guy whose surname is pronounced like 'fail,' she figured she had to live up to it. I wonder if her maiden name is Pass."

"Ha!" Marian exclaims. She sits up with a clap. "So it's my turn. What topic to pick, what to pick . . ." She taps her chin, but it's pretty clear she knows exactly what she's going to ask. And that I probably won't like it. Usually I can spot a Gleason trap a mile away. Not this time. "Oh, I know! Neil! As in, thoughts regarding Neil."

I internally beg my face to not betray me by turning crimson, although I know it'll be a lost cause. Of course Marian would've figured out that there's something going on. Or not going on. It's hard to keep anything from her. It isn't like I don't want to talk about it, but she used to take baths with him as a kid. I doubt she wants to hear about her best friend thinking about him in such non-innocent ways.

"Okay," I say as my mind races to think of things to say about Neil. It's pretty easy: he's sweet, he makes butterflies swirl in my stomach, his forehead crinkles in this swoony way when he's concentrating on something. But what can I say about him to Marian? "He's currently my favorite Gleason," I start, even though I'm not sure whether that's a truth or lie at this point.

"Hey!" Marian says. "I'm just going to stop you right there because I know for a fact that's a lie."

I feel relieved for only a split second, because there's no way she's going to let me off that easy.

"Anyway, I really want to do this. Ready?" she asks, and I'm not sure if I am. "He refuses to eat green M&M'S, he's bungee jumping this summer, and he's going to ask someone out this week."

My heart plunges at the last one. Do I want that to be a truth or a lie? I know that there's something about his older brother telling him as a kid that green candy was snot-flavored, so I think the green thing might be true. The Gleasons and their hang-ups on candy. Neil isn't the bungee-jumping type, but his family does like to dare one another. "The lie is asking someone out?"

I realize I'm holding my breath as Marian studies me. "Do you really think that boy is going to jump from anything while tethered by his ankles?"

"Well, your family loves its crazy bets," I reason.

"Let me break it down for you," she says as she raises her eyebrows. "It's clear Neil has been pining away for a girl. We all have our theories on who said female is." I swear she's looking more pointedly at me. Or I'm imagining it. Because I want it to be me. Or maybe that's why she tried to bring up boys? So, yeah, I clearly have everything figured out.

Marian continues, "We felt he needed some motivation, so

there is a bit of a dare for him to step it up already and ask this mystery girl out. He has until the end of next week."

Neil is asking someone out next week. What if it isn't me? What if when I've finally come to admit my feelings for him, I'm going to have to watch him with another girl? What if she's going to join us for lunch and everything else and I'm going to have to have it shoved into my face?

So basically, next week is either going to be awesome or the worst.

Chapter

FIVE

Here goes nothing.

With a deep breath and silent prayer, I focus on the one thing I do have control over and hit submit on my application to UW–Green Bay. I redo the application for my backup options to the campuses at Eau Claire and La Crosse.

I did it. I applied to college. Next up: financial aid and more scholarships. Fun, fun, fun!

"It's almost game time," Dad shouts from the living room. "I need my good luck charm with me before kickoff."

I love all my daily routines with Dad. We don't just have Taco Tuesdays; we have Chinese Food and Classic Movie Mondays, Bad Movie and Pizza Wednesdays, Game Night Thursdays, and, my favorite: Football Sundays. There's something about living in Wisconsin that makes cheering for the Green and Gold seep into your DNA. Over the course of the past few years, Dad and I have developed our own complicated and precise game-day traditions.

I throw on my ratty Donald Driver jersey, pull on my green, white, and gold striped Green Bay Packers socks, put my hair up into a ponytail with a green hair tie, and finish it off with a Packers bow.

When I get to the living room, Dad is wrestling Baxter into his Packers jersey.

"You know he hates that," I say, although Baxter's growling and squirming make that pretty obvious. However, the Packers haven't lost a home game since Dad bought it at the start of the season, so Baxter has been forced into the insanity.

Poor dog.

I take my place at my designated couch position—left side—while Dad takes the right. In front of us at the coffee table is our first-half spread: cheese, crackers, and summer sausage. Dad has his Spotted Cow beer while I drink Sprecher root beer. At ten minutes left in the second quarter, we fire up the grill. We eat burgers, brats, and potato salad during the third quarter and finish off the bingeing with frozen custard in the fourth. It takes a strong and flexible stomach to be a Packers fan. Oh, and we can only use the bathroom during commercial breaks.

"Everything looks good," Dad says with a satisfied nod as he surveys the room.

Since there's a commercial break and four minutes before kickoff, I know this is my only opportunity to tell him my news before we both get swept into Packers madness.

"It's official! I put in my applications for UW."

"That's great, honey." He holds out his beer bottle to cheers me. "Congrats!"

"Thanks."

"I still can't get over the fact that you're growing up. In a few days you'll be a full-blown adult." He cocks his head. "Which is odd since I haven't aged at all." He rubs his face, which is weathered from working outside all these years.

"Especially mentally."

"Hey!" he objects before piling three cheese slices and two pieces of sausage on one cracker. "Speaking of the upcoming big day, what do you want to do on Thursday?"

"The usual," I reply with a smile.

There should be no surprise that Dad and I also have a tradition on my birthday. We first go out for butter burgers and cheese fries. Then we go home, put our pajamas on, and eat frozen custard from the container while watching one of the first Star Wars movies. And I'm not talking about those Episode I to III crap ones. No, the real first movies: *A New Hope*, *The Empire Strikes Back*, or *Return of the Jedi*.

For most of my childhood I had dressed up as Princess Leia for Halloween—even when I started growing out of the costume and the white dress was up to my calves and the bun headband was stretched to capacity. Dad always dressed up as Han Solo. Still does.

"Works for me!" He puts another piece of cheese in his mouth. (Yeah, we also like cheese. A lot.)

"Even though my applications are in, I still have to apply for the scholarships and financial aid. So I have a bunch more forms for you."

He nods while chewing, pointing at his full mouth, but I know he's stalling.

I didn't realize how extremely disorganized my dad is until there was all this paperwork. Our house isn't messy or anything. We clean it on the weekends, trading off the kitchen and bathroom each week. But he didn't have most of the forms I need for financial aid. He had his social security number, but I need his last two federal tax returns and bank statement. When I told him that I also needed to know his untaxed income, he froze. Probably since a lot of Dad's work is under the table. I don't really see anything wrong with that, since I don't report my babysitting income.

"I want everything to be in before Christmas break," I press.

He gives me a thumbs-up before finally swallowing. "Remind me again what you need?"

"I sent you an e-mail with everything."

"You know I don't like e-mail."

"I also left you a list on the counter."

He takes a swig of beer. "Okay, okay. I'm on it."

"Because—"

"Ally, I said I'm on it." He cuts me off, which isn't like him. But the game is about to start. "I know it's important, so I don't want to rush it. Okay?"

I nod as he turns up the TV. Dad starts talking about the

offensive line, and I sit there in silence. Occasionally I'll laugh at something or cheer when we progress down the field. But I know what's really bothering him. It's not about a bunch of silly forms.

As much as it's also been Dad's dream for me to go away to college, I know he's upset I'm leaving. How can he not be, when it's been at the front of my mind as well?

I'm growing up. Things are going to change us. Neither of us is going to like it.

And he's really, *really* not going to like the conversation I want to have with him at halftime.

~

I slide open the screen door that leads to our tiny backyard. Dad is standing over the charcoal grill, an intense look on his face.

The man takes his grilling very seriously.

I hand him a beer.

"Ah, I've trained you well," he says with a smile.

I also want him in as good a mood as possible. The Packers have done their job—we're up twenty-one to nothing after the first half.

"Can I ask you something?" I begin cautiously.

"Of course," Dad replies.

Ever since Marian brought her up, thoughts about my mom have been swirling around in my mind.

Maybe I should talk in my essays about losing her. How growing up without a mother had an effect on me. Dad's done everything a mom would do, but there were times when he had to call in for backup, like when I got my period for the first time and when I needed a bra. Grandma Gleason (well, Marian's grandma) is usually the one on speed dial for "Female Stuff," as Dad likes to put it.

He eyes me suspiciously for a moment. "Oh God, this isn't the *talk* talk. Didn't we have that once? I'm fairly sure we did, and I went to work the next day and took a hammer to my head to forget it."

"It's not," I reassure him. Both of us would like to banish any reminder of that moment of awkward pauses, stuttering, and the fact that we both went to our rooms afterward and couldn't make eye contact for three days.

"Are you dating Neil?" he asks.

"No!" At least at this current moment in time. We'll see in a week.

"Okay, okay." He holds out his hands in surrender. "I had figured something was up with how he's always loitering around here in the mornings."

"We walk to school together."

"Oh, is that what the kids are calling it these days: walking to school?"

"Ew, gross, Dad!"

He laughs, proud of himself for making me sufficiently horrified. "I'll give you that Neil's a nice-looking kid. He's got a good head on his shoulders. But you're still my baby girl." He flips the burgers and closes the lid to the grill. "What's on your mind, Ally Bean?"

It should be simple. But I know deep down it isn't. I don't want to upset Dad, but I need this. I don't know why now, but I do.

"I wanted to talk about . . . Mom."

There. It's out there. But the second I say the word, I see the anguish on his face. His jaw clenches.

He nods for a few moments before he speaks. "What about your mother?" he says in an even, too-controlled voice.

"It's just that I think maybe I might want to write about her for one of my essays. But I don't really remember that much. Honestly, I don't remember anything. Like, do I have any of her traits? Do I remind you of her?"

Dad turns his attention back to the grill. He opens the lid, and smoke comes out and covers his face for a second. He flips the burgers and turns the brats. The only sound between us is the sizzle of the grease hitting the coals.

Other questions begin to flood into my head. It's as if I finally removed the stopper that had been placed years ago, and now everything is rushing out. "I know that she died of cancer, but was it sudden? Did I know she was sick? Did she try to hide it from me? Was I different after?"

How had I never wondered about these things before? It could be because Dad is always focused on the future. "Let's look straight ahead," he used to say when we would pick up and move to a new place. But he also does that with everything else: we rarely talk about the past. Everything is looking ahead.

Maybe that's what happens when you have a painful past: you can only assume the future will be better. The old wounds are too painful—there's no point in picking at them. But I know that's exactly what I'm doing. I'm digging into the most tender part of Dad's past and asking him to relive his pain. For years, I've tried not to bring up Mom because I didn't want to hurt him, but now I have so many questions I can't stuff them back inside me and pretend they don't exist.

He rubs his eyes. "Where's this coming from?"

"All these big questions I've been thinking about for these essays . . . I guess they've made me examine my life in a different way. Then I realized there's a lot about my past I don't know."

Dad looks defeated as he puts the burgers and brats on a plate. He covers the grill and heads inside. I follow him. He pauses at the counter that separates the living room and kitchen. His back is to me and I'm afraid to move. I should've known better than to have this conversation with him. He's done so much for me, and how do I repay him? I open up the oldest, deepest wounds, all so I can write a silly essay.

But it's more than that. I want to know these things. Then maybe when people ask me about my mom, I'm not so distant and cold about the woman who gave birth to me. Who raised me for my first three years.

"I really don't know what to tell you," Dad finally says. He turns around and all the color from his face has been drained. He looks tired. He looks old. "Your mom got sick, then she died. You were so young I didn't know what else to do. So we moved. I needed to get away from the memories."

"Was I close with her?" I ask. I can't imagine I could ever have the kind of bond like the one Dad and I share with anyone, but usually girls are closer to their moms.

"Not like you and me," he states with an aggressive edge to his voice that I don't recognize.

"I didn't mean . . ."

He holds his hand up. "Listen, you've been driving yourself senseless with applications and scholarships. Why don't you wait until you see if you even get accepted?"

I suck in a breath. Dad doesn't think I can get into college? It takes him a few seconds to realize what a slap that comment is to me.

"Ally Bean . . ." He comes over to where I'm standing and reaches his hand out to me. "Of course you're going to get in. Of course you will get scholarships. We will make this work, but dredging up the past isn't going to help either of us. Especially me."

"I'm sorry," I say, my voice barely audible.

In the background, the second half begins.

"I know, sweetheart. Listen, I'm going to take Baxter for a walk. Be right back."

Baxter, who usually jumps up anytime Dad grabs his leash, stares blankly at him like it's a cruel joke. Dad never leaves the house when a Packers game is on.

"Come on," Dad says roughly to Baxter.

Baxter gets up and cautiously approaches Dad without a wag in his tail. He lets out a whimper as Dad grabs his collar too abruptly.

"Be careful," I say before he slams the front door behind him.

How could he get so short with me for asking some basic questions about my own mother? The person with whom I share half my genetic makeup. I feel an ache inside me that I've never experienced before.

As the Packers take the field, I don't know what to do. I don't feel like cheering. I don't feel like watching the second half and eating brats like everything is normal.

Dad keeps talking about lasts with me: last birthday or Homecoming.

But this was a first. Not simply Dad walking out of the house in the middle of a football game, but him seeming truly upset with me.

I hate doing that to him, but I deserve to understand my past. To know who I am and where I come from.

Because how can I go anywhere if I don't know where I've been?

Chapter
SIX

I kept imaging that this week had the potential to be pretty awesome. I thought I'd done everything right: studied, volunteered, joined school activities, and studied some more. It was all supposed to fall into place, but then everything came apart once I woke up.

"Hey!"

I jump at the sound of Neil's voice greeting me in the morning. Oh, right. And to make matters worse, Neil may be asking someone out . . . someone who isn't me.

"Hey, hey!" He holds up his hands as he approaches our front door with caution. "Are you okay?"

"Yeah," I lie, feeling foolish at my reaction.

My plan had been to be quiet during our walk to school in case, you know, he wanted to ask me something.

Now that's the last thing on my mind.

"Do you want to talk about it?" Neil throws out into the silence.

"It's . . ." My mind is still trying to figure it all out. "I applied to schools yesterday."

"Congrats," he says as he nudges my elbow. "It's hitting you, huh? We're going to college."

I shake my head. "No, I got an automatic reply from all three schools."

Neil raises his eyebrow at me. "Oh, is that how it is? They don't even need to look over your application. They see that *the* Allison Smith from Valley Falls has applied and *boom!* You're automatically accepted."

I wish.

I guess I should just be grateful I didn't check my e-mail last night.

Yesterday was weird enough, even though when Dad came back after his walk he acted like nothing had happened. Our conversation and his agitation had been erased like any memory I had of my past life.

So I had collapsed into bed with Baxter and tried to sleep. Even though I slept poorly, I wouldn't have gotten any if I'd been aware that there were three e-mails in my in-box that were going to unravel everything.

"No." I take a deep breath. "My social security number was rejected. They said it's invalid. My applications didn't go through."

Neil doesn't miss a beat. "You probably put the wrong number in. I do that with numbers all the time. I switch digits around."

"That's what I thought, but it's the right number. I double-checked."

"Did you ask your dad for the card? Maybe it was copied down wrong."

"He was already gone by the time I got up." Not like I feel I could ask him anything regarding college applications after yesterday.

"It'll be okay. It's probably a glitch with the university's system." Neil pats me on the shoulder, his hand hovering a beat longer than normal. "You should talk to Ms. Pieper."

"Yeah, that's what I'm assuming. I'm going to her office as soon as we get to school. I'm more frustrated than anything at this point."

I spent so much time filling out all those forms and answering these big questions about my life. Getting all the paperwork and tax forms. Ensuring everything is filled out exactly so. Meeting every single deadline.

Man, adulting totally blows.

"It's going to work out fine. It has to be on their end."

"What's on whose end?" Dana approaches us from the sidewalk that intersects our route.

"Nothing," I say. Dana is the last person I want to know about my problems.

The corners of Dana's lips curl ever so slightly before she turns her attention to Neil. "So how was your weekend?"

I keep my head down but can still feel Neil's gaze on me.

After it's sorted out, tonight Dad and I can have a good laugh during Chinese Food and Classic Movie Monday. Obviously he was onto something when he said I'd let this get to me. Applying to colleges has caused me to lose my mind.

"My weekend was good," Neil replies to Dana.

"Oh?" Dana says, her voice sounding strained. "I figured you were swamped since you didn't return my texts."

"Yeah . . ." I quickly glance up and see Neil rubbing the back of his head. "It was really busy."

I bite the inside of my cheeks to stop from smiling. Neil was ignoring Dana. He wouldn't be doing that if he was asking her out, right? RIGHT?

It's not like I have anything against Dana, per se. Her quest to topple my top ranking in class honestly helps. It motivates me. I probably wouldn't be close to a 4.0 grade point average if she weren't so aggressive about, well, everything. It's the way she approaches things—like everybody has to know about each little achievement she gets. Her online profiles (all in her real name because why post something if she can't get the credit?) are a stream of her daily accomplishments. The only reason the entire school knows about my GPA is because Dana is constantly talking about her score and how close she is to beating me.

At the end of the day, it's probably not only about being number one. She wants to get up on that stage and give the valedictorian speech at graduation. Honestly, she can have that. My goal has always been about the scholarship money.

But now there's this Neil factor. Dana usually gets what she wants. And I don't want her to get Neil.

"I heard about Lee's party," Dana says with a hint of envy.

Who *didn't* hear about the party? It's not uncommon for people to show up to one of the Gleasons' many parties uninvited. It happens often, and that person is greeted with open arms. What's one more person when there are so many of them?

But there's no way I'm going to share that piece of information with Dana.

"Well," Dana continues, "I spent Saturday in De Pere, where our debate team took first place."

She pauses so Neil and I can congratulate her. We both oblige, albeit unenthusiastically.

"Thanks. We're undefeated this year."

Another pause from Dana, but Neil and I both remain silent this time. "Yes. Then yesterday morning I volunteered at the nursing home."

Pause.

Good Lord. Don't people volunteer to do something good for other people instead of waiting to be congratulated? Although I doubt Dana would even wake up in the morning without praise or a filtered selfie.

"After that I applied to a few more schools. I've got ten applications down. Only five more to go."

Fifteen schools? How does she have the energy? Or the time with all her debate team wins and volunteering and apparently saving the world? Or the money? You have to pay to even apply. And if you get accepted . . .

"Did you apply to any UW schools?" I ask, wondering if it was, in fact, an issue with the university system.

"Of course. Madison is on the top of my list. Why?" She flips her hair.

"Only curious." I start walking faster to the school and wave them goodbye. As much as I hate leaving her alone with Neil, just in case, I need to get to Ms. Pieper's office stat.

⟿

"Come on in, Allison," Ms. Pieper calls to me from inside her office.

The cinder-block walls behind her desk are covered with inspirational posters, and there's an overstuffed floral couch that lines the opposite wall. As usual, I make myself comfortable on the couch as she sits in the red armchair next to it.

"How's the application process going?" she asks with her usual quiet, soothing voice. "Still focused on the UW system?"

"Yes. It was going well until I decided to submit last night. My applications were immediately rejected because they say there's an issue with my social security number."

"Oh." She looks surprised, which suddenly worries me. Ms. Pieper has been at this school for over twenty years. She's had to come across every issue possible when it comes to college applications.

"I got this automatic e-mail from all three schools." I hand her the e-mails I printed out this morning, along with a folder that has all my application information.

Ms. Pieper puts on her reading glasses as she examines the letters. She looks up and gives me a reassuring smile. "Well, let's see what we have."

She gets up from the chair and sits at her desk. She types into the computer for a few minutes. Her eyes go back between her computer screen and my folder, her frown lines deepening.

"Is something wrong?" I ask.

She takes off her glasses and leans back in her chair. "I think I found the issue. You have a different social security number on your college applications than what we have in your school records."

I can only nod since I'm not exactly sure what that means or how that even happened.

"Where did you get this?" She holds out my college application and points to the number I'd used.

"It's what I had from when I got my driver's license. Oh wait." A memory starts to resurface in my head. "There was something with my number back then. Dad told me that I had to get a new number, which is why I had to wait a month to take my test." That must be it. But why the new number doesn't work now still doesn't make sense.

"You mean you had to get a new card, not number."

I shake my head. "I'm pretty sure I had to get a new number."

Ms. Pieper looks blankly at me. I can't read what she's thinking, which makes me feel worse.

"Isn't that what happens when you lose your social security number?" I ask, because frankly I have no clue how it all works.

I've only needed that number to get a driver's license and apply to college. Dad always handles that stuff.

After a few uncomfortable seconds, Ms. Pieper stands up. "Well, I'm sure this is nothing. There has to be an explanation. I'll call up admissions offices at the campuses and figure it out."

I bite my lip. "Because I'm not sure if this means I have to start over. Or if I can continue to apply for scholarships if I don't know where I'll even be going."

She gives me that smile that she reserves for the most troubled students. "Allison, this is my job. You shouldn't be stressing over it. Why don't you take a few days off from college and scholarships while I figure this out?"

It was the same thing Dad said to me yesterday: take a break.

He was right. Ms. Pieper is right. I'm becoming unraveled. For the next week, I'll be mellow and chill. All the other things can wait.

"Sounds good?" she asks.

I stand up and nod. "It sounds great."

Chapter
SEVEN

Since my meeting with Ms. Pieper yesterday, I've been walking around with a considerable weight off my shoulders. I'm going to enjoy the next few days of not having to worry about anything but my homework. And, well, the whole Neil situation.

But I'm slowing my roll when it comes to college. There's a part of me that hopes it'll take her even longer to straighten everything out. I didn't realize how much I needed a break until I was given permission to take one.

Even last night with my dad (and some chicken with broccoli and an old black-and-white movie) was relaxing. He and I are back to normal. Instead of fretting over every little thing, I'm going to appreciate all that I have.

Which is a lot.

We'll see how long this mellow version of me lasts.

"Morning," Neil greets me as I step outside my house to go to school.

"Hi," I say with an extra bat of my eyelashes. *Way to be subtle, Ally.*

"So, I wanted to talk to you about something," Neil says.

"Oh, okay," I say coolly, because this can only mean one thing.

He gives me a weird glance. "Yeah, listen."

I find myself holding my breath. Maybe this is it. He's going to confess his love to me. Or he's going to tell me he likes someone else. That I must have a really high opinion of myself to automatically assume it's me he likes. Or, you know, I could woman up and ask him out. But if he does like someone else, I'd feel like an idiot.

So five minutes. Super-Chill Ally lasted all of five minutes.

"I heard a rumor about you," he states with a crooked smile.

Oh God. What did he hear about me? I haven't told anybody about my feelings for him. But he probably figured it out. He's going to tell me he's asking Dana out and he just wants to be friends.

I'm going to die.

Yeah, Super-Chill Ally has completely exited the solar system.

"Did you really tell Rob to shut his big mouth in English yesterday?"

Oh *that.* "Well, he was being Rob and went into this long explanation that made anybody with a brain realize he hadn't read any of *Fahrenheit 451.* Ms. Reali couldn't get a word in edgewise, so I'd kind of had it." Oddly enough, I didn't get in trouble at all. Probably because I said what a teacher probably shouldn't. I even got some applause from my classmates.

"Nice!" He held out his hand for a high five. "Besides, you didn't really need to have a reason. I'm sorry I missed it, especially since you're supposed to be the nice one of our group."

"Really," I say with a laugh, and tilt my head back. Isn't this how being flirty works? "So if I'm the nice one, what's your role?"

The cute one, I want to add. *The sweet one who brings me brownies when I'm babysitting. The one who remembers when I have a test and checks on me. The one who cares.*

"The sole male Gleason cousin still in school? That's easy: the manly one."

I'm going to be real for a hot second: if Neil ever had to draw a self-portrait, he could get away with doing a stick figure. The guy is tall and skinny. But it suits him.

And I like it. I like *him.*

I do my best to give him a come-hither smile, but it probably looks like I'm about to have a stroke. "Yes, of course. You're a very manly man."

He cocks his eyebrow. "So you noticed."

"Kind of hard with those muscles." I reach out and grab his arm and give a squeeze.

"Ha ha," Neil replies with a grimace.

He thinks I'm making a joke. I guess I am because Neil's not some bulky guy. But . . .

I scramble trying to think of what I can do to turn this back around. I thought we were being all cute and flirty, and then I had to make him self-conscious.

"I'm glad everything's cool with your applications," he says as we round the corner to school.

"Me too. And hey." I nudge him, looking for any excuse to touch him lately. "Thanks for being so great with everything."

"Of course."

"And bringing brownies."

"Ah, I see how it is." He nudges me back. "You just want more brownies."

"Oh, I'm always going to want your brownies."

Oh my God. What did I just say? *I'm always going to want your brownies.* You'd think with all the telenovelas I watch, I'd be able to come up with better lines than that.

"That can be arranged," Neil replies with a shy smile.

What is even happening right now?

Neil takes a deep breath. "So you have the weekend free of applications?"

"Yes, thank God." And thank Neil for preventing me from making any more horrendous sugar/hookup analogies. I'm probably five seconds away from saying something like, *I'm getting a cavity being around someone as sweet as you.* For real. I need help. "A weekend of freedom."

A whole weekend. I don't even know what I'm going to do with myself.

"And your birthday's on Thursday."

I smile that he remembers. "Indeed it is."

"So I feel like this should call for some sort of celebration. We should do something this weekend."

"Yeah." Then I stop in my tracks. Wait. Who does he mean by "we"? Is he talking about just him and me or the group? The group usually figures out our weekend plans at lunch on Friday if there aren't any Gleason events. If he's going to be vague, then so will I. "Sounds good."

"Saturday?" he asks as he opens the front door of the school for me.

"Okay," I reply. "I'm babysitting during the day."

"Saturday night, then?"

"Sure."

"Great!" He's nodding to himself. "Okay. We'll figure it out. I should head to my locker." He gives me one final look, but he lingers for a small beat. "Okay, Ally. It's a date."

I try to not burst into a full-on song-and-dance number in the hallway. Because that's it. It's settled.

Best. Week. Ever.

Chapter
EIGHT

Something's happening.

Two days later my Gleason shenanigan radar is starting to go off because Marian is stalling before heading into the cafeteria for lunch.

"It's just, do I want to keep working at the grocery store or should I get a job somewhere else?" Marian asks as she makes herself comfortable leaning against my locker.

This is exactly the kind of stuff we talk about on our way to lunch or at lunch, but she hasn't moved an inch toward the cafeteria. This isn't normal. And today of all days, I've got to have my defenses up.

"I mean, I like working there. But will it look bad on my future job applications that I've only worked for my uncle? It's not like I can't deny there's a family connection; my last name is on the sign. I guess it's better than working for my dad at the gas station."

I take a step closer to the cafeteria, but Marian remains glued to my locker.

"You work really hard," I say, because it's true and just in case she is having some kind of work-related crisis. Anytime I'm at Gleason's Grocer when Marian's working, she's always unpacking boxes or putting labels on food. Sometimes she's at the register or slicing meat and cheese at the deli counter. "I guess it depends on if there's another job you want to do."

"There aren't a lot of options here," she states.

"Yeah, but you're a Gleason." Pretty much anybody would hire her. Her father *is* the mayor.

She looks thoughtful for a moment, while my stomach grumbles.

Her phone buzzes in her jeans pocket. After glancing at it, she pushes off the locker. "Well, anyway, let's go eat."

"Do you want me to recommend you for babysitting gigs?" I offer.

"Huh?" She looks at me as if we didn't just talk about jobs. "Oh, no. That's okay."

It's official: I'm walking into a trap. Before I couldn't wait to get to the cafeteria because I'm hungry, but now I'm thinking I'll skip it.

All becomes clear as we turn the corner to the cafeteria. There it is. A huge sign on the back wall.

Marian starts to cheer as Neil, Rob, Jan, and Julia join her.

I am going to straight up murder each and every one of them.

And what a surprise, it's Rob's loud mouth that kicks them off.

"*Happy birthday to you . . .*"

I hide my face in my hands as one by one, my fellow classmates in the cafeteria join them, like people who feel obligated at restaurants when someone has a birthday.

This morning, Marian gave me a birthday muffin and a very cute beaded bracelet, so I thought that was it. But clearly, I'm not so lucky.

While it's a wonderful, sweet gesture, everybody and I mean *everybody* in the cafeteria is looking at me. I try as discreetly as possible to walk over to the table, even though every fiber in my body is telling me to run out of the building and head to Canada.

I finally slink down in my seat as they end the song and there's a smattering of applause throughout the cafeteria.

Rob holds up his hands. "For the record, that was *not* my suggestion."

"True," Marian says as she sits down next to him. "Rob did think you'd be horrified, but I wanted to do something special. You're eighteen! It's a big birthday and you've chosen to spend tonight hanging out with your dad instead of us. Now, let's get to the presents."

"You guys didn't need to get me anything," I protest.

"Wait until you open them," Rob states.

Fair point.

"First, this is from Grandma." Marian hands me a red envelope. Inside is a card with a fifty-dollar bill and a note that reads,

I'm so proud of you and wish you nothing but happiness. Love, Grandma.

Even though Grandma Gleason isn't technically my grandmother, she's always treated me like I'm one of the family. I even call her Grandma, which she loves.

So do I.

Marian pulls out a folder. "Now that you're eighteen and an adult, there's a whole new world open for you. Here are all the forms you can use to register to vote, open a bank account, get a credit card, or, you know . . . get married."

Good Lord. I haven't been able to look at Neil since sitting, and I certainly can't now. Although everybody else seems to be looking between us.

Can you also have the power to turn invisible when you're eighteen?

"Maybe this is a good time to remind you that as an adult, you can also sue someone," Neil offers.

"Oh!" That perks me up. I look right at Rob. "Good to know. Yes. Good. To. Know." I raise my eyebrows at him, to which he winks back.

Ugh. Boys.

Jan and Julia both hand me lottery tickets. "If you win, we want half," Jan says with a nod from Julia.

"You guys got it."

Rob cracks his knuckles. "Now that all the boring stuff about being an adult is out of the way"—I have to admit, there is a lot of paperwork—"let's get to the fun stuff. You can skydive."

"I'm not jumping out of a plane." I've never even *been* on a plane.

Rob nods. "I had a feeling you'd say that. So you and me. Green Bay. Next weekend. Let's do it."

"Do what?" I ask, even though I don't want to know.

He hands me his phone. There's a tattoo parlor pulled up.

"No."

"Oh, come on. It doesn't have to be anything big," Rob insists. "I'm thinking something along the lines of 'Rob BFF forever,' but with the number, like"—he holds up four fingers—"evaaaah."

Rob is laughing at himself, while the rest of the table groans loudly. Remind me why we put up with him again? Oh yeah, right, because Marian really likes Rob. And he has a car.

"Rob."

"Ally." He mimics my serious tone.

"There's no way I'm getting a tattoo with your name on it since I am going to do my best to forget you once I go away to college. It will probably take a team of shrinks, but by God, I will make it happen."

He gestures at his face. "You won't ever be able to forget this."

"Yes, it will haunt my nightmares."

"Neil, you're next!" Marian says with a wink.

I finally get the courage to look at Neil. He's smiling at me and there's a small flutter in my heart. He looks down shyly. "I'm going to wait to give it to Ally on Saturday."

A chorus of *oooohs* erupts from the table.

Rob makes a kissy face at us. Then starts singing, *"Love, exci—"* before Marian kicks him loudly under the table.

So, yeah, I guess I can be more horrified.

There really is only one thing that can save me now.

"Is that cake?" I point at the box in the center of the table.

"Of course," Marian replies. She opens the box and there's my favorite cake from Gleason's Grocer: carrot cake. It has HAPPY 18TH BIRTHDAY, ALLY written in purple script that matches the ginormous sign taking up an entire wall in the cafeteria. "And we're eating it the proper way."

Marian hands each of us a fork, no plates. We dive into the cake from outside and start eating. Marian and I used to do this when we'd have sleepovers. We'd get a sheet cake, sit on the floor of her bedroom, and eat while we watched a movie.

I'm not a sweets person; I prefer cheese fries over chocolate, but damn, do I love a good grocery store sheet cake.

My bag lunch (and any discussion about my upcoming date) is forgotten as we all sugar up.

Cake for lunch? Maybe being an adult won't be that bad.

Chapter

NINE

"Oh, come on! Unbelievable!" Dad protests the next evening.

Even though it's Friday, we're having our usual Taco Tuesday festivities since I had to babysit this past Tuesday. We just found out that in our latest telenovela obsession, the aunt is actually the mother of the main character.

"You honestly didn't see this coming?" I ask. "She kept looking longingly at Monse with dramatic close-ups, especially whenever Monse mentioned family. There had to be something fishy going on. Have we learned nothing from *Perdóname, Padre*, when the priest was actually the baby daddy? Nobody is ever who they seem."

"Okay, but *this* priest seems on the up-and-up."

"The apt word there is 'seems.'"

He wags his finger at me. "You are starting to become a conspiracy theorist."

"I believe the word you're looking for is 'realist.'"

He grimaces. "Okay, but if Ceci and Pato don't end up together, I give up."

We both laugh that we've become so invested in these characters, particularly since Dad can only piece together the plot from the mannerisms and the few words he's picked up. Every once in a while he asks me for clarification, but it's pretty scary how much he can get from studying people.

Our living room is suddenly flooded with red and blue police lights.

"I wonder what's going on." I pause the TV and walk to the front door.

Baxter follows and starts barking at the door, assuming we have visitors. "Baxter, it's not for us."

"What is it?" Dad asks.

"It's Sheriff Gleason and . . . someone, I don't know who." A black woman with short, dark hair gets out of the car. Then I see her jacket. "Oh, she's with the FBI."

The FBI in Valley Falls? This is huge, and a little bit exciting. Everybody in town is going to lose their minds over this. It's just like watching a movie.

Sheriff Gleason sees me watching from the window. I wave at him and he nods.

"Someone must've done something really bad. Sheriff Gleason looks all serious and professional."

My mind races through the past few episodes of our favorite crime show, its topics ripped from the headlines. What could it possibly be? Drugs? Money laundering? I can see the headlines now: Small Town, Big Murder.

Sheriff Gleason and the FBI woman talk for a few seconds before walking up the sidewalk. I keep waiting to see which neighbor's house they are going to. I notice both the Paffords and Rosses across the street are also looking out their windows.

The whole town is going to know about this in ten seconds.

My heart stops when Sheriff Gleason and the FBI woman turn in to our walkway. They're heading to our front door.

"They're coming here." I step away from the door, scared of why they'd be visiting us. I mean, it's Sheriff Gleason. He comes over all the time, but never with his lights flashing. Or with an FBI agent.

Wait a second. "Dad, is this some belated birthday prank?"

When he doesn't answer, I ask again. "Dad?" I turn around and instantly know this isn't a joke. Dad's as white as a fresh sheet of paper, with tears cascading down his face. I run to him. "What is it? What's wrong?"

He lets out a loud sob. "I'm so sorry. I'm so sorry, Ally."

I feel sick. "Just tell me, what did you do?"

There's a knock at the door. "Ally, can you open up?" Sheriff Gleason's tone is stern.

Dad's voice is a whisper. "I always knew they'd find out, and I'm sorry. You have to believe I did it for you. Everything I have ever done has been because I love you."

Chapter
TEN

"Ally? Ally?" Sheriff Gleason kneels in front of me.

I'm on the floor.

I don't know how I got here. But at some point in the past few minutes, I simply collapsed.

It's as if my body can't handle what's happening.

I know my mind can't.

I don't understand what's going on. What I'm being told.

"Are you okay?"

No words can escape my mouth. I can't even think straight. Or breathe. All I can do is shake my head, try to get rid of the accusations.

He places his hand on my shoulder. "Of course you aren't okay, honey. That was a silly question."

The FBI agent with Sheriff Gleason approaches. "We really need to go down to the station and get everything on the record."

"Please, Agent Kinblad," he pleads in a soft voice, "I know these people."

She snorts. "Apparently not well enough."

I try to open my mouth to speak, but I am too numb.

I know I have to snap out of my catatonic state and discover the truth.

"Can you . . . ," I say, my voice near a whisper. "Can you begin again?" I haven't been able to fully process what I've been told. I probably never will. It's just too much. And impossible. It has to be. "Sheriff Gleason, who am I?"

Who am I? It's such a ridiculous question. I always thought I knew who I was, the kind of person I've always been. That still has to count. I'm the same person, deep down, as I was ten minutes ago.

But can that really be true if what Allison Smith was built on is entirely false?

Sheriff Gleason rocks back to his heels, still next to me on the floor, while Agent Kinblad stands over Dad, her hands on the cuffs that are clipped to her belt. "We're investigating a tip we received. We believe your real name may be Amanda Linsley. You were born in Tampa, Florida. The allegations are that your father, whose real name may be Daniel Linsley, took you from your mother when you were three."

"He took me," I say slowly, as if the words can sink in better that way. "What does that mean?"

"Kidnapped," Agent Kinblad states bluntly.

"Kidnapped?" I echo. *There's no way. He wouldn't . . . He's my father. How can a father kidnap his own child?*

I look over at Dad. Why isn't he telling them it's a lie, that they're wrong? "Dad?"

He doesn't look up. He hasn't spoken a word since the officers came in. "DAD!" I scream, which finally lifts him out of his haze. "Tell them it isn't true," I beg as my voice cracks. "Tell them."

He stands up, and Agent Kinblad puts her hand near her gun. "Settle down," she commands him, as if he's some criminal.

My dad couldn't hurt a single soul. When he was laid up from an accident at work three years ago, we had to scrimp to get by. Yet Dad never stopped buying Baxter treats. Dad was the one who deprived himself. He took a smaller portion at dinner. He made sure I had plenty of food for lunch. I'd come home to a freezing house, but he would turn up the heat as soon as I walked in. He's always cared more about other people. How could they think that he would even be capable of doing something like kidnapping?

Dad rubs his head—what was once a nervous tic has now turned into something more desperate. "I'm so sorry. I'm so sorry . . ."

He spins around to look at me, and as he meets my eyes, I find myself frightened of my father for the first time. His face softens in defeat. "I never wanted to hurt you. I love you. I did this for you, for us."

"What did you do?" I ask, trying to make sense of what this all means.

Dad couldn't have done anything wrong. Look at me. *I'm fine.* I'm more than fine. I'm healthy. I've got a great education and a home. What more could any child want? How is that a crime?

Dad takes a hesitant step toward me, but Agent Kinblad holds her arm out to stop him and steps between us. "I have to ask that there be no more contact between the two of you. We shouldn't even have you in the same room until we get full statements. This is highly unorthodox." She glares at Sheriff Gleason.

"I understand. I do." Dad's shoulders are slumped. "I knew it would eventually catch up to me." Dad looks at me. "Ally, sweetheart, you have to know that I did it for you. She was going to take you away from me."

I want to ask him, *Who?* But I'm unnerved that Dad would . . . confess. Is that what he's doing? Is he saying that these allegations are true? They can't be.

They simply can't be.

"Dad," I barely croak. My mind is spinning with so many questions. *Who was going to take me away from you? Who would do that to a daughter and her father?*

Agent Kinblad puts handcuffs on Dad.

"That's really not necessary," Sheriff Gleason says.

"I'll go," Dad replies. "Brian, please take care of Ally for me."

"Of course," Sheriff Gleason replies.

Agent Kinblad puts her hands on Dad's back as she leads him to the front door. "Daniel Linsley, alias Jason Smith, you are under arrest for the kidnapping . . ."

I put my hands over my head. I can't watch. I can't hear these horrible accusations against my dad.

But I also heard what Dad said. That it's true.

It can't be. It just can't be.

Agent Kinblad can have her charges, Sheriff Gleason can say what he wants, but I know the truth. I know what my life has been up to now. It's been good. Because of Dad.

How could he be punished for that?

How can they think arresting my dad is the right thing?

I watch in horror as my father, my only family, is pulled out of our home in handcuffs.

This isn't happening. This isn't happening. You're going to wake up soon. This will all be over soon. Just wake up.

If I don't, my life will never be the same again.

Chapter ELEVEN

I wait in Sheriff Gleason's office. It's been nearly two hours, and I can no longer tell myself that it's only a nightmare.

It's my new reality. I still have no idea what that is or what's really happening. I'm absolutely terrified.

"Hey, Ally." Officer Basini pops her head in. "Sheriff will be here in a couple minutes. They're just finishing up." She gives me a tight smile since "finishing up" means that they're almost done questioning my dad. "Do you need anything else? Chips? Another soda?"

"No thanks." I haven't touched the soda and sandwich they gave me when I first arrived.

"Sure I can't get you something to read? Or turn on the TV?"

I shake my head. It's impossible to concentrate on anything.

It's almost ten o'clock at night. There's a part of me that wants this day over as soon as possible. There's another part that dreads what tomorrow may bring.

Photos of Sheriff Gleason's family fill every space on his desk and nearby bookshelf. I try to find some solace and normality in Jan's and Julia's smiling faces, but I can't help feeling a twinge of spite that they're in their home untouched. They'll wake up tomorrow with their family. The only worry they have is whether or not they'll get into their top college choices.

All I want at this moment is to talk to Dad. At first, it was so he could comfort me. That's always been his job. Now what I want, more than anything, are answers. *Kidnapping.* Why would he do this? Why would he lie?

Why? Why? Why?

There's also a sickening feeling taking over me. While I had tried to block out all the charges Agent Kinblad flung at Dad, one of them was social security fraud. *My college applications.* My meeting with Ms. Pieper. Is that what led us here?

Kidnapping. Is this my fault? Would we have continued living our wonderful life if I had talked to Dad about the issue with my applications instead of Ms. Pieper?

Kidnapping. The word keeps echoing in my head. Kidnapping connotes that I've been held against my will, which couldn't be further from the truth.

I want to be in the safety of my home with Dad. But I'm the reason we are here.

My questions. My applications. My needs.

Me. Me. Me.

I can hardly breathe.

Dad is being questioned by the police, and it's all my fault.

I lay my head on the cool surface of Sheriff Gleason's metal desk.

But . . . Dad has lied to me. For at least fifteen years.

He *kidnapped* me.

He forged documents. He did work that paid off the books.

The only thing he was ever strict about was oversharing on social media. *He didn't want people to find us.*

If all of that is true, what does it mean? When can I see Dad again? Are we going to be able to go back to our life like nothing has happened?

Tears burn behind my eyes. It's all too much.

The one person I've relied on my entire life is not at all who I thought he was. I'll never be able to look at him the same way.

"Hey, Ally." Sheriff Gleason comes to sit in his office chair. "Sorry you had to wait so long." He looks tired. "Your dad's doing okay. He's told us everything we need to know. And I need to talk to you about a few things."

He opens a manila folder and places a few photos in front of me. One of the photos is me, covered in cake, from my first birthday. It's the one that's on Dad's bedside table. The other is a photo of me from a year or two later, I guess. And then there's another image of a girl about my age. We share the same green eyes, dimpled chin, and light brown hair. There are certain features that look like I'm staring into a mirror.

I'm about to be sick. "Who is that?"

Sheriff Gleason shows a paper with two of the photos—the one of when I'm probably around three and then this other one, which features a big MISSING sign above the name Amanda Linsley. The other photo has AGE PROGRESSED written across the bottom. I start looking at all the information they have on this Amanda Linsley person.

"Wait a second." I have a small glimmer of hope that this has all been one big misunderstanding. I point at the date of birth on the flyer. Amanda's birthday is January twenty-fourth. "That's not my birthday. Mine is December eighth. Yesterday."

Yesterday feels like a lifetime ago.

Sheriff Gleason rubs his eyes. "January twenty-fourth is your birthday. Your real birthday."

"What?" That can't be possible. We just celebrated my birthday. "I can't—" The look on Sheriff Gleason's face tells me it's the truth.

An exhaustion I didn't know was possible takes over me. "When can I go home? When can Dad come home?" As soon as the words come out of my mouth, I know that isn't happening tonight.

"I've called Marian's mom. I think it's best that you stay with them for a while. Is that okay?"

"Baxter." It's all I can muster, but Sheriff Gleason nods.

"Marian is already at the house getting Baxter and packing a bag for you. Listen, Ally, it's been a long night. Now that we've talked to your dad, our next step is for him to appear before a judge in federal court, which he'll do on Monday. Because we didn't have time to get an indictment, he's going to be advised of the charges and the judge will address the bond. From there, a case will be presented to the grand jury for an indictment."

"What does that . . ." I put my head in my hands. "Federal court?" That's the only thing that stood out. Federal court sounds bad.

"He took you across state lines, so this is a federal matter."

"There'll be charges?"

"You have to know that your dad is making it easier on himself—and you—by coming clean. This is good."

A cold laugh escapes my throat. I can tell you two people none of this is good for: Dad and me.

"So can Dad come home on Monday after the charges?" I know the bond will probably be a lot of money, but I'll give every cent I have so he can return home. Return to me.

Sheriff Gleason sighs. "The prosecutor is going to recommend against a bond. I don't see the judge granting him one."

"Why not?"

"He's a flight risk."

"Flight risk? My dad isn't going to go anywhere. He's—" I stop myself. It's because he's done it before. He fled. With me.

I have to keep reminding myself that everything I thought I knew is wrong.

Although I don't feel like I can truly believe this new version of the truth until I hear it directly from Dad. I'm sure there's a part of me that never will.

Sheriff Gleason shifts uncomfortably in his seat. "You should prepare yourself for what happens when this becomes public on Monday."

A bitter laugh escapes my throat. "Are you kidding? The entire town has to be in a gossip frenzy by now. *My dad was dragged out of our house in handcuffs by an FBI agent.*" Even though I say it, I still can't believe it.

"I'm talking about the media."

"The media? Why would they care?"

"Listen, we are going to protect you the best we can. The charges will only have your birth name, Amanda Linsley, so hopefully that will help with your privacy. I've made it clear that nobody in this station is going to talk. My family will do whatever we can to make sure you aren't hounded. And it's probably best if you don't go to school for a couple days."

So I can't see my dad. I can't go home. Now I can't even go to school.

It's probably best to remain numb to it all.

"Sheriff Gleason, how much trouble is my father in?"

He hesitates for a minute before answering. "A lot."

I've got to fix this. I don't care what they think Dad did or even if he confessed. This is about me. I should get some say.

"But what if I don't want to press charges? That's how this works, right? He took me, but I don't care. He's my father." A thought suddenly comes to me. "He *is* my father, right?"

"Of course."

I exhale loudly, grateful for one thing in my life to remain the same.

"Can't you do something?" I beg. "You know my dad. You've seen how he's raised me. Doesn't that count for something?"

Sheriff Gleason clenches his jaw. "I wish I could, but the law is the law." He leans back in his chair. "Ally, I know this is a lot to process, but I don't think you fully understand what this means."

My mood shifts once again from confused and tired back to angry. "Of course I know what this means. My father is being taken away from me. I have no idea when I can see him again. Oh, and to top it all off, I have no clue who I am."

"That's not what—" Sheriff Gleason stops himself and takes a deep breath. He shifts in his seat. "There are more people affected by this." He pauses, realizing the weight of what he's about to say. "Your mother is alive."

Chapter

TWELVE

How much can one person take? One heart? One mind?

This can't be happening . . .

"Ally?" I hear Sheriff Gleason's voice, but it's as if he's underwater. I suddenly yearn for the safety of being submerged. Where my hearing and vision are muted. Where I can duck down and be comforted by water hugging my body. "Ally? Did you hear what I said?"

"I don't have a mother."

I can't possibly have a mother.

Yes, everybody has a mother, but all this time . . .

All this time . . .

Sheriff Gleason tries to get me to focus on him to steady myself. I can't look at him. I can't do anything.

"I understand that—"

"You can't," I spit out. *I* can't even comprehend it. Maybe it's easier for someone on the outside of my life to put everything back in order, but I can't.

I *won't.*

"You're right, you're right." Sheriff Gleason holds his hands up in surrender. "But you should know how relieved and grateful she is. She's been looking for you all these years, Ally. She never gave up hope that she'd find you."

I lean forward and put my head in my hands.

All this time . . .

Dad has lied.

Your life is a lie.

YOU are a lie.

I start hitting my head, hoping I'll wake up from this nightmare. That I can find something that feels real to hold on to. None of this is real.

But it is real.

Even though I don't want it to be.

"Ally, please don't."

I feel Sheriff Gleason's grasp on me as he tries to stop me from doing any damage to myself. I jerk my hands away from him and abruptly jump up from the chair. "I don't understand. I don't want to understand. Please make this all go away."

Maybe if I stubbornly refuse to acknowledge this, it will disappear. The last agonizing and confusing hours will flutter away with it. I can go back.

Dad made this life for us because he did what was best. I don't know this woman claiming to be my mother. I do know my dad.

If he decided I shouldn't be with her, there must be something wrong with her. Maybe she was abusive. Maybe she didn't love me.

The thought that my mother is out there should give me comfort. I should be yearning to learn about her, but instead it absolutely terrifies me.

Her existence is the final blow to life as I knew it.

"Listen, I have her phone number." Sheriff Gleason puts a small piece of paper on his desk. "Your mother is desperate to hear your voice. Maybe she can answer some questions for you. I'm sure you have many."

"No!" I scream.

I beg my mind to stop processing all that's happening. I can't concentrate on whatever Sheriff Gleason is saying to me now. I can't focus my eyes. I can barely breathe.

This is what it must feel like to lose your mind.

Another person enters the room, and I can make out Sheriff Gleason gesturing them to leave. I think he's telling them everything's fine. But it's not. I don't feel right. I want to go back to feeling nothing. I want to be numb.

I want this to all go away.

I finally make out a few words from Sheriff Gleason. "Breathe, just breathe."

I try, but my breath is caught in my lungs. It comes out in fits and starts.

You're hyperventilating! my mind screams at me. *Start breathing.* It wants me to fight what's happening to my body. I want to give up.

But I can't. Dad needs me.

I focus on a picture on Sheriff Gleason's desk. It's from the last Gleason family reunion. I see Neil, who stands out with his bright red hair and pale skin. I focus on his smiling face as I try to breathe.

In and out . . .

In and out . . .

I will my mind to conjure a happier time—hell, even a miserable one—to focus on anything but the present. Every moment that surfaces features my dad. The one constant source of joy in my life.

No, I have other people, other things. Concentrate on them.

A memory flashes in my head from this past summer. Marian, Neil, and I took a ride over to Green Bay to tour the UW campus. We went for frozen custard afterward. I was craving turtle custard. They were out. Before I had a chance to pick another flavor, Neil smiled at the cashier. "You have hot fudge, right?" She nodded. "And caramel? And I assume you have pecans since the flavor of the day is butter pecan?" The woman confirmed that they did, indeed, have all those items. Neil continued, "Okay, you have all the elements to make this amazing friend of mine a turtle sundae. So tell me, Judy, what do I need to do to persuade you to put a smile on her face?"

At the time, I was horrified of his making a fuss. But as soon as I took a bite of the sundae with the cool vanilla custard, the combination of hot fudge and caramel, the saltiness of the pecans, I gave Neil that smile he wanted.

There are good things in this world, like turtle sundaes and friends.

My breath steadies.

"See," Sheriff Gleason says. "It's going to be okay."

I realize that a small smile has spread on my face, but it quickly vanishes. "No, it won't. Nothing is going to be okay ever again."

I truly believe that. I can't, I won't, ever get past this.

"Sheriff Gleason." I look him in the eye. "I need to see my dad."

"I'm sorry. I can't make that happen tonight. He's still talking to the FBI. Maybe tomorrow?"

I nod. I'm too exhausted to fight anymore.

"My brother is here to take you to his house. Whenever you're ready. It's probably best if you get some rest. I'll stop by tomorrow and we can talk some more. This will give you time to figure out what questions you may have for your dad. I know you've had a lot to process."

I collapse back in the chair, unsure how I'll make it to the parking lot. Every time a new thought forms in my head, it gets shoved away by another one. Now there's only one thought, one word, that keeps repeating in my head.

"I already know what I want to say to him," I announce in a voice that sounds steady for the first time in hours.

"What's that?" Sheriff Gleason bends down so he's close to me.

"Why?"

After a few beats, Sheriff Gleason realizes I'm not going to say anything else. "Why . . . ?"

"Just why? That's all I want to know. Why?"

Chapter
THIRTEEN

"You can stay as long as you like," Marian's mom, Janet, says as we enter their quiet house.

"And let us know if you need anything at all," Dennis replies. He places a cautious hand on my shoulder as if I'm breakable.

I blink in my surroundings. I'm not really sure how I got here. There are snippets of the car ride over. But if I had to recall any specific moment, I'd fail.

"We made up Susan's room for you, unless you'd prefer to sleep in Marian's," Janet offers.

Usually when I stay over, Marian and I both sleep on the floor of her bedroom in sleeping bags. Even after Marian's older sister went away to college, we kept up our tradition. I'm not sure how long I'm going to be here. A night on the floor whispering secrets to each other would be a welcome comfort, but not a good long-term solution.

Dennis and Janet exchange looks since I haven't spoken in . . . I don't know how long.

"You don't have to decide now. No rush."

My reply is to stare blankly back at them and then look around. Even with Susan gone, their house is rarely this quiet. Whenever I come over, Marian usually bounds down the stairs to greet me, but it's only her parents and me in their kitchen. The yellow walls and pristine white cabinets always made this room cheerful and bright. It's hurting my eyes now.

"Do you want something to eat? Or drink?" Janet opens the stainless steel refrigerator, which is covered with photos and invitations. "I have some leftover lasagna that always tastes better the next day. Or I can make you a sandwich."

The thought of food makes me sick to my stomach. I can't imagine ever having an appetite again.

My silence is deafening, so Janet keeps talking to fill in the void. "Or I can cut up some fruit. Pete got in some ripe avocados at the store. I could make you some avocado toast or guacamole."

"Honey." Dennis nods at her. She closes her mouth, and then gives me an embarrassed smile. He turns to me. "Why don't you go up and see Marian? If you need anything, just let us know. But help yourself to whatever you need. We'll be here."

"Thanks," I finally say while they exchange relieved glances that I can speak.

I take the familiar stairs to Marian's room slowly. Each step is a painful reminder of why I'm there. Going to Marian's house and sleeping over is one of my happiest memories from growing up. Is it now going to be tainted like everything in this nightmare?

Marian's door is open, music playing softly. The second stair to the top squeaks. We'd skip it if we had a late night, but today I put my foot down firmly so she can hear me approaching. As the stair groans, I hear Marian shift.

"Ally?" she calls from her room. Her head pops out, and before I can even register the look on her face, she embraces me. It's the first welcomed touch I've received in hours. I lean into her. "I'm so, so sorry." She takes me by the hand and closes her bedroom door behind her. My duffel bag is on the floor beside her bed, along with Baxter's favorite chew toy.

"Where's Baxter?" I ask. I'm used to him greeting me when I'm home, but I almost had forgotten that he was going to be here.

"Neil and I took him for a long walk, and he's passed out in the basement. Do you want me to go get him?"

"In a minute," I reply as I sit next to her on the bed. As much as I want the comfort of my dog, I need a few moments to collect myself. For some reason I don't want Baxter to see me unraveled. At least one of us should live in ignorant bliss.

"Do you want to talk? Or not talk? Or we can talk about anything else?" she offers. "Two truths and a lie?"

Maybe confiding to Marian will make me feel better. Not like I could ever feel great about this, but it could keep me from drowning.

"I'm angry. I'm scared. My life."

She waits for me to continue.

I throw my head back. "I'm doing two truths and a lie. The lie, of course, being my entire life."

She rubs my arm. "That's not true."

"How much do you know?" I ask, both embarrassed that this will all be public soon and yet hopeful I don't have to relive it all again right in this instance.

"A little." She looks down at her colorful floral rug. "Enough, I guess."

"Do you know that I have a mom?"

It's such a foreign word to come out of my mouth, "mom." There's something not right about it.

I, of course, knew at one point that I had a mom. Everybody has or had a mother. But this fact—that the woman who gave birth to me is alive and has been looking for me—is something I can't ignore. Her phone number burns in my back pocket. Only ten digits away from being connected to a voice that may have some answers, a voice I didn't even know existed.

I try to place myself in her shoes. How she's probably waiting by the phone to talk to me, her daughter. How she is happy I've been found.

I know I'm a total asshole for refusing to call her right now. For asking that she give me time. Time to figure out what to do. To see what I can even do. To see Dad. To get answers.

"Ally?" Marian's waving her hand in front of my face. It's a familiar gesture. Usually she has to get my attention when I'm busy thinking about a class assignment or my to-do list.

"Sorry," I reply.

"You don't need to apologize for anything. So . . . you have a mom?"

"Can we talk about something else?" While I brought her up, I realize that I want to shove her back down again. Just like I don't want to talk about what my father did. If I concentrate too long on him, anger starts to bubble up.

"Of course." She bites her lip. I've never seen her so unsure of herself. "Ah, so this probably isn't a surprise or anything, but Neil is a nervous wreck right now. He really wants to talk to you. I had to shut off my phone because he was texting me every two minutes to see if you were here. It was everything to get him to go home so he couldn't bombard you when you arrived."

"So everybody knows."

Marian flinches.

It was a stupid question. Of course they do. I knew it the second the police showed up on our block.

"Can I ask a favor?"

"Yes, whatever you need," she replies.

"I know it's going to be hard, but I don't want this to change anything."

A serious look spreads on her face. "We've already talked about it." She didn't need to clarify that the *we* is the Gleason clan. "And lives have been threatened if anybody even thinks about talking to the press."

Her answer surprises me. I'm not worried about the media. I'm worried about this second family I've built over the years. "I don't understand why the media will care."

"Well, as my dad said, people can get obsessed about their fifteen minutes of fame. But my family takes care of our own, and you are family. This town also takes care of its own. I mean, everyone practically thinks you're a Gleason anyway. Oh!" Marian's hand goes up in front of her face.

"What?" I ask, afraid of the answer.

She shakes her head. "Nothing, I just realized something." She studies me for a second before continuing. "I know you don't want to talk about your mom, but you know what this means?"

"That my life has been a lie," I reply, the constant echo inside my head.

"You probably have aunts and uncles, a grandmother and grandfather. Cousins!" Marian's face lights up, ignoring the dread that has enveloped my entire body. Marian has been surrounded by a large family her whole life. It's the only thing she's ever known. There might be this other huge family out there that I belong to, but they are strangers to me.

Shouldn't I feel like there's this part of me that's missing? But I feel nothing. I'm empty inside.

Marian looks confused at my nonreaction to having a family. I should be happy that there's a piece to the puzzle of my life that will be put into place.

But I'm not.

I don't want any of this.

Chapter
FOURTEEN

I've never been the type of person who needs to be entertained. If Dad has to work late, I stay in my room and read. Or watch TV. Or just stare out the window and daydream.

I wish I could just think of something now to take me away.

But I can't. No matter what I try to do to distract myself, the truth comes crashing down around me.

I let out a loud groan in frustration, and it echoes throughout Marian's empty house. It isn't even noon on the longest morning of my life. Marian is babysitting while her parents are out running errands. At least that's the story I was told, although I'm convinced they're probably at some emergency Gleason meeting to discuss yours truly.

Baxter has been happily running around the backyard barking at squirrels or, at one point, his own shadow. I took him for a walk earlier, but it was unsettling. People I've known since the day I moved here would either greet me with an especially cheery disposition or they'd give me a look of pity.

I can't escape the truth anywhere.

So I decided to stay inside, to confine myself to the Gleason house. Just like a prisoner. Although unlike Dad, I'm innocent.

Even homework, which can usually occupy hours of my time, isn't helping. I try to work ahead in every subject, but I find myself reading the same sentence over and over again. Nothing sticks.

I'm staring blankly at the ceiling when there's a knock, followed by the front door opening. My protective instinct makes me duck behind the kitchen counter. Most of the people in town don't lock their doors, but Dad and I always have.

"Ally," Sheriff Gleason calls out. "I've brought in reinforcements." When he sees the worried look on my face, he clarifies, "Donuts. Not to be a cliché, but yum."

He sets down a bag from Dunkin' Donuts. The closest one is over a thirty-minute drive from here. He's trying to make an effort, so I give him a forced smile. Plus, he's the one who can decide when I get to see Dad again. I also wonder if he could be a character witness or something. I don't know how this kind of stuff works, but everybody knows my dad is a good person.

You'd think that with all the courtroom and police shows I've watched I would have some kind of understanding of the legal process.

"Thanks." I open the bag and pull out a chocolate-glazed donut. I place it on a napkin and pick at it. I haven't been able to eat since, well . . .

He pulls out a stool from the counter and sits down. He takes a swig of coffee as he studies me. "How are you feeling? Were you able to get any sleep last night?"

"A little," I lie. I tossed and turned, staring at the ceiling and then the clock, wishing that the night would be over, but dreading what fresh hell today would bring.

"I wanted to give you an update. After your father's court appearance, the sheriff in Tampa is planning a press conference."

"Tampa? Why?" I ask.

"You've been a missing child from Tampa for years. There will be a lot of people there relieved you've been found."

"Yeah, great." Too bad I'm miserable that I've been found.

"I know you're upset, but I think you need to understand how serious this is."

"Sheriff Gleason, no disrespect, but my father is in jail. I have no idea what's going to happen to him or to me, so, yeah, I think I get how serious this is."

He takes a long sip of his coffee. "Have you called your mother yet?"

I shake my head.

"I understand, I really do." He puts out his hand hesitantly near mine, but then draws it back.

"What's her name?" I ask.

"Paula."

"Paula," I reply. It doesn't feel right calling this virtual stranger Mom.

"I'm going to be honest here, Ally. You have to talk to her. For over fifteen years, she's been searching for you. You're her daughter. If Jan, Julia, or Don went missing for even a day..." He clears his throat. "Well, it's been hard to persuade her to stay away so far. She wants to be on the next plane here."

"Wait a second. You talked to her?"

He nods. "She asked to speak to someone who knew you. She was so happy to hear what an amazing young woman you've grown into. But she really wants to see you. I told her that you'd call her today. She's waiting by the phone."

I can't call her. I can't. Talking to her would mean that I'm somewhat accepting what's happened.

Sheriff Gleason sighs. "This has to be incredibly tough, but your mom—"

"She's not my *mom*," I bark.

"I understand—I can see your side," he clarifies. "But she is also innocent in this."

"Is she really?" I fire back. "There must have been a reason my dad took me from her. Maybe, just maybe, she's not this completely innocent person. Besides, this is my home. I've never even been to Florida. Oh."

I keep forgetting that I was born there. I lived there for my first three years. I try to picture life in the sun. There has to be a memory of being there. A memory of her.

But there's nothing.

"Sheriff Gleason, I really, really need to talk to my dad."

He takes a deep breath. "I've got one more piece of bad news."

"Jesus Christ," slips out.

"On Monday at the hearing, the prosecutor is going to request a no-contact order."

"What does that mean?"

"That you won't be able to communicate with your father. No talking, no letters, nothing."

"For how long?" I ask.

"I don't know. Probably not until the trial is over and he's been sentenced."

"How long can that take?"

"A few months."

I grab my jacket. "Well, then, let's go talk to him now." I open the front door and stare Sheriff Gleason down. He hesitates a moment before standing and following me out the door.

I don't care what a judge says. I need to see my dad. I need to look him in the eye, and I need him to tell me what happened.

I deserve answers. I need the truth.

Chapter

FIFTEEN

I jump at the buzzing sound as the doors open to the room where I'll be talking to Dad.

The room is concrete, with bright fluorescent lights overhead. Based on my TV-and-movie-watching experience, I'm surprised there isn't two-way glass on any of the walls.

I pick at my nails as I wait. Any sound coming from the hallway causes me to bristle. There's another loud buzz, and I nearly fall off my chair. The door clicks open, and Officer Dash offers a tight smile as he escorts in my father.

This entire time I'd been picturing our reunion with tears and hugs. But now . . .

Dad is in handcuffs. He's sporting more stubble than usual, and his face is drawn.

He's been in here for a little over twelve hours, and he already looks defeated.

Neither of us speaks as Officer Dash starts undoing Dad's cuffs.

Officer Dash who is on Dad's baseball team.

Officer Dash who once came over to our house to make large batches of chili for a fund-raiser when the police department needed new sirens for the three cars in their fleet.

Once the cuffs are off, he leads Dad to the chair across from me. "No physical contact, understand? I'll be right outside the door if you need me."

I realize he's saying the second thing for my benefit. As if I need protection from my own father.

Officer Dash, whose two small children I babysit for, no longer trusts my dad.

He nods to the camera in the corner of the room before being buzzed out.

We're being watched.

The entire Valley Falls police department, including Sheriff Gleason, no longer trusts my father.

And I hate it, I absolutely hate it, but I don't know if I'll ever be able to trust him again, either.

Dad's eyes are glued to the table. There's a moment of uncomfortable silence, neither of us knowing what to say. This has never been a problem before. There'd be times when he'd be fishing that we'd both enjoy the silence that being in the middle of a lake gave you, but this is different.

"Are you okay?" I finally ask, even though, I don't know, maybe he should be a little concerned about how *I'm* doing.

He moves his head a bit. I'm unsure if it's a nod or a shake. Then he looks up at me, his eyes wet. "I never meant for this to happen. I'm so sorry."

"Stop apologizing," I snap.

There is only one person here responsible for what's transpired. I'm not sure what's going to happen once I leave this room or when the next time I'll be able to talk to him will be. So I have to get answers. Now.

"I need you to tell me everything," I say, my voice cold. "Everything. I need to know the truth. Who am I?" My voice wavers on that question.

Yeah, I'm pissed. I'm also scared. The reality of the situation hits me—I'm seeing my father as a criminal.

"You're my daughter, and I love you very much." He looks at the floor.

"Why did you take me?" I ask, trying to understand how we got to this place.

"I never meant for it to get this far. You have to believe me."

I wait for him to say more, but he remains stubborn with his silence.

I stare him down, but still he refuses to even look at me. According to Sheriff Gleason, Dad was chatty enough last night. Telling him and the FBI agent everything they needed to know. But me, his daughter, his "pride and joy," the person he's put in this mess? He won't tell me a damn thing.

The chair beneath me makes a loud scratching noise as I stand. Dad finally looks up as I hover over him.

"I need you to tell me what happened. I need you to tell me why."

He shuffles in his seat. "It's complicated."

"Well, *no shit*, Dad."

"Language," he scolds me.

I laugh bitterly. "Oh, no. No. You don't get to lecture me on a single fucking thing ever again."

He clenches his jaw shut.

"You know that this affects me, right? *You* did this. *You* are the reason this is happening. So I have every right to ask you a few questions. Do you even realize? I'm a child you took away from her mother. So you better start talking, and I only want to hear the truth. NOW!"

The door clicks open, and Officer Dash sticks his head in. "Everything okay in here?"

"Not if he doesn't start talking." I point at my father with the anger that had been simmering now boiling over.

"Okay, okay," Dad relents.

"Then I guess we're okay." I sit back in my chair, cross my arms, and wait for Dad to speak.

Officer Dash pauses for a minute before shutting the door.

"Talk," I command.

"Things weren't going well with your mother."

"How did you meet? Were you married?" I don't know where the deceit begins, so I'm not sure if there's even a shred of truth in what little I've been told about my parents.

"We met in a marketing class back in college, Florida State. But everything I told you about our marriage was true."

"You went to college?" This entire time he's made a fuss about me going since he never went. About how I'd be the first one in the family and how proud he'd be of me. Yeah, that's what I was led to believe. Add it to the list of the BS he's been spreading. "Why would you lie about that?"

"I never meant to lie to you, it's just . . . you started asking questions and I got worried that you'd start looking things up and realize that a Jason Smith never went to Florida State. I also didn't want you wondering why someone with a business degree was working construction."

"I didn't even know we lived in Florida."

He nods. "That's where I'm from—and Paula . . . your—your mother. We got married young, right out of college, and then we had you. You were a bright spot in our lives. But we . . . we grew apart. We would have these epic fights about the smallest things."

"Did you hit her?" I ask, although I couldn't picture my father ever being violent.

"Of course not. But our marriage was never going to last. After a particularly bad fight—and what's crazy is I can't even remember what it was about—your mother and I decided to separate. I moved a few blocks away into a studio apartment, still holding out hope that maybe we could reconcile. Your mother had primary custody—courts usually favor the mother. So I got you every other weekend. Then I got laid off. I worked for a marketing consulting firm and they downsized." He speaks slowly, probably sensing that I'm going to need time to process this all. "The good news in losing my job was that I was able to look after you while your mother worked."

"What does she do?"

"Back then she worked long hours in the marketing department for a hotel. It was amazing for me, getting to spend all day with my little girl. You were so inquisitive. Always asking, 'Why, Daddy?'

"Every day, you'd learn a new word or discover something. And you loved animals. We spent hours poring over books with animals, or I'd sit you on my lap and go on the internet and look at whatever animal you were obsessed with that day. You went through a really long koala stage and kept saying, 'We go Australia.'

"We developed such a strong bond. I'd come get you every morning at eight and then return you when your mother got home. Sometimes that wouldn't be until seven, and you went to bed soon after that. You started crying when I'd pull up to your mom's house . . . Sometimes Paula had to call me in the middle of the night because you would wake up and scream for me. Paula wasn't happy about that. She didn't like that you only wanted to be with me."

He pinches the bridge of his nose. "It got to the point that I didn't want to get another job, because it would take me away from you. I saw how the time apart from your mother affected your relationship. As soon as I'd start working again, I'd see you much less, and, well, that wasn't going to be enough.

"Things got tense between Paula and me. She thought I was poisoning you against her. So she decided she wanted to put you in day care instead of letting me take care of you. The day that was supposed to be my last weekday with you, I took you to Busch Gardens. You ran around all day. You got to feed a flamingo and see a giraffe. When we got into the car, you were so happy, holding the stuffed giraffe I bought you."

My stomach plunges as if the floor has crumbled underneath me. I still have that giraffe—I named her Ginger. There's a relic of the pivotal day of my past sitting in my closet, and I had no idea.

"You asked where we were going once I started up the car, and when I told you that I was taking you home, you asked *which home*. When I said your mother's, you started crying uncontrollably. I had to pull over to comfort you. So I told you we were just going for a drive. I missed the exit to your mother's and kept driving. I was an hour late. Then two hours. I got you some ice cream and saw the missed calls and messages from Paula. At first, she was worried we'd gotten into an accident. Then the messages became accusatory. I didn't know what to do. I wanted to keep you with me. I didn't want you at some strange place the next day, surrounded by people you didn't know. I'm your father; I should take care of you. I wanted to keep you with me. So two hours turned into three. I couldn't bear the thought of dropping you off and not seeing you again for nearly two weeks. You kept saying, 'I want to stay with you, Daddy.' It broke my heart. I couldn't bring myself to take you home."

He hangs his head while the realization of what he's implying hits me.

"So you took me away from my mother because I threw a fit? All of this was because I was crying? Jesus Christ, Dad." I can't count the number of times that a kid I'm babysitting has had a breakdown when their parents start to leave. Do the parents stay at home? No. They leave, and the kid eventually gets over it because they're kids. Kids bounce back way better than adults. Clearly. "I was a toddler."

"I know!" The anguish on his face grows. "You have to understand, I kept telling myself that in ten minutes I was going to turn around. Then I wanted another ten minutes because I knew how much trouble I was going to be in once we returned to your mother's. I was planning on going to Paula's. Once you were asleep in the back, I took out my phone to call Paula to tell her where we were. But my phone was crazy with more messages. I listened to the last one first. Your mother was furious . . . and she had every right to be. But she told me she had called the police. She said she'd make sure that I would never get to see you again. I realized at that moment that if we went back I could lose you forever. I'd be lucky to even get supervised visits.

"I knew I was making a mistake, and it would eventually catch up to me, but I got back in the car and kept driving. And driving. With every mile, I was digging myself into a deeper hole that I couldn't get out of. So I made the decision to keep digging. I kept driving. At one point, I took out all the money I had, traded in my car for another, and kept heading north. When you woke up in the middle of the night, you asked what we were doing. I told you it was an adventure. Eventually you stopped asking questions altogether. We stopped in Cleveland since I figured we could hide in a bigger city."

"We lived in Cleveland?" I have absolutely no memory of Cleveland. Chicago was the first home I can recall.

"Yes. For only a couple months. The longer I kept you away, the more lies I had to tell, the more trouble I knew I was in. So I kept us moving. I was anxious those first few years. We never stayed more than six months in a town, especially when someone would start asking questions. My plan was to eventually get us to Canada. That's where we were headed when we stopped in Valley Falls. I found a temporary job and was waiting on a contact to get us passports that hopefully would've worked. We were only supposed to be here for a few months, but you really took to it . . . and so did I. So we stayed."

He leans back in his chair. "After a while, I started to believe my lies. I'd been lying for so long that it had to be true. I couldn't face what I had done. What I did to you. What I did to your mother. But all it took was one look at you, to see how happy you were here, to convince myself that it was for the best."

As furious as I am at him for what he did to us, this part rings true for me. I liked our life. But it doesn't change the fact that none of it was based on reality.

"I thought that it was behind us, then the college applications started happening."

And there it is. The real reason we're in this position.

"Oh, so first it's my fault you took me and now it's my fault you got caught?"

"No!" He holds up his hands. "No, not at all. My love for you made me do something foolish. My fear of what your mother was going to do kept me driving. This is all on me, and I've been running from that mistake ever since. I should've told you. I should've done a lot of things. But now the truth is finally out and I'm going to take responsibility for my actions. All I can say is that I'm so sorry, Ally."

"Don't you mean you're sorry, *Amanda*?" I don't feel like an Amanda. But in this moment I want to punish him as much as I feel *I'm* being punished.

"Amanda . . ." He looks off in the distance as if he forgot that was my real name. "We called you Mandy. I thought I could easily switch you to Ally without you asking too many questions."

Now questions were all I had.

"Didn't I ask about my mother, miss my other family?"

"You were so young," he says. "You did ask about her at first, but then as time went on, you adjusted."

"By 'adjusted' don't you mean you told me she was dead."

He flinches.

"She's alive. She wants to talk to me."

This surprises him. "You haven't talked to her yet?"

I return his question with a glare. How could he think that it would be so easy for me to go from thinking I don't have a mom to being totally cool talking to her?

"Honey, you should. She really loves you. I'm sick thinking about what I did to her."

"What you did to her? What about what you did to me?"

Tears begin streaming down his face. "I know. I know. This is all my fault. I'm so sorry."

"You keep saying that. Everybody keeps apologizing to me, but it doesn't fix anything. Is saying sorry going to change the fact that the past fifteen years of my life have been one big lie?" My entire body is vibrating with anger and frustration.

"Ally Bean—"

"Don't you *dare* Ally Bean me," I spit out.

"I'm sorry. I'm going to make this right, please believe me. I'm not lying anymore. I'm going to serve my time. The only thing I hope you can do is forgive me. Can you forgive me?"

I don't know what to say. He's the only parent I've ever known. He also really screwed things up. And he's going to pay for it.

But so am I. So have Paula and her family. Along with every person we know in Valley Falls.

"Ally?" he pleads with me.

I don't know if I can do it. I don't know anything anymore.

It's all too much.

I need time.

I need space.

"Ally?"

The walls are closing in on me. I try to call out for Officer

Dash to get me out of here, but my voice fails. I try again, but nothing.

"Ally?" Dad pleads.

I can't.

I just can't.

It would be so easy to tell him that I forgive him, but it's impossible. At this moment, I'm confused, I'm angry, and I'm hurt.

I love my dad, but he has deceived me. The person I thought he was, the person I thought I was, doesn't exist.

I can't.

"GET ME OUT!" I scream.

Officer Dash opens the door. "Is everything okay?"

I shake my head. "No, it isn't. I need to get out of here." I turn my back on Dad.

"Ally," Dad says one last time. "I love you so much, honey. Please look at me."

I lock eyes with him. The eyes I've been staring at my entire life. The ones that had greeted me every day when he came home from work. The ones that had comforted me when I was upset. The ones that had looked into mine while he lied to my face.

Every day.

For fifteen years.

I shake my head. "I don't know who you are."

I rush out of the room. I don't even flinch when I hear the door buzz, locking him in.

Chapter

SIXTEEN

Minutes later, I find myself alone in Sheriff Gleason's office.

And I am completely broken inside.

There's something I can do to begin to put the fragments together again. Something I have to do.

I pick up the phone in his office and stare at the receiver.

Before I can talk myself out of it, I start dialing. My hands shake, and I press a wrong number. I hang up and try again. Taking each digit one by one. I slow my breathing down in an attempt to calm my nerves.

She picks up before the first ring can finish.

"Hello? Hello?" The voice is unsteady, a desperate note to it.

I can't seem to find my own voice.

"Hello?" she says again.

It's her.

It's . . . my mom. Although I can't really wrap my head around that concept. *No, it's Paula*, I tell myself. It'll be easier on me if I think of her solely as a person from my past.

I try to reply, but only a croak comes out.

"MANDY?" she pleads into the phone.

I hear a male voice in the background say, "Is it her?"

Huh. I've been so focused on everything happening to me I never really stopped to wonder about her. Is she married? Or I guess remarried? Does she have other kids?

"It's not a prank call, is it? Or a reporter?" the male voice asks with a tone seeping of irritation.

I clear my throat and finally speak. "It's me."

A wailing sound comes from the other end. Not like she's in pain or hurt, but like a person who has had a tremendous weight lifted off her shoulders.

Of course. She's your mother. Remember that.

I have to constantly remind myself that this woman, even though I didn't know she existed until yesterday, has been looking for me this entire time.

All this time . . .

The sobs slow down. "I knew we'd find you. I never gave up. Please know that, Amanda. Oh, wait. You don't go by Amanda, do you? We named you after my mother, your grandmother. But now you go by Allison, right?" I'm glad I'm not the only one nervous about this. She keeps talking faster and faster. "Allison is a nice name. One of my college roommates was named Allison. Or do you prefer Ally?"

"My name is Ally."

"Okay, Ally, sweetheart. Whatever name you want. How are you? I talked to the sheriff last night, and he said that you're a really good student and smart. That makes me so relieved to hear that you've been doing great. Are you doing okay?"

Of course I'm not doing okay! But I bite my tongue and lie.

"I'm okay." Although it might not technically be a lie since I have a feeling she's more wondering what kind of person I turned into. As angry as I am at Dad, he was a good father.

If only I could find the courage to tell Paula about Dad. About how I feel. A daughter should be able to open up to her mother, but Paula is a stranger.

"I am thrilled to hear your voice." I can practically hear her smile. "We've had so many false tips over the years. Even though it hurt to get my hopes up, I knew you were out there. I just knew we'd eventually find you. I don't want you to think that I'd forgotten or moved on. Not a single day went by without me thinking of you."

"Honey, take a deep breath," the guy says.

"I'm sorry. I'm not giving you a chance to talk. I've just been imagining this moment for so long. I know you must be confused and scared, but, Mandy, I mean, Ally, please know that I love you and am here for you."

Love.

She loves me.

But she doesn't even know me.

She's quiet now. Is she waiting for me to tell her that I love her? How can you love someone you don't know?

"I want you to know that Dad has taken great care of me," I blurt as I try to hold on to the good memories. "I'm one of the top students in my class. I'm going to get a scholarship. I don't do drugs. Ah, I don't even have a single cavity."

She laughs at my babbling. "It's so good to hear. Oh, honey, I have missed you so much. Do you . . ." She takes a deep breath. "I know you were so young, but do you remember me?"

I search my brain again for any glimpse or memory of my mother.

I've got nothing.

When I think of a mom, I think of Julie Andrews. When I was little, I'd come home from school and Dad would still be at work. We couldn't afford day care, so I would just lock the door and put on *The Sound of Music*. I used to want to be part of the von Trapp family. I'd even sing along.

Maria was something special. The love and care she had for those children—that's what a mom represented to me.

Besides, beating Nazis is always a plus.

"Mandy?"

"I—I—" I stutter. "I don't remember you. Sorry. I thought you were dead."

She sucks in her breath. "Oh, no. No, no, no . . . I can't believe your father told you that." Bitterness creeps into her voice when she mentions Dad. "All this time you thought I was dead?"

All this time . . .

"Cancer."

She starts crying. First it's quiet sniffles, like she's fighting it. Then the floodgates open and I can hear her sobbing.

Okay, maybe I shouldn't have told her that. *Hey, Mom, I know we haven't spoken in fifteen years, but I thought you died from cancer.*

She pulls herself together and starts talking again. "I know Sheriff Gleason said that you need some time to adjust to everything happening. I'm sure it's a shock, but I can't wait to see you with my own eyes. To hold my baby girl again. I've waited too long and can't wait a single second more. So we're getting on a plane as soon as possible. And when you're ready to see me, I'll be there. I've always wanted to be there for you, honey. Please know that."

I nod, even though she can't see me. I'm not sure I'll ever be ready.

There's no way I'll be able to live up to whoever she has in her head. I'm just a boring, normal girl. Or maybe she'll be disappointed with how well I turned out, if it seems like I didn't really need a mother. Maybe she's expecting to swoop in and save me.

I don't need saving.

I meant what I said: my dad had taken really good care of me. I like the life I have.

But last night was like a split in my universe. Every moment from my life will, from now on, be identified by whether it was *before* or *after.*

"Honey?" she says. I think she's given up trying to remember that I'm not Amanda. "Is there anything you need me to do? I'll do anything."

And the weird thing is, I believe her. She would do anything for me. At least, I hope she will.

But can I really ask her to let me continue my life here uninterrupted? To let me live this lie of a life in semi-ignorant bliss.

"No, I'm okay," I reply.

"I'm so happy to hear your voice. It's like a piece of my life is back."

Well, I guess I should be glad someone is happy.

Chapter

SEVENTEEN

I don't believe in ghosts.

I've always been too practical about life and trusting of science to get freaked out by ghost stories or urban legends.

But now that I'm walking around my home, I feel as if I'm being haunted.

Everywhere there are memories of my dad, our former life, *before*.

"Let me know if you need anything," Sheriff Gleason says as he pops his head into my bedroom. "Take your time."

I nod as I shove more clothes into a bag. I have no idea when I'm going to be back here. I've been warned that there may be journalists outside the home when the story goes public, although I can't really fathom why on earth a journalist would care what's happened to me. It's really nobody's business but my own.

A photo of Dad and me at the lake catches my eye. We both

look so happy and calm. Dad, holding up a big fish, and me, covering my nose with a book. I always had to take a shower immediately after we went fishing. Especially since Dad insisted upon cutting the fish as soon as we got home. "It keeps them fresh," he used to argue. I'm pretty sure he did it because he knew it grossed me out.

I put the photo facedown on my nightstand. Every happy memory is now tainted by the fact that Dad was hiding something from me. Every moment we had has been tarnished, and there's no turning back.

All this time . . .

I stomp out of my bedroom and go directly into Dad's.

"Can I help?" Sheriff Gleason calls after me.

I scan Dad's room. He took the smaller of the two bedrooms, saying he only needed a place to rest his head at night, while I required my own space since I was growing up. His bed is still made, with a navy blue plaid comforter. The only other pieces of furniture are a chest of drawers and a nightstand, with a lamp and a book of crossword puzzles on it. I go to the drawers and start rummaging through his stuff.

"Ally?" Sheriff Gleason asks. "What are you looking for?"

"I don't know."

I have no idea, but I hope to find some answers.

There were plenty of times I could've gone through Dad's things, but never had a reason to snoop around. Or doubt anything he'd told me.

Not anymore.

There are only clothes in the drawers. Next up, I open the door to his small closet. A variety of button-down shirts and pants hang. Sneakers and work boots are on the floor, but there are a few shoeboxes above. I grab them and pull them down.

They are really light, practically weightless.

Bingo.

One box has the year written on it and is filled with receipts. (God, being an adult seems so mundane.)

I open the second box and dump out the contents. More slips of paper. Some have numbers written on them. Then my breath catches as I see Dad's old driver's license from Florida. No, it's Daniel Linsley's driver's license. It's been hard to believe my dad was this other person—Daniel Linsley—but here it is. The name, the photo, the address, and his birthday.

His *real* birthday. A month and year earlier than he told me.

My eye catches on two small photos, which were probably in his wallet when we left.

One is a photo of my dad and a woman I can only assume is Paula at their wedding. I've never seen this before. I've never seen her face before. Dad has always said that it hurt to look at her, so I never pushed him on it. The one picture of my mom and me in my bedroom is from right after I was born. The mother's head is turned and looking down at a very pink newborn baby.

I trace her face with my hand. We have the same green eyes. *I have her eyes.*

That simple fact alone makes me feel closer to her.

The other photo is a younger version of Dad on the beach.

There are two older people. His parents? And a woman who looks a little older than he is. Could it be a sister?

Oh my God, my dad's parents might be alive. And his sister. *Of course they are.* I've been so focused on Paula, but I probably have family on his side as well.

I sit cross-legged on the floor and stare at the two photos.

"Ally?"

"I've never seen these," I say as I hold up the photo of Dad and his possible family. "He kept these from me."

He had kept the truth from me. Kept my family from me.

I go back to the wedding photo. Paula is wearing a white lace dress and Dad is in a gray tuxedo. They aren't looking at the camera because they only have eyes for each other. They are holding hands and laughing.

What happened to them? It's hard to believe that kind of love can turn sour.

Maybe I am the reason?

Sheriff Gleason comes from behind me and sees the driver's license with all the scraps of paper. "Oh my God. We're going to need the contents of that box. This saves us a search warrant."

These memories are now evidence. Everything has been tainted by this mess.

Sheriff Gleason kneels down next to me. "Are you okay?"

"I really wish people would stop asking me that," I say angrily. "Sorry."

I stagger to standing, my head swirling. It's a combination of everything I just uncovered and the fact that I haven't eaten in almost twenty-four hours. I go back to the living room and sit in my normal spot on the couch.

Looking around at the place I have called home for eight years, I wonder what's going to happen to it. Every piece that has been added throughout the years tells a story from my life with Dad. I unsteadily get back up and head over to the shelf above the fireplace that is lined with the Precious Moments figurines that Dad had gotten me for my birthday every year.

I hold a figurine in my hand and trace the outline. It's of a girl in a blue dress, blowing out a candle on an oversized cupcake. It's from my first birthday in Valley Falls. We'd only been here a few weeks, but twenty people came over for cake and ice cream, all thanks to the Gleasons.

That night, when he tucked me into bed, Dad told me that we were going to stay put. No more moving every few months. He liked it here. I liked it here. I slept really well and felt so safe that night. So happy.

And it was all a lie.

I take the figurine and throw it across the room. It smashes into pieces.

Sheriff Gleason flinches in shock. "Ally?"

I grab another figurine and hurl it against the wall.

Then another.

And another.

Sheriff Gleason backs away, knowing I need this release.

It feels good. With every sound of shattering porcelain, I feel some of the hatred and betrayal lessen.

Once all the figurines lie in pieces, I stagger back and look at what I did. There is only so much I have left, and I decided to destroy one of the good memories.

They are gone. I did that.

"Ally?" Sheriff Gleason steps toward me.

That's when it happens.

This entire time, I've been holding on to small scraps of the past. I've been trying to convince myself of so many different things. My emotions have bounced back and forth.

Now they have finally settled into despair.

I collapse on the floor. The tears and anguish I've been holding back release in a torrent of screams and sobs. I don't recognize this person I've become. I'm utterly destroyed. I've been thrown against the wall and shattered.

Sheriff Gleason wraps his arms around me as I cry and cry.

And cry.

"It's going to be okay," he says to me.

But that's just another lie.

Chapter

EIGHTEEN

There is now only one constant left in my family life.

Baxter licks my cheek as I hug him tightly. He tries to wiggle from my grasp, but I won't let go. I desperately need to hold on to him.

A low growl radiates from Baxter as he breaks free. He takes a few steps to grab a ball and then drops it in front of me. His tail is wagging; his legs are poised to run to catch it.

I place the ball in my hand and throw it in the backyard. Baxter happily yelps as he runs after it, then brings it back. He drops the ball at my feet and barks.

What it must be like to be a dog. He has no idea what's happening. He doesn't even seem to be upset that my dad's not here. Of course, he also now has Marian's family spoiling him rotten. Even their grumpy cat, Gizmo, has been hiding, so Baxter truly rules the roost.

"Hey."

I turn around to see Marian standing near the sliding glass door that leads into the house. "It's freezing out here." She wraps her arms around herself as she sits down next to me, wearing a coat.

I hadn't really noticed the cold, and I only have my oversized UW sweatshirt on. I'm still feeling numb from my visit to the house.

"How was seeing your dad?"

I shrug.

"Did you speak with your mom?"

I nod.

"Do you want to talk about it?"

I pause for a moment. "Not really, but I'm just so angry. At everything. Especially my dad."

"That's understandable. I mean, I cried when I found out my parents lied about the tooth fairy and Santa. And that's nothing. If you can't trust your parents, you know."

I do. I really do.

She rests her head on my shoulder. "You can trust me. And you can trust my family, who is really your family, too."

"I just, with everything . . . I mean, I can't thank you guys enough."

"Of course."

I lay my head on hers as we look out at the backyard. A quiet peace falls over me for a moment, and I'm wondering how I can hold on to the best part of my life.

"This is nice," I comment.

"Yeah. Quiet is good, especially after today."

"So I take it babysitting went well."

"It was fine. Although it was very clear from the start that I'm a very poor substitute. Annie, Thomas, and Liz kept reminding me of all the fun stuff you do with them."

"Oh God! You were at the Dorns'?" I stand up, jolted from my brief moment of tranquility. I knew she was babysitting, but I didn't know where. I completely forgot that I was supposed to babysit for them today. It's Saturday. I'm supposed to have my date with Neil tonight. I want to keep living my *before* life, even though that feels impossible right now. "I can't believe I forgot."

"It's okay." Marian pats the seat next to her. "I've got you covered. Nobody expects you to do anything with everything going on. You just have to . . ."

What? I want to ask. What exactly am I supposed to do? I can't go to school. I can't concentrate on anything.

I close my eyes and feel the sun on my face, the warmth fighting its way through the frigid air. I try to not think about anything. The past is too painful, the present too confusing, and the future too scary.

"Ah, so," Marian begins. "There's one other thing."

Of course there is.

She continues, "I could only keep him away for so long."

I open my eyes to see Marian gesturing her head to the door, where Neil is peeking out from behind the blinds. He takes a step back when he sees me and gives me a little wave.

"Believe me, I tried to give you some space, but he's been freaking out. He doesn't have to come out here. All he wanted was to make sure you're okay. Apparently my word—as his flesh and blood—is useless. Besides, you haven't been responding to any of his texts."

I have no idea where my phone is. It wasn't like Dad needed to know where I am. There's probably a part of my subconscious that knew I didn't want to deal with the texts that were coming in after last night.

"Do you want me to tell him to leave?"

Neil is not even discreetly hiding now. "No, it's okay."

I call for Baxter, but he's happily chewing on a branch that has fallen from the large oak tree in the backyard. I let him have his happiness while I follow Marian into the house.

"I've got some homework to do before Rob picks me up. Oh." She shakes her head. "Never mind. I'm going to stay home tonight."

"Go out. Please. I'm exhausted. You have fun." Someone should.

Marian gives me a hug and pauses before she heads upstairs and leaves me alone with Neil. He's standing on the other side of the kitchen table, looking at me like I'm a dangerous animal.

Maybe I am.

"Ah," he says as he rubs the back of his head. "I've got my mom's car. Do you want to go somewhere?"

I look around the Gleasons' home. This might be the only

view I have for the foreseeable future. But there really isn't any-place I want to go, or more importantly, anybody I want to see.

"Not really." I pull out a chair and sit down. "Sorry that we can't go out tonight. I'm not really in a social mood."

"Of course, of course! I wasn't—that's not why—I mean, I just—" he fumbles.

"It's okay," I assure him.

Although right now I'd love to have a date be the only thing I have to stress over.

Neil nods for a bit. He then goes around the table and pulls out the chair right next to me and sits down. He puts out his hand for a minute before tapping my hand with his. He's overthinking every move, every word. Is this how it's going to be now between us? Is this how everybody is going to treat me? Like I'm some delicate flower who could turn into a Venus flytrap at any moment?

"What do people know?" I ask.

Neil grimaces. "Enough."

It's exactly what Marian told me yesterday, which is entirely too much for me.

He opens his mouth, and then closes it. He rethinks what-ever's going on in his mind before he opens it again and finally speaks. "I can't believe it."

Me neither.

He reaches into his jacket pocket and pulls out a present wrapped in "Happy Birthday" paper with balloons printed on it. "I wanted to give you this."

A birthday present. Even though my birthday isn't until January . . . something. I don't even remember the date.

I take the rectangular-shaped gift and open it. It's a leather notebook with *AS*, my initials, stamped in silver on the front.

"I figured since you prefer to take notes by hand, you'd need something fancy for college."

It's not like I prefer to write by hand, but my old laptop weighs a ton and I don't want to lug it around school. I rub my initials. But *AS* isn't me. It never was me.

"Thank you," I manage to barely croak out.

I stare down at the notebook. Not sure what to say. It's such a sweet and thoughtful gesture, 100 percent Neil, but it's for Allison Smith.

Neil fills the silence. "I don't know if you want to talk about it . . . Or we can talk about something else?"

"Something else," I reply, even though every time I try to focus on anything it brings me back to here. But then my mind goes to the one moment of peace I'd had in the past twenty-four hours. "Hey, Neil, do you remember when we went to Green Bay and you got that woman to make me a turtle sundae?"

He appears taken aback by my abrupt change of subject. "Yeah, of course."

"I thought about that the other day. Actually, it was last night." I can't believe something that seemed so long ago was yesterday. "And it was the only time I wasn't miserable about what was happening. It was a good memory. It made me smile." I'm startled by a lone tear traveling down my cheek. I had thought I'd used up all my tears at home. I wipe it away, embarrassed that a memory of an ice cream sundae can unravel me.

He puts his arm around me. I feel his breath on my neck. Neil has always been by my side. Always close to me, but never this close. It's comforting.

I lean into him. He brushes back a strand of hair that has fallen in front of my face. I turn to say something to him, but before I can get the words out, his lips are on mine.

I make a noise of surprise as his hand reaches up to cup my chin.

Neil van Horne is kissing me.

It's nice. Really nice. But . . .

I pull away.

"Sorry!" he says, slightly out of breath. "Sorry."

"My life is falling apart so now you decide to finally kiss me?"

"Sorry!" He gets up from the table. "I'm sorry. You looked so sad, and I wanted to comfort you."

I stare at him dumbfounded. I mean, yeah, it did comfort me a little, but still.

"You know, I never said I had great timing." He gives me his embarrassed crooked smile.

A laugh escapes my throat. I almost forgot what it was like to laugh.

Neil begins to pace in front of the table. "I'm sorry. I know that was stupid. Oh God, I'm an *idiot*. I've been so worried, and I wanted to do something for you, and I wasn't sure what I could do. Clearly, I screwed up. Don't hate me."

"I don't hate you." I could never hate Neil.

I stand up and walk toward him.

He gives me a worried stare. "What?"

I don't know how I look, but I do know what I want.

I want silence. I want to escape.

I want Neil.

Before I can talk myself out of it, I grab him by the shoulders and pull him to me. I kiss him. And keep kissing. There's a hunger inside me. I wipe my mind clear of anything but Neil. All I want is to feel his lips on mine. How his hand tightens around my waist, protecting me.

I pull him in closer so there isn't a millimeter between us. We are pressed against each other, our limbs entwined, our mouths connected. I don't even need to breathe, all I want is—

He pulls away abruptly. "Are you okay?"

Everything I've been pushing down comes flooding back. I grab my head, wanting it to all go away. "I was."

"I don't—I mean—I just," he stutters. "Don't get me wrong, that is one of the *greatest* things that has ever happened to me, but I want to be sure it's something you want and you're not . . ."

He doesn't finish his thought because we both know what he's about to say. And we both know he's right.

He takes a step toward me, but I take a step away.

"Ally?" The look on his face is a mixture of confusion and pity.

I don't want to look at it anymore. I don't want to be reminded of what got us to this awkward place. It makes all the memories of the past twenty hours come crashing down all around me.

I don't say anything. I simply turn and walk away. I've been doing that a lot lately. First to Dad, now to Neil. I take the stairs two at a time and lock myself in Susan's room. I fall onto the bed and put a pillow over my head.

Wishing, praying that all the screaming and confusion swirling around my mind will silence.

Chapter

NINETEEN

It doesn't.

Chapter
TWENTY

I finally slept.

And slept. And then slept some more.

My body shut down and gave me hours of some peace.

I spent all of Sunday in bed. Anytime the bedroom door opened, I pretended to be asleep. There was food placed on the nightstand. It remained untouched.

I didn't have the energy to talk to anybody. I was tired. I was embarrassed. Two members of the Gleason family have seen me at my worst. First Sheriff Gleason with my total breakdown and then Neil with my . . . whatever that was. I basically attacked the poor guy.

Even though I got some sleep, there were the occasional flickers in my subconscious. Memories of Dad. Of being in a car with him as a kid.

And then there were flashes of the sun. The smell of the ocean. Was it a long-buried memory of living in Florida?

I woke up after ten o'clock on Monday and stayed in bed for another hour. I knew the house would be quiet—Marian would be at school and her parents at work—but I didn't want to get up and face the world. So while I stayed cuddled under my blankets, my dad was in court.

My stomach rumbles for the first time in days so I venture down to the kitchen. I'm hungry. No, hungry doesn't convey the emptiness I feel. I start eating. Cereal. Toast. More toast. I heat up a frozen pizza.

Nothing is filling me up.

I'm on the couch polishing off an entire bag of potato chips when the doorbell rings. I don't move. Not solely because I'm still in my flannel pajamas and haven't showered since Friday morning, but because I don't want to see anybody.

After a few moments, the door opens.

"Hello?" Grandma Gleason calls out. "Ally?"

I wonder if she'll go away if I don't move or make a sound.

Her footsteps come closer so I realize I have no choice. "In here," I call out as I shove the empty bag of chips under the couch.

She enters the room and stops when she sees me. She looks exactly like Neil's mom, but a little older and with bright white hair she wears in a bun. She glances up and down and grimaces at my chest, where I notice several broken potato chips rest.

"When's the last time you've eaten a fruit or vegetable?" she asks.

I reply by staring blankly at her, because I honestly can't recall.

She walks over to the kitchen, which overlooks the living room, and opens the refrigerator. She pulls out some grapes, an apple, and an orange. She takes out a bowl, cutting board, and knife and starts making a fruit salad.

I don't have the heart to tell her that I'm full from all the processed food I just inhaled.

"You are going to eat, then we'll talk about a shower."

I know better than to argue with her. "Have you talked to your son?"

She pauses mid-cut. "Yes. He says your father has been advised of the charges. The judge didn't grant a bond, so he's being transferred to a jail until his hearing. And the no-contact order has been issued."

"So it's out."

"Yes." She looks up. "It's out. There'll be a press conference in a bit from the sheriff down in Florida. I came over in case you wanted company when you watch it."

"Oh." I hadn't even thought about watching it. But I guess I should know what people are saying about Dad. "Do you think we can find it online?"

Grandma Gleason doesn't answer. She finishes making the fruit salad, then comes over to sit next to me on the couch. She hands me the bowl and a fork.

She finally speaks. "I think we should turn on the TV." She grabs the remote, and the TV glows to life. A game show is playing, but then she switches to CNN, where we watch a commercial.

I eat an apple slice. When the news comes back on, there's a BREAKING NEWS graphic. The news anchor appears, and I almost choke.

"For those just joining us, we are following a breaking story from Wisconsin. A teenager who was kidnapped by her father when she was three has been found. Amanda Linsley, the missing girl . . ."

There's a ringing in my ears as the two images from the MISSING poster fill up the screen.

While I understand they're talking about me, they aren't using my face or name.

Grandma Gleason takes the bowl from my shaking hands and places it on the coffee table. "Are you okay?"

Can people stop asking me that? I'm going to start wearing a T-shirt that says, No, I'm Not Okay and It's Not Going to Get Better.

Instead, I remain silent. It's difficult to focus on any one thing that's being said. I will myself to listen, to be present, since this affects me, but I can't. It's too much.

The screen goes to a podium in a sunny courtyard. That brings me back. A bald man in a suit comes out with two police officers behind him. A voice comes on over the picture. "We are now going live to where Sheriff Hunt of Hillsborough County, Florida, will make a statement and then answer questions from the press."

The sheriff swaggers up to the microphone. "Thank you for coming. I am happy to report that Amanda Linsley, who has been missing for over fifteen years, has been found in northern Wisconsin. Her father, Daniel Linsley, took Amanda from her home when she was three and has been on the run ever since. We received a tip six days ago that Amanda may have been found. We were able to confirm with the FBI and the local police in Valley Falls, Wisconsin, that the person in question is Amanda. Daniel Linsley will face multiple counts, including kidnapping and forging documents. Amanda's mother has been notified, and I can tell you that, as a father, it was one of the greatest moments in my life to inform her that her daughter is alive and safe." The sheriff pulls out a handkerchief and wipes away the nonexistent tears on his face. Camera shutters drown out any other sound for a moment.

"Well, it seems like someone is going to milk his fifteen minutes," Grandma Gleason says.

"Has Amanda spoken with her mother? Have they seen each other? When will Amanda return to Florida?" a voice calls out.

"Yes, I can confirm that Amanda has spoken with her mother, who is currently on her way to Wisconsin. I do not have any details about when Amanda will be returning to Florida. As she's a minor, we expect that she will move back with her mother."

I stand up. Who the hell is this guy, and why does he think he has any say over me? He's never met me. He's never met my dad. He has absolutely nothing to do with the case. It was the people here who figured it out. Yet there he is, taking credit and acting like he has any idea what's going on in my life.

My gratitude for the Gleasons grows even more. Sheriff

Gleason could be doing this same thing. He could be posing for pictures and talking about Dad and me, yet he's remained silent. He's letting the court speak for itself.

I grab the remote and change the channel. But there he is. The sheriff's face is on Fox News. I press another button and he's on MSNBC. Another button, BBC World News.

"Sit down." Grandma Gleason pats the seat next to her. I oblige since I don't know what else to do with myself.

"Why did he say that they expect me to move back to Florida? How can someone who is a stranger make a decision like that for me? This is my home." I find myself shaking. It's difficult to breathe.

Grandma Gleason puts her hand on mine. "It's unfair. But in the eyes of the law, you're still a minor."

"I'm eighteen!" No. God dammit, I'm not. Dad lied about my birthday. I'm only seventeen. "Okay, but I'll be eighteen in . . . Do you happen to know when my official birthday is?"

"January twenty-fourth."

My mind is reeling. "Okay, I'll be an adult at the end of next month. That's what? Six weeks? Seven weeks?"

She nods. "Brian is seeing what he can do. But your mother is set on you moving back to Florida with her."

"What?"

Just when I think there's no possible way things could get any worse.

"No. No," I say forcefully, as if by protesting enough I can make this all go away. "I'm not going anywhere with her. She can't make me."

"You've spoken with your mother?"

"Yes, we talked for like ten minutes."

"And?"

"Well, at no point did she drop that bomb. How convenient." I fold my arms.

"But how was it?"

It was . . . I haven't really discussed my conversation with Paula. I tucked it away, not wanting to deal with it. But this reality is cruising toward me and there's nothing I can do to prevent myself from getting run over by it.

I take a deep breath. "It's weird. I know she's technically my mom, but you're more of a mother figure to me," I state. "Jess down at the grocery store is more of a mom to me." Whenever I'm buying groceries, Jess always makes sure I'm getting some fruits and vegetables. She does it in such a sweet and kind way that I can't argue with her. "It's not that I don't want to meet her, it's just . . . How can she expect that I'd be willing to pack my bags and leave everything behind?"

"So you're going to see her?"

"Yes," I say without an ounce of excitement. Besides, I don't have a choice. Not about this. Not about where I'm going to live.

It's such bullshit.

Grandma Gleason starts to rub my back. "I can only imagine

how excited she'll be to see you. She's been waiting all this time. Poor thing."

I grimace. Every parent who's spoken to me—Grandma Gleason, Sheriff Gleason, and Marian's parents—have this compassion for Paula I don't share. They imagine losing one of their children. I get it. I do, but . . .

I. Don't. Know. Her. And I'm supposed to leave my entire life behind to live with her? AND I HAVE NO CHOICE? It's hard enough dealing with the fact that Dad is gone and now everything I know, *everybody* I know has to go away, too?

No. That can't be happening. (How many times have I thought that in the past few days?)

I won't let it happen.

My mind starts trying to come up with a plan to make this all go away. I've always been able to come up with a list of tasks to achieve a certain goal. But this feels impossible.

"Will you go with me to meet Paula?" I ask. I can't imagine facing her alone.

"Of course." Grandma Gleason kisses my forehead. "Of course I will. And how are you feeling about your father?"

I lean back on the couch. Thinking about Dad is another topic I've been avoiding. God, is there anything in my life that I'm willing to face?

"I'm confused," I admit. "I don't have any clue what I'm supposed to do and how I'm going to handle this. I'm so furious at him for what he did, but then I think about my life and I feel like I can't get too mad because I was happy. I loved my life.

I loved him. I *love* him. Then I wonder if I have Stockholm syndrome."

"Your father cares greatly for you."

"I know." I do and that's the problem. "He's my dad, he's supposed to protect me. He made this horrible mess, and I'm left to deal with the fallout on my own." I gesture toward the TV, where reporters are discussing me. How could anyone ever be prepared for this?

"You're not on your own," she reassures me.

"But I feel like I am. People keep telling me that they understand how I feel, but how can they when *I* don't even know how I feel?"

It's too much. It's all too much for one person.

"You are allowed to feel however you want. I'm not going to sit here and tell you that it's not going to be difficult, because it is. But it'll make it easier if you talk to us about it instead of bottling everything in."

I think back to being at the house and what happened when I decided to unleash all I was feeling. How I destroyed nearly a decade's worth of memories. "I'm scared of what I'm feeling. I'm terrified about how much this is going to change everything. Not just my future, but what I think about my past." I glare at the TV.

"Maybe I should change the channel," Grandma Gleason says as she puts on the local NBC station out of Green Bay. We both gasp. A reporter is outside my home. Not the home of Amanda Linsley, but of Allison Smith. Me. The real me.

They know. Everybody knows now.

". . . it's in this house that Amanda Linsley and her father lived under aliases for the past eight years."

The screen splits from the young male reporter standing outside my house to a female anchor sitting behind a desk. "And do we know what names Amanda and her father have been using?"

The reporter nods for a minute. "Unfortunately, Andrea, nobody in this small, tight-knit community is talking at this time. But we do know that she goes to the local high school and is regarded as an excellent student. Her father worked in construction, and they are, allegedly, well liked. But no specifics have been given."

I let out a breath that my real name, well, not my real name, but the name that I know—Allison Smith—is secret for now. I once googled my name and couldn't find me. There are way too many Ally Smiths to choose from.

Oh. Right. Dad chose our last name —doesn't get much more common than Smith. Huh. *Well played, Dad.*

"Don't you worry, nobody here will talk. If they do, the full weight of the Gleason family will descend upon them like hellfire," Grandma Gleason states with a scowl.

Grandma Gleason is the sweetest lady you'd ever meet. Unless you cross her family and then the claws come out.

I give her a smile because I appreciate it.

Even though I'm not a Gleason.

I'm not even a Smith.

I'm a Linsley. Whatever the hell that means.

"But the press can be relentless. This is a juicy story, so they won't really leave you alone until there's a statement."

"From Sheriff Gleason?" I ask.

She gives her head a little shake. "No, honey, they need to hear from you."

Chapter

TWENTY-ONE

Once again, I'm staring down my computer, willing the words to come.

This time the stakes are higher. It's not scholarship money I'm looking to earn. I'm trying to regain control. This is about my life. My family.

There's been nothing—no test, no class—that has prepared me for this.

After Grandma Gleason left, I looked myself up online. Not "Ally Smith," but "Amanda Linsley." The search results were flooded with stories about my . . . kidnapping. It's still such a foreign concept. I wasn't held against my will. But there are those same two images—the one of me as a kid and the age-progressed one. There are statements from the FBI and the Florida sheriff. The only statement made by Sheriff Gleason was asking for my privacy.

His plea has fallen on deaf ears. The media are stationed outside the police station, the high school, and my house.

Those reporters aren't interested in knowing me. They're chasing a sensation, a way to garner clicks and ratings.

I type in "Daniel Linsley," and the same articles pop up. I refine my search to "Daniel Linsley family," and the same thing. I try again, add "Florida" and filter out any stories from the past year.

There are a few articles from when I was first reported missing, and I scroll through them all. I notice one link for an obituary for a Franklin Daniel Linsley. I click on it and read about a man who passed away from cancer. My heart plunges when I see "he is survived by his wife, Sandra; his daughter, Sharon; and his son, Daniel; as well as his granddaughter, Amanda."

My grandfather, who died. I scroll up to see the date: three years ago on March fourteenth. Something about that date rings familiar. Why?

Oh my God. That was when Dad fell off the scaffolding.

My father, who was always so careful, wasn't paying attention and hurt himself.

My father, who was dealing with the loss of his own father.

My father, who was in mourning and couldn't tell me about it.

I remember how sad Dad was at the time, but I thought it was because he was hurt and we didn't know how we were going to pay our bills. He had to hide a lot from me.

I get up and pace the room. When I have to really think about

Dad now, only fury bubbles up. I think there will always be a layer of disappointment and anger with what my father did and, what hurts the most, the lies he's told.

The last time I spoke with him—which might've been our last conversation for years—I turned my back on him as he begged for my forgiveness. He's going to jail. He's alone. And he's in there because of me.

This isn't how I want to leave things between us. Before I can move on and make sense of everything, I have to forgive him. That doesn't mean what he's done will ever be okay, but it's not helping me to hold this anger so close to my heart.

Because of the no-contact order between us, I don't have a lot of options. None, really. But I do have Sheriff Gleason, and maybe he can help.

I take a small piece of paper and write down three things:

I'm sorry.
I love you.
I forgive you.

I fold it into a tiny piece, hoping I can persuade Sheriff Gleason to give this to my dad. Or tell him these things.

What if he can't? Or refuses?

I can't have Dad sitting in jail thinking I hate him.

The only thing I can control at this moment is my statement. If the media reports on it, maybe Dad will see it.

Writing those essays had been like pulling teeth. Every word a struggle. But as I start to type, the words pour out.

⌒

In the past few days, my world has been turned upside down.

That disruption, in part, has been caused by the media. While I appreciate the concern that has been shown about my well-being, I wish to be left alone. I want to go on living the boring, normal, and wonderful life that I've been leading.

It's important for me to let everybody know that I love my father. He made a horrible decision that has impacted many, but whatever happens in court will not change my feelings for him.

My focus will be to finish out school and get to know my mother and my family.

I'm asking that the media respect my privacy—and that of my family and community—during this difficult time.

⌒

I sit back and examine what I've written. I put in the part about Paula because—while it's mostly true—a plan has begun to form in my head. I need her on my side.

As for the rest, especially about my father, I don't think truer words have ever been written. At least by me.

Chapter
TWENTY-TWO

It doesn't work.

Even though my statement has been read by countless reporters, more are now standing outside my home and school. A few have been camped out at the police station.

So much for giving me my privacy.

The past twenty-four hours could best be described as a media tsunami.

And because I've turned into some kind of masochist, I can't get enough of it.

I refused Marian's offer to stay home from school to keep me company, because I don't want anybody to see how I live now. Despite Grandma Gleason's request yesterday, I haven't showered. I haven't gotten out of my pajamas.

Last night at dinner neither Marian nor her parents had the heart to tell me how disgusting I must be. I shoved food into my mouth without tasting. I woke up today to find pockets of acne had popped up on my chin and forehead.

I look nothing like that age-progressed image of me that has been dominating the news cycle. Granted, I don't really look much like myself from a week ago, either.

And I keep googling. Oh, how I keep googling. Since this girl they talk about, this Amanda Linsley, doesn't share anything with me—especially a name or face—it's easier to believe it's not me. It's like watching a telenovela, with the absence of cleavage and hot men.

Ugh. "Hot men" leads my mind to wander to Neil. I've been ignoring his e-mails and texts. I've made it very clear to Marian that I don't want to see anybody. I do mean *anybody*. If Neil came over, I'd lock myself in my—well, Susan's room.

Yeah, the fact that I'm not an adult has been very apparent the past couple of days.

Fox News was outside the school trying to get people to comment about me. Dana, of all people, approached the reporter with her hair done and full makeup.

"What can you tell us about the student?" the reporter asked as he shoved the microphone in Dana's face.

She smiled at the camera like she was enjoying herself. "You know, there always was something off about her dad."

Discovering this scoop clearly excited the reporter. "How so?"

"Well—" But Dana never got another word out. Neil showed up in the frame and pulled Dana off camera.

"Hey!" the reporter called out.

"Interview's over," Neil shouted at him. His hand obstructed the view of the school, and it appeared as if he tried to knock the camera down. The feed was quickly cut, and they've avoided going live ever since.

The clip has gone viral, and I keep replaying it.

The front door opens without a knock. I sit up, expecting to see one of Marian's parents, but instead it's Sheriff Gleason and Grandma Gleason.

Their disappointment in my physical state is clear on both of their faces.

Grandma Gleason clears her throat. "I didn't realize that grunge is still in. Maybe you should shower and freshen up before we go."

They're taking me to see Paula. I am going to meet Amanda Linsley's mom. My mom.

"Do you need help picking out what to wear?" she asks.

God, what does one wear when meeting one's mom for the first time in fifteen years?

"I'm okay," I reply as I stand up. "But before we go, I've been thinking and there's something I need to ask you both."

Chapter

TWENTY-THREE

"Ready?"

I duck down in the back seat of Grandma Gleason's car as we exit the garage, not wanting to risk being seen by reporters.

"It looks like the coast is clear," Sheriff Gleason says. He changed out of his police uniform and instead has on jeans and a sweater so as not to draw suspicion. Grandma Gleason is in the seat next to him.

The sedan slows as we get to the corner of Elm, where you'd take a right to get to where Dad and I live. Or is it "lived"? *Had lived*, before.

"Oh my," Grandma Gleason calls out under her breath.

I take a peek at my block and duck back down. There are news vans lining the entire street. Bright camera lights are focused on my house.

I can't help but feel sorry for my neighbors. How they're being hounded and questioned. Then I feel a twinge of gratitude that they aren't talking.

God, all it will take is just one person, *one person* saying my name or giving them a picture. I'm so relieved for my Erin Rodgers alias and private online life.

As we hit the highway that leaves town, I start to relax a little. I've never been so grateful to get away.

We're meeting Paula at her hotel in Green Bay. She's staying there because, well, first of all, there isn't a hotel in Valley Falls. And, most importantly, it will give us some privacy.

The car is mostly silent on the drive to the hotel. I get comfortable enough to fully sit up in my seat. I watch the farmland pass by. Do they even have farms in Florida? Or is it all palm trees and beaches?

I realize my hands are gripped in tight fists. All I can do at this point is pray my plan works out.

Bile rises in my throat as we pull into the Hyatt Regency. Sheriff Gleason parks the car, and nobody moves. "Whenever you're ready."

"Okay," I reply without moving a muscle.

The car is still as we wait for me to give a signal that I don't plan on giving anytime soon. I look out at the hotel. Somewhere inside is my mother.

A woman whose help I desperately need.

The silence is shattered when Sheriff Gleason's phone rings. "Hello?" He glances back at me. "Yes, we're here. We . . . Yes, she needs a couple more minutes. Got it."

I look down at the car floor. I feel like such a bitch for not rushing in to greet my mother with open arms. It's just . . . hard. How can I switch off a part of my brain that has always put my father first? How can I simply accept this new version of my life?

Maybe I should treat this like ripping off a bandage. Get it over with. Once it's off, it won't be so painful.

I open the car door and start walking toward the entrance of the hotel. Sheriff Gleason and Grandma Gleason follow behind me. I go straight to the elevator and press the up button.

"What floor?" I ask, my voice robotic.

"Fourth," Sheriff Gleason responds. "Room 402."

I nod as I hit the button.

"Hold the elevator," a voice calls out.

Sheriff Gleason reaches his hands out to stop the door from closing. A man gets in the elevator with us. I feel the blood rush out of my face when I realize it's that young male reporter from Fox News.

"Thanks." He gives us his big white-toothed smile. He's scribbling in his notebook, and it takes everything I have not to look over his shoulder to see what he's writing.

If he only knew who he was standing next to.

"A little cold out there," Grandma Gleason says to the guy.

"Yes. I'm not used to it."

Why is she talking to him?

It's then that I realize Sheriff Gleason has his head tilted away from him. He's been ducking reporters as he goes in and out of the station all week.

Grandma Gleason is simply trying to distract the reporter. "You're not from around here, I take it."

"No, I'm in town for a story. Have you heard about the missing girl who was found?"

I can only stare at the door.

"I did. How wonderful!"

Wonderful?

She continues, "We're up here from Milwaukee to look at schools, and of course see Lambeau Field. Are you a Packers fan?"

"Not a big football fan," the reporter replies as we finally reach the fourth floor.

I don't breathe until the three of us get off the elevator and the doors close, leaving the reporter behind.

At least that nerve-racking encounter made me forget for thirty seconds why we were in the elevator to begin with.

"Not a word," Sheriff Gleason whispers as we walk to the room. "We don't know who's listening."

I nod as we approach the door. On the other side is Paula. His hand hovers to knock, but he looks to me for confirmation. I nod.

His knocks echo the beating of my heart. The door flies open, and there she is.

My own eyes are staring back at me.

Her hand flies up to her mouth; tears begin to brim. "Oh my God."

Before I can say anything, she grabs me tightly.

Sheriff Gleason guides us into the room and closes the door behind us.

"Oh, my sweet girl," Paula sobs as she puts my face in her hands. "I have missed you so much." She pulls me in again. "I don't think I'm ever going to be able to let go."

I can't move a muscle. My arms remain limp by my side, but there's a familiar smell to her. Maybe it's the same perfume that Marian's mom wears.

Or perhaps I hadn't completely forgotten her.

I glance over at Sheriff Gleason and Grandma Gleason, who have their backs to us, wanting to give us some privacy, I guess.

"Hello," a male voice says.

We finally break away, and a man whose voice matches the one I heard on our phone call stands before us. He's wearing khaki pants and a black-and-white collared shirt under a peach sweater. He has neatly combed brown hair and wire-rimmed glasses. And he's wearing penny loafers. Dad would definitely call this guy a square.

Paula wipes away her tears. "Oh, Amanda, this is my husband, Craig. I guess that makes him your stepfather."

Craig laughs a bit, obviously uncomfortable about this. Which makes *all of us*. "I can't tell you how happy I am to finally meet you, Ally." He extends his hand, then stares at it. "Oh, that's so stuffy. Come here." He gives me a quick, almost formal hug.

After a round of introductions, we're invited into the sitting area of their two-room suite.

"I have something for you," Paula says as she goes over to a bag and pulls out a teddy bear with a red ribbon tied around its neck. It's not a new teddy bear; it looks used, loved. "I don't know if you remember Snuggles."

I take the bear and put it in my lap. His black beaded eyes stare back at me. There's something familiar about this bear. But it could be that I'm desperate to remember something. Anything.

"I need to thank you," Paula says to Grandma Gleason, taking her hand. "She is extraordinary. Thank you for taking care of her."

"It's Dad," I find myself saying. Everybody looks at me; the mood in the room shifts when I mention him. "He raised me. Although Grandma Gleason is like a grandmother to me."

"Thank you," Paula says again to her, ignoring my comment about Dad. She turns to me. "Your real grandmother can't wait to see you again. The whole family is chomping at the bit to throw a big welcome-back party for you."

"That sounds wonderful," I reply with fake enthusiasm. This is it. This is the moment I need to start buttering her up. To start the plan in place that will let me hold on to a glimmer of my real life. "I'm looking forward to meeting them. Did you bring pictures?"

This excites her. She takes out a huge photo album and starts flipping through the photos. I try to remember all the names and ask the right questions. But it's surreal to see these faces and know that somehow, in a different life, I belonged to them.

"And this is Sarah." Paula points to a picture of a maybe-ten-year-old girl with curly brown hair and dark brown eyes. "She's your sister."

"Half sister," Craig clarifies.

"I have a sister," I say in a near whisper.

"Yes. She wanted to come, but we thought it would overwhelm you. You'll see her soon enough."

And there it is again. This automatic assumption that I'll be with her in Florida. And "soon."

"I can't wait," I lie. "We were actually talking." I nod to Sheriff Gleason and Grandma Gleason, who both straighten up in their seats, getting ready for their parts. "Christmas is in a couple weeks, and I thought I'd come down for the break. Then we have a long weekend for Martin Luther King Jr. Day in January, and winter break in March. I'd love to come stay with you then, if that's okay."

Paula and Craig exchange a look.

Shit. This can't be good.

"Oh." Paula's bottom lip starts to quiver. "But I've missed so much already."

"And we have plenty of time to catch up," I reply cheerfully, hoping it will stop her from crying. "We have years and years."

I don't want to hurt her. I really don't. But I can't just up and leave my entire life. It's going to be hard enough to continue without Dad, but at least I'll have the Gleasons.

"We are happy to have Ally stay with our family through her senior year," Sheriff Gleason says on cue. "She's been doing so well in school, it would be a shame to take her out when she only has a few months left until graduation."

"And, of course, we would like to invite your entire family up for her graduation," Grandma Gleason chimes in with a warm smile. "We'll have a big family party—the Gleasons and the Linsleys."

"It's McMullen now," Paula states. "My last name is McMullen. My maiden name is Cardiff."

"Well, whatever name, we're happy to have you." Grandma Gleason piles on the charm.

It doesn't work.

"The last thing we want is to take you away from your friends," Craig starts as Paula breaks down in tears. He rubs her back.

"No!" Paula says through sobs. She regains her composure and takes a few measured breaths. "I've missed fifteen years of your life. It's a miracle you've been found, and I came here with every intention of bringing you back with me. We have a room ready. We have wonderful schools near us. It's time for you to be with your real family."

Both Grandma Gleason and Sheriff Gleason wince at this.

"I know, and I'm so sorry, it's just . . ." Is she really going to make me say it? "I don't really know you, and you can't really expect me to just leave everything I know behind."

"Do I need to remind you it's your father's fault that we're strangers?" Paula snips.

Fair point.

"I know, I'm so sorry." I keep apologizing to her.

"My own daughter doesn't know me," Paula cries out. "And she doesn't want to." She holds on to Craig tightly.

God, I'm a selfish asshole.

Okay, plan B.

"I do want to get to know you. Truly." There's a part of me that even thinks I'm telling the truth.

Paula's sobs slow so she's simply sniffling. Craig hands her a handkerchief from his pocket.

"Would it be okay if I at least finish out the semester?" I beg. "It's only two more weeks." This is the worst-case scenario for me, but, I feel, a totally reasonable request. It gives me some more time here.

"Isn't your school currently surrounded by reporters?" Paula asks.

"They'll go away eventually," I reply. There has to be a bigger story to chase. So Amanda Linsley has been found. Let's all move on.

Paula sits for a few moments, while it feels like the entire room is holding its breath. Will she see that I need time to get adjusted to all of this . . . whatever the hell you want to call it?

Paula wipes her nose and then stands up. "You should know, the law is on *our* side."

Sheriff Gleason follows suit and rises. "We know, and please let's not start making threats about what's legal."

"Nobody's doing that," Craig butts in, even though Paula was making a threat.

"I'm simply stating the facts," Paula says with her jaw set. "She has to come back with us. I'm her rightful guardian."

Sheriff Gleason grimaces. "Believe me, I'm fully aware of the law. But we need to do what's best for Ally. She's been through a lot, and taking her away from everybody she knows might not be the wisest move right now."

"The reason she doesn't know her real family is because Dan stole her from me."

"But why should Ally be punished?" Sheriff Gleason counters.

"Yeah," I say aloud.

"I don't see how her living with her own family is punishing her," Paula replies, a stubborn determination on her face.

The room is silent again as the tension continues to rise. I didn't think today was going to be easy, but I definitely didn't think it would go this badly. I ball my hands into fists and let my nails dig into my palms.

Sheriff Gleason studies Paula, probably thinking about his hostage negotiation training. I certainly feel like a hostage at this current moment. I have absolutely zero control over what's going to happen to me. "Okay, I hear you. I simply think we need to take a minute—"

"No." Paula cuts off Sheriff Gleason, her face crimson. "Enough!"

My entire body goes numb. I collapse down on the couch. This can't be happening.

This can't be happening.

It can't.

I thought my so-called mother would do what's in my best

interest and let me stay here. I would come visit. In a few weeks when the weather will be so cold here you can feel it in your bones, I'd look forward to going to Florida.

"I'm sorry," she continues. I notice the bags under her eyes. She looks tired, defeated. "I really am sorry, but I have been living in hell for fifteen years not knowing where my daughter was. I want to know her. I have that right. I want my daughter to live with me. And that's what's going to happen." She gets up and heads to the bedroom, slamming the door behind her.

How can someone who doesn't know me be able to make these demands of me? If she really cared, she'd let me stay here.

"Ally?" Craig says in a soft voice. "I can't imagine how difficult this is for you. But do you understand where we're coming from?"

I can't move. I can't speak. And would it matter if I did? I have no choice in this matter.

Once, in health class, we learned that one of the reasons drunk drivers often walk away from car crashes is because they're relaxed when they're in the accident (which yes, causes said accident in the first place). It's bracing yourself that causes one to break limbs.

So I relax and accept the oncoming collision. Accept my fate, even though it absolutely terrifies me.

I move my head as much as I can, assuming he'll take it as a nod.

They're in charge, and there's nothing I can do about it.

"Great," Craig replies with a clap of his hands.

So it's settled. I'm moving to Florida.

Everything that I've worked for. Everybody I know and trust.
It's all gone.

Chapter

TWENTY-FOUR

"Is this the right one?" Marian holds up my ratty, but lucky, Donald Driver Packers jersey.

I nod. She and her mom had gone over to the house to get a few more things for me to pack. They were able to dodge reporters by cutting through our neighbors' backyard and using the back door to get into the house.

I'm leaving tomorrow. *Tomorrow.* Paula didn't feel the need to allow me to stay even an extra day. They argued that the press would catch on. I don't care what their excuse was.

Tomorrow, I'm getting on a plane for the first time in my life and flying to Florida. With my new family.

I can't say goodbye to Dad. I can't leave the house because of the media. I can't go to school.

Maybe it's best for me to go away. Maybe everybody in Valley Falls will be better off without me.

I fold up the shirt and put it in the suitcase, the third one I've packed for this trip. It sits on top of the ragged teddy bear Paula gave me yesterday. The rest of my stuff is going to be boxed up and sent to me. All of Dad's belongings will be put in storage.

Ms. Pieper is working with administrators to transfer all my credits and transcripts with my correct social security number. Next week, I'll be going to a new school in Florida.

It's all happening too fast.

Isn't the law supposed to protect its citizens? Instead, it's taking me away from my home and placing me with a stranger.

"Do you want some flip-flops or something?" Marian digs through her closet.

I nod. I've realized while packing that I don't have a lot of warm-weather clothes. Even in the summer we rarely get above eighty. It's currently eighty-two degrees in Tampa. In December.

That doesn't seem right.

"Are you going to talk?" Marian prods me.

I shake my head again.

"Well, you're probably going to change your mind when you find out what I have to say next. But, honestly, at this point, I'd take you yelling at me over the silent treatment."

I groan and fall back on her bed. I know what this means. I know exactly what this means.

Since I came home with the news yesterday—and my subsequent freak-out and breakdown, which kept me in tears and locked in Susan's room—the house has had a steady stream of visitors and phone calls. People wanting to see me before I leave.

I don't want to see anybody. I don't want to say goodbye. Saying goodbye when I have no idea when or even if I'll ever be back is going to be impossible.

The one person who has been a constant my entire life is gone. I'm not allowed to talk to him. I don't even know when I'll see him again.

What good would it be to take a daughter away from her father?

Although what good would it be to deny your mother your company? the angel on my shoulder whispers into my ear.

But I am going, I remind it. *I am fucking going.*

"Ally?" Marian says as she bites her lip. "There are a few people downstairs who want to say goodbye to you. Please let them."

I cover my face with my hands so she doesn't see the tears I've been fighting. Once I start, the floodgates will open and I won't be able to stop.

I'm going to leave the real hysterical sobbing for when I'm in Florida.

I'm Paula's problem now.

"Who's downstairs?" I ask, but I already know. It's going to be Rob, and Jan and Julia, and the whole Gleason clan.

Including Neil.

"It was pretty much impossible to keep any of them away. And I know it's hard for you, but they've also had your back. Nobody is talking. Every person in this town is protecting you. You're one of us. It doesn't matter where you live. Plus, you'll come back here for college."

"True." Even though I won't be eligible for most of the scholarships I was going to apply for since I'll no longer be a Wisconsin resident. And there goes that Academic Excellence Scholarship, which is all Dana's for the taking now. I'll also have to pay out-of-state tuition, which will be even more expensive. "I hope. That's what I want."

"If it's what you want, then it's going to happen," Marian replies with a confident nod.

Yeah, like what I want makes a difference anymore.

"We also have pizza downstairs. Good pizza." Marian wiggles her eyebrows at me. "And frozen custard."

"From Culver's?"

Marian scoffs. "Of course. Do you think we're going to skimp on your last night here?" She laughs before she turns a little sad.

"Hey." I go over and hug her. "I know I've been a tad, um . . ."

"Withdrawn? Moody? Sullen?"

"Yes. I appreciate everything. And I will see you again."

"Oh, if you think some huge scandal is going to tear us apart, you don't know me at all. Now, let's go downstairs. If you get uncomfortable, the safe words are 'Rob's an ass.'"

"Aren't safe words supposed to be things that aren't likely to be uttered?"

"Right." She holds my hand as we start walking toward the stairs. I can hear familiar voices in the kitchen. "So I guess it should be 'Rob's a genius.'"

"Do I hear my name?" Rob bellows from below. "Can't stop thinking of me, huh?"

He greets us at the foot of the stairs, his cocky grin on full display. "Yeah, so listen, Ally. I really don't like it when others take attention from me. And you created some huge national news story that has distracted people from the fact that I got a B-minus on my trig exam. That's right, B-minus." He pats himself on the back.

Same old Rob.

And I couldn't be more grateful for it.

The Gleason cousins are gathered around the table, eating pizza, and gossiping like the rug isn't about to be pulled from under us. This is what I want. For things to be normal. To not be the center of attention. To hear the family bickering and to understand the inside jokes.

The only person acting different is Neil. He's sitting on the other side of the table, quiet. He picks at his pizza and refuses to look at me.

Can't say I blame him.

"Oh God, can you just get over the fact that I can dance better than you?" Jan says to Rob.

"Have you seen my moves?" Rob gets up and starts to do something that I think is supposed to be the robot but honestly looks like a seizure. "They better reserve a section of the dance floor at prom for me. Nobody can get near my moves."

"That's because nobody wants to lose an eye," Marian says as she tries to take cover from his flailing limbs.

"Aw, man, prom is going—" Rob stops his dancing as he looks over at me. "Oh, nothing. Never mind."

The room gets quiet when everybody realizes I won't be here for prom. Or graduation. For most of high school, we talked about the big moments of senior year. I'm going to miss them all.

Rob clears his throat. "But for real, I think I should enter one of those dancing reality shows."

The room erupts into laughter and taunts at Rob, who gives me a little nod.

Neil leaves the table to get more soda.

I need to make things right between us before I leave.

I follow him to the refrigerator. "Hey," I say.

"Oh, hey." He gives me a shy smile. "I'd ask how you're doing but . . ."

"Yeah. This is nice, though. Sorry I haven't returned any of your messages."

He shrugs. "I get it. But it sucks that you have to go away."

"I know. I don't want to."

"Yeah . . ."

There's that awkwardness that we didn't used to have before. I did that. I ruined everything.

"And I'm also sorry for . . ." Is he going to make me say it in front of everybody? I wonder if they even know about our little tryst the other day.

Neil's cheeks redden. "Oh, no. You don't have to apologize for that. Like, ever. It was, um . . . It was pretty great, and I just wish I would've had the guts to do it sooner, that's all."

"Yo, Neil!" Rob calls out. "Can you grab me a Coke?"

Neil opens the fridge and gets out a can of Coke. He turns to walk away, but I grab his hand. "I don't regret it, either."

It's true. With everything I'm leaving behind, there's a pain in my heart each time I think about not being around Neil anymore. My lips tingle at the memory of his lips on mine.

"It's only for a while," Neil reminds me. "You'll be back for college."

I really hope that's true.

He studies me for a minute, then a smile spreads on his face and my stomach does a little flutter. "And, Ally, I've waited this long. I can wait a little longer. You're worth it."

Chapter

TWENTY-FIVE

"I have something to tell you," Sheriff Gleason says to me the next day. "I gave your message to your father."

"You did?" A foreign feeling swells in my belly: hope. I haven't felt hopeful in what seems like forever. Even though I can't say goodbye, I need to have some kind of word from him before I leave.

"Yes. He thanks you for the message, but most of all he wants you to know that he loves you. He made it easy so I couldn't forget." He gives me a wink. "He also said that he wants you to give your mother a chance. He knows he's deprived her of getting to see an incredible young woman grow up. And I agree with him. Paula and her family deserve a chance. They've been punished for years. So please try."

I nod. Dad has a point, even though, you know, *this is his fault.* I can't deny that Paula is my mother and I should try. It doesn't really matter, does it? The law says I have to go with my guardian.

Sheriff Gleason says I have to go. Even my dad wants me to go with them. So I'm going.

But I can be sad about leaving. All through packing and even now, I'm still in disbelief that I'm really moving. That this IS happening.

"Please give them until at least graduation." He says it as if it doesn't feel a lifetime away. "Then you can come back here. You'll be so busy with your last semester of senior year it'll fly by."

"Sure," I reply unconvincingly.

"Well, I better make sure there aren't any prying eyes around."

"Thanks, truly." I give him a quick hug before either of us tears up.

He nods at me one last time before exiting the house.

I head to the living room and sit on the couch, my packed bags by my feet. Marian and her mom wait with me for Paula and Craig to show up. Baxter's lying on the floor, his sad eyes looking up at me. He can tell there's something wrong. Dogs always have a sixth sense about these things. He whimpered when Marian took him out this morning, stubbornly pulling on his leash. I have a feeling he thinks I'm leaving him behind. He's probably going to hate being on the plane. He'll probably hate Florida, too, but at least I'll have him.

"They're here," Marian's mom says as she pulls the drapes down again. "Now, remember, call if you need anything."

"And I'll see you in a couple weeks," Marian replies.

Marian's mom called Paula last night to see if it would be okay if Marian came to visit me during Christmas break.

It's making an impossible situation just a tiny bit easier knowing I'll get to see a familiar face soon.

Baxter starts running in his little circle. He started doing this his second day here. I think he's waiting for Dad to walk through the door.

"Come here," I call to him. For some reason I don't want him enthusiastically greeting Paula and Craig. They haven't earned that yet. "Baxter!"

He yips in protest as I pick him up and place him in my lap. He tries to wiggle out, always wanting to be the welcome wagon, but I hold on tight.

"They know you have a dog, right?" Marian asks.

Oh my God. Did I forget to tell them Baxter was coming? Does he need a plane ticket?

"We'll figure it out," Marian's mom says as she opens the door.

There's a little bit of tension as Marian and her mom meet Paula and Craig.

"Hi, honey. You look great." Paula's eyes flicker down to Baxter. "And who is this?"

Baxter finally has had enough. He gets out of my grip to greet them. He jumps on Paula, who takes a step back. "Oh, goodness, he's lively."

"This is Baxter. I think I forgot to tell you I have a dog."

And there it is again. That look between her and Craig. That look isn't good.

"Oh, honey . . ."

"It's Ally," I snap, knowing full well she can't bring herself to call me by my name. My real name.

"Ally, sweetie, we can't have a dog. I'm allergic. Your sister is allergic."

Baxter's tail is wagging happily, despite Paula's refusal to pet him.

"Baxter can't come?" My lip starts to quiver as I fall back down on the couch.

If I have to leave Baxter behind, it will be my complete undoing. I'm desperately trying to hold on to something of my former life. Baxter is the most innocent creature in all of this. They are going to take him away from me.

"We can look after him," Marian offers.

"Well, that would be nice," Craig says. "And, you know, we can figure something out. Plus, we don't even have a ticket for him. Maybe he can visit at Christmas."

"I don't get to keep my dog," I state, not hiding the anger in my voice.

"We'll see what we can do. We don't want to keep you two apart," Craig says with a friendly nudge of his elbow, like he's on my side. Like he's my pal.

"Yes, we wouldn't want to take me away from the things and places I love," I say with every ounce of spite I can conjure.

The air goes out of the room. I'm not going to pretend this is okay. I may have no say in what's happening, but I can make my feelings perfectly clear.

"You know, we can maybe build a doghouse in the backyard and Baxter can stay there?" Craig offers.

I stand up. "Let's just go."

I'm done. I'm finished. I want to take one step after the other. Get on that plane. Get to Florida. Get to my new home. And do what Sheriff Gleason says: start counting down the days until I graduate and then I can return here.

I bend down and pet Baxter, who licks my cheek. "I'm sorry, buddy. Marian will take really good care of you. Be a good boy." Baxter barks and turns around again in excitement, thinking he's going somewhere with me. A tear trickles down my face, and he licks it. "I'll see you soon. I will."

I make quick with my goodbyes to Marian and her family. I feel if I stay another second in this house, I won't have the courage to ever leave again.

"I'll see you in two weeks," Marian whispers in my ear as she hugs me goodbye. "And I'm bringing Baxter with me."

"Thank you," I reply.

Sheriff Gleason checks for any reporters, and then we walk out to Paula and Craig's rental car, a fancy SUV. After one more round of hugs, I get in the back seat and take one last look at my friends, my family. I wave to them as Craig pulls out into the road.

Paula looks back at me. "It means so much to have you back with me, honey. I know this is hard on you, but don't think of it as an ending. Think of it as a new beginning."

Chapter
TWENTY-SIX

I can't stop staring, mouth wide open. I've never seen anything like it.

High above the clouds, the world looks surreal. Peaceful. Beautiful.

My heart raced when the plane took off from Green Bay. I spent the short flight to Chicago mesmerized by how blue Lake Michigan was and tried to spot certain landmarks in Milwaukee, but we were too high up for me to recognize my life from the past.

Now, as we get closer to Tampa, the feeling of wonder evaporates as I realize that with every passing second, I'm going farther and farther away from home.

I close my eyes now and lean back in my seat, letting the sun's warmth comfort me.

"Are you feeling okay?" Paula asks as she reaches for the sick bag.

"Amanda?" Craig says from the aisle seat. "I'm sorry, Ally. Ally," he repeats before he lets out a laugh. "There's a lot to get used to."

No shit, Sherlock.

"Are you okay?" Paula asks. Both she and Craig are studying me.

"Yeah," I reply. "I was wondering . . ."

"What do you need, honey?" Paula asks.

I've been forced to submit to Paula's demands so far, but there's one thing that I want—no, I need—so I don't completely come undone.

"I don't want to make waves, but I would really like you to call me Ally. It's what I'm used to."

She grimaces. "I understand, sweetheart, *Ally*. But Amanda is my mother's name. It's a family name. My mother, your grandmother, can't wait to see you again. All the family is just bursting with excitement."

"We couldn't keep them away if we tried," Craig says. "Believe me, I'm someone who has tried." He snorts as he playfully jabs Paula in the ribs.

"I'm excited to meet them," I say as Paula grimaces. "See them again," I correct myself, even though I have no recollection of my grandmother or anybody I've seen in the new album of photos Paula showed me during the first part of this flight.

I spent extra time looking at my baby book. It hurt to see pictures of Paula, Dad, and baby me as one happy family. There were countless photos of people holding me. Complete strangers.

"I know I'm named after your mother, which is great, but Ally is what I respond to. Plus, the media knows me as Amanda. All I want is to live a normal life, if that's even possible anymore. I don't want any special attention. If I go by Amanda Linsley, everybody will know who I am."

"Amanda McMullen," Craig corrects me.

Oh, right. They want me to take Craig's name since he, Paula, and my half sister, Sarah, all have the same last name. The word "adoption" has been thrown out, but I don't have the capacity to even comprehend that. So like with everything else, I bury it deep inside.

"Ally McMullen sounds just as good," I reply unconvincingly, giving Paula another win.

I'm trying to give her what she wants to stay on her good side. She's the one in charge of me. She decides when, or even if, I get to visit my friends again. But there are some concessions I refuse to make, starting with my name.

"Well, we need to sort out your name because we have to get you a new ID," Paula says. "We can't be having the police escort you every place you need one."

My driver's license, while valid because I did pass the test, was taken away since it had a fake name. Oh, and, you know, it was obtained using forged documents. Sheriff Gleason was required to escort me through airport security with my birth certificate since I didn't have a valid photo ID to fly. He must've called ahead because everybody was very polite about it, but we did get a few stares from other people waiting in line. Like, *Who is this teen getting a police escort?* They probably thought I was some troubled youth being hauled off to juvie.

If they only knew the truth.

Which is an odd thing to think, because I still feel as if *I* don't know the truth about me.

"Speaking of your grandmother." Paula pulls out her iPad and starts showing me more pictures. "There she is with your grandfather at our Fourth of July barbecue."

"You can see the fireworks over the water from our backyard," Craig adds.

She swipes her finger to another picture. "And who is this?" she quizzes me.

There's a photo of an older man and woman with two grown kids. I know this. "That's my aunt Eileen and uncle Fred."

"Correct!" Paula beams. "And they are with . . ."

The names of my cousins on Paula's side—I have five!—can't seem to stick in my brain. Since Paula is the youngest of her siblings, Sarah and I are a few years younger than our cousins, all of whom are either in college or have graduated and have real jobs.

I shake my head as Paula explains that the cousins in the picture are Mike and Mary. Mike works in IT and has two kids, and I begin to blank out as she tells me about Mary.

I'm never going to remember this.

How rude would it be to ask family members to wear name tags for the foreseeable future?

There's a chime as the seat-belt sign illuminates. We're told we are starting our initial descent into Tampa. I look out the window and see palm trees and the sun reflecting off the crisp blue waters of the Gulf of Mexico.

"I've never seen so much water before," I say, and then close my mouth. Of course I've seen this before, when I was little. There's this part of my life I can't seem to recall. Maybe being in Tampa will help me remember that these people I'm about to see aren't strangers. They're family. My family.

I wonder if remembering my past will stop me from being so uneasy about my future. But that's the thing: the future is scary because there are so many uncertainties. What helps people cope is having people there with them that they can count on.

With every second I'm on this plane, the distance is growing between me and the people I could rely on.

I've never felt more alone.

I take a deep breath so I don't break down in tears on the plane. Paula assumes my nerves are about the landing.

It's everything after that has me terrified.

"It's okay. It'll be just like Chicago, maybe a few bumps." She hesitantly rests her hand on top of mine. "We're going to try to not overwhelm you, but it's hard. There are so many people who are grateful you've been found. Nobody wants to wait another minute to see you again."

"Who will be there tonight?" I try to hide the dread in my voice. These two new people already have my brain at capacity. I don't know how much more I can take.

"Most of the family will be there."

"Dad's family, too?" I ask. I'd been so overwhelmed with Paula's family I'd forgotten to even ask about Dad's.

"No," Paula states flatly.

"Are they—"

Paula cuts me off. "It's going to be nice and casual."

So no getting answers about Dad's family from Paula. Guess that's another item on the list to tuck away until later.

"We're getting some Mexican food delivered." Paula puts her hand to her heart. "I didn't even think to ask if you liked Mexican food."

"Who doesn't like Mexican?" Craig asks. "Plus, in Florida you get authentic Mexican."

My thoughts go to Taco Tuesdays and watching telenovelas. It made Tuesday one of my favorite days of the week. Am I really never going to eat tacos and watch TV with my dad again? That's impossible. He'll eventually be let out of jail, and then . . .

Then what?

Can I go back? Can you ever go back once everything has been upended?

Craig, oblivious, continues, "You get a nice, long weekend to relax. We can do whatever you want. Sundays we usually go to church."

I raise my eyebrow. "What religion are you?"

Paula seems shocked. "Catholic. And so are you."

"I am?" Funny, I think I'd know that. Dad and I went to church on Easter and Christmas because everybody else did, but I never thought of myself as particularly religious.

"You were baptized," Mom states.

"Okay."

"I have pictures." She flips through my baby book again.

"I believe you." It doesn't matter that water was dumped on my head when I was a baby. I'm not a religious person. And let's be real: with all the shit that's been happening in my life, I really doubt the existence of some greater good in the universe.

Craig jumps in, sensing an argument brewing. "Hey, maybe tomorrow we can head to the beach, although it's a little chilly. I think it's in the midseventies."

A laugh escapes my throat. "Midseventies is cold?"

"Well, not compared to where we just came from. But the water will be cold. Our pool is heated, though, so if it's swimming you desire, we will make it happen."

Their house has a *pool*? Although looking out the window up here makes me think everybody in Florida has one. *It's your house now*, I try to remind myself, but it feels false. It's like I'm going to live somebody else's life. But I guess I am. This is Amanda McMullen's life.

Ally Smith is slowly being erased. She was the illusion. That life was a fabrication. This is the one that I was meant to have. Maybe someday it will even feel like mine.

"So what would *you* like to do this weekend?" Craig asks.

I'm grateful he seems to want me to have some sort of say in my new life.

"Anything you want!" he offers.

If I could do *anything*, I'd stay on this plane and fly right back to Wisconsin.

I flash back to my old life. What would I be doing this weekend? Hanging out with Marian. Going on a date with Neil.

I can't do any of that stuff. But there is one thing I can do.

"I'd like to watch the Packers game on Sunday. We're playing the Bears, and I don't want to miss it."

Craig shakes his head as he laughs. "We've got to get you into the Buccaneers. We have season tickets. Have you ever been to an NFL game? Nothing beats seeing it live."

I nod. "Yeah, my dad and I went to Lambeau last year for a preseason game." I pretend to not notice Paula bristle when I mention him.

That day was the best. We arrived at the stadium early to tailgate. Everybody was decked out in green and gold. Dad and I made burgers and brats on the grill. As we looked at the spreads around us—people grilling lobsters and steaks, one group had a long table full of only appetizers: dips, sausages, cheese, maybe a vegetable (probably not)—Dad declared us "amateurs." He went over to the "pros" to get some tips, and we were invited to join them.

"I'll distract them while you steal the rest of the pan," Dad joked when he noticed that I'd devoured almost the entire batch of this one dip. I don't know what it was, but it was cheesy and gooey and possibly the greatest thing I've ever eaten. "Your ability to put away food is definitely one of the top five reasons why I'm proud to be your father."

"What's number one?" I had asked.

"Putting up with your pops."

"I really should be given some medal for that," I had fired back, to which we both laughed, as we did, indeed, finish the rest of that dip.

"Ah, Lambeau," Craig replies to me now, taking away a good memory and forcing me back to this painful reality. "I've heard that you haven't seen a game until you see one in Green Bay."

"Yeah. It's amazing."

He smiles. I'm starting to warm up to him. He's trying, so I'm going to make an effort. "Well, I guess we'll have to go sometime."

"I don't think that's a good idea." Paula continues her role as General Buzzkill.

Does she really expect me to not go back to Wisconsin at some point?

"Anyway"—she changes the subject—"we don't feel that you should go to school right away. Maybe once the new year starts. Whenever you're ready."

I look out the window as bitterness slowly creeps into my veins. Sure, sure, I can take my time. No rush. *Whenever I'm ready.* Where was this patience before I was forced to move to Florida?

Not like I would ever be ready for this, but still.

The ground gets closer and closer. The wheels touch down on the runway. My heart begins to race as the plane slows. We're here.

Nothing is ever going to be the same again.

Paula turns her phone on. "This reminds me—we need to get

you a new phone." She has the latest iPhone and didn't hide how horrified she was by my phone. I don't want a new one. But if I get a smartphone, it'll be easier to stay in touch with everybody. Although the thought of seeing pictures of my friends continuing their lives without me may be a bit too much to handle.

How long before their lives go back to normal? How long before they forget me?

Every time we left for a new city, before Valley Falls, I'd had a friend or two who said they'd keep in touch. It would last for a few weeks before it would eventually fizzle out. Distance does that to relationships.

But I was so young and only knew those people for a few months. Things with the Gleasons would be different.

It has to be.

Paula's phone begins to chirp nonstop. "Goodness." She silences the ringer, but I can see the messages popping up on her screen. "Oh, no."

"What is it?" Craig asks.

Paula looks at me, concern etched on her face. "It's the media. They found out we're coming in today. The airport is surrounded."

TWENTY-SEVEN

"I am going to kill whoever did this!"

"Don't make a scene. It's going to be okay." Craig attempts to calm Paula down as she paces outside the arrival gate for our flight.

For nearly a week, I've been in a tiny town where *every single person* knew I was Amanda Linsley. There were reporters everywhere and not one person talked. Not a single one.

I've been in Florida with my new "family" for less than five minutes, and the media has swarmed the arrivals area.

Someone talked.

Craig steps away as he takes a phone call. I don't know what to say to Paula. I should probably comfort her, but I'm also pissed. It's my face that's going to be plastered all over the news. Most of what I want is impossible, but I should have the right to salvage an attempt at a regular life. While I realize that's somewhat impossible, a girl can still dream.

"Okay." Craig comes up to us with a confident nod. "Here's what we're going to do: Paula and I are going to go ahead and deal with the media. If they corner us, we'll simply say you're coming next week. We will ask, once again, for your privacy. We'll also tell them you're only here for a visit. Hopefully that will throw them off. I've also talked to the sheriff, who will have police at our house in case there are any issues. Luckily, we live in a gated community, so only authorized people can enter. The reporters won't be able to get near us. Ally, are you okay waiting here for about thirty minutes until we have everything sorted out? Paula's mom is going to meet you and take you to our house."

"No." Paula shakes her head, and tears start streaking down her cheek. I glance around the boarding area and see we're attracting some attention. My defenses immediately pick up. How much have they heard? What if someone figures out who we are? A single click of a camera phone could have everything crashing down.

Even though it's warm in the airport, I put the hood of my jacket over my head.

"It's fine. I can wait," I reply. I'm almost relieved to have a little more time before I step inside their house.

"No," Paula says more defiantly. "I can't. I can't let her go." She reaches for Craig. "Don't take Mandy away from me again. I can't bear it." She buries her head in his chest.

He brushes her hair. "It's okay. It's over. The nightmare is over. She's here now. She's not going to be taken away from you."

I keep forgetting about what this has been like for Paula.

While I have no memories of her, Paula had three years of my life engraved in her mind and heart. She carried me in her womb for nine months. I was once a part of her, and then I vanished.

I put my hand on her shoulder. It's the first time I've reached out to her—in any way. "It's okay. Nothing is going to happen to me. I'll be right behind you. I really don't want to be on TV, so this is for the best."

Paula sniffles for a few seconds before peeling herself away from Craig. She wipes her tears. "I'm sorry for blubbering. I'm just so scared . . ." She reaches out and touches my chin gently. "I don't want you to disappear from me again."

"I'm not going anywhere," I tell her. It's true. I'm legally in her custody now, and I couldn't leave even if I tried.

I'm slowly becoming resigned to the fact that Paula deserves to spend time with the daughter who disappeared. Maybe I shouldn't think only about myself for a while.

Craig holds her hand. "We've got to go. We don't want the journalists to be suspicious."

"I bet it was Randy," she says. "He's always so desperate for attention. I can see him blabbing. Makes him feel big, important. The jackass."

"We'll figure it out," Craig says as he rubs her back. "But we've got to go."

"Maybe Man—Ally should go first?"

"Too great a risk for her to be recognized," Craig counters. He reaches into his back pocket to get his wallet. He pulls out a twenty-dollar bill and hands it to me. "Why don't you get yourself a treat while you wait? Your grandmother is going to text you so you have her number and then let you know when the coast is clear."

I nod as I look at the twenty-dollar bill. It's like nothing to him. Dad and I could make twenty dollars stretch to feed us for an entire weekend if we needed it, and sometimes we did.

Paula rummages through her bag. "Do you remember what your grandmother looks like?" She hands me a photo of a woman with graying hair holding me on my third birthday, right before I went away.

In the photo, I'm smiling with cake smeared on my face. Grandma is laughing. As I look at this photo, it feels like it could be anybody else. Not me.

"I'm going to text you every ten minutes," Paula says. "And please respond right away. I want to make sure you're okay."

"I will," I reply.

"Okay." Craig gives me a smile. "All you need to do is take this train here to baggage claim. We'll get your bags, so don't worry about that. Your grandmother will be waiting for you, and we'll see you in about an hour or so."

"Great!" I try to muster some enthusiasm. I'm suddenly nervous about being left in this giant airport alone. What if I get lost? What if I can't find my grandmother? What if I get in a wrong car? What if I actually get kidnapped?

Paula puts both hands on my shoulders and looks up at me. It's the first time I've noticed that I'm a few inches taller than she is. Must've gotten my height from Dad. "I will never let anything bad happen to you, ever again."

And just like that, the nerves go away. I believe her. And it's weird that she knew what I was thinking without my having to say it.

Maybe moms and daughters have a bond that can't be ripped away by distance and time?

I see a Starbucks up ahead. "I'll be there." I try to sound nonchalant about it, but I've never been to a Starbucks. *I know.* Valley Falls is too small to have any coffee place, let alone a major chain. There are a few in Green Bay, but I've never been able to justifiably cough up five dollars for a coffee. But now I have twenty dollars. I can get a large! And maybe a cookie or something.

And like the emotional pendulum I seem to be on, I feel guilty that going to Starbucks with money from Craig makes me excited while Dad is rotting in jail. Am I really that easily bribed?

(That answer, it appears, is yes.)

"See you soon." Paula grips me in a tight hug before she walks off with Craig, looking back every few seconds. Once they board the train to baggage claim, I get in line at Starbucks.

I begin to analyze everybody ahead of me, a game Dad and I used to play: guess the person's life story, like the guy in a business suit in front of me. He's probably on his third coffee of the day, heading home after some very important business meeting.

We didn't have many strangers back home, so we could only play this when we were at some diner on our way back from fishing. Or when we were in Green Bay. It shouldn't be surprising that after we became hooked on telenovelas, the simple observations turned into full-blown conspiracies. Dad would automatically assume that this guy, who just looked at his watch, was late to meet up with his mistress, who also happened to be his sister-in-law.

Come to think of it, this guy does look a little anxious. He's shaking his right knee impatiently. What's he hiding?

I look around again and realize nobody is giving me a single glance. Why would they? I'm simply a girl getting coffee. They have no idea how much I'm hiding or who I am, how I am doing something as mundane as getting something to drink but on the inside I'm torn apart. I don't know what's ahead of me or, really, what was behind me. I don't know who I am or what I want. My life has been ripped in two, but to anybody else I look whole.

My mind flashes back to last week. My birthday, with cake for lunch and dinner with Dad. Even though it wasn't really my birthday. How could that have been only a week ago?

"What can I get you?" the girl behind the register asks me.

"Oh," I say with a start. "Ah, yeah. Sorry. Um, can I have one of those frozen drinks?"

"A Frappuccino?" the barista clarifies. "What size? And which flavor?"

"Oh, um . . ."

Who knew ordering a coffee could be so complicated? After proving to everybody behind me that I'm new to Starbucks and don't know the proper way to order a drink, I pay for my Venti Mocha Frappuccino and brownie and sit down.

My phone buzzes with a text from Paula. I tell her I'm inhaling sugar. Then another text comes from an unknown number. And it's a long text with proper spelling and punctuation, which signals that it's from an adult.

Hello, it's your grandmother. I can't wait to see you. I'll let you know when you can come out. Should be a few more minutes. Love you.

OK, I reply, unsure what else there is to say. I can't comprehend saying I love her back. I mean, I don't really know her, so how do I know if I love her? It's weird.

I spend the next twenty minutes looking at all the travelers on their way to unknown destinations. I usually have a book with me when I'm out by myself since I don't have a fancy phone to distract me. I didn't bother packing a book in my backpack because I knew I didn't have the mental capacity to get swept away into a fictional universe, even though that might be what my brain needs the most: diversion.

There are a few more texts from Paula:

Are you all right?

Is anybody giving you trouble?

Is everything okay?

Do you need anything?

How are you feeling?

I reply to each right away. Then the text comes from my grandmother saying that the media have left and I can meet her.

I'm uneasy getting on the train. It's not that I'm afraid of getting lost; it's that I'm nervous meeting this woman. When I think of grandmothers I think of Grandma Gleason.

I wonder what she's doing right now. And Marian. And Neil.

I get off the train and follow the signs to baggage claim. I pass by security and stop as soon as I see her.

It's not that I recognized her from a memory or the photo Paula showed me, but it's the look on her face. A warm smile and pride in her eyes. It's a look for someone you love. It says I'm safe. It says I'm wanted.

"Hello, my sweet granddaughter," she says as she takes a few hesitant steps toward me. "You've grown so much." She has on coral capris and a matching cardigan over a flowered shirt. Her bright white hair is short, and she has makeup perfectly applied. But there are those eyes. The same eyes that I have. That Paula has.

"Hi . . . Grandma."

I can't seem to bring myself to call Paula "Mom," but for some reason I'm compelled to be more at ease with this woman. Maybe it's because I had a grandmother in Grandma Gleason, so it's not a completely foreign concept to me. Not like a mom.

She steps closer to me while I'm frozen in place. She takes my hands and stares into my eyes. "You have grown into such a beautiful young lady." She puts her wrinkled hands gently on my face. "Now, let's get you home."

Home.

Grandma Amanda wraps her arms around my shoulders as we walk toward the exit. "Yes, it'll be good to get you home."

There's that word again: *home*.

I nod and smile along, even thought I feel empty inside.

I don't know if I'll ever feel at home again.

Chapter
TWENTY-EIGHT

"Ah, here we are." Grandma Amanda pulls into a crowded driveway.

The house in front of me is a giant two-story, light yellow, stone-like house with blue shutters and a big dark blue door, which has a WELCOME HOME sign hanging above it. This house looks shiny and new compared to where I used to live. There are cars lining the curb and in front of the two-story, three-car garage down the driveway.

She gets out of the car and I follow her. We were quiet most of the drive. She'd occasionally mention a favorite restaurant or the exit toward the beach. I stared out the window, with my nose practically pushed against the glass, just like Baxter used to do. A pang in my stomach happens when I think about Baxter. He must be so confused and wonder where I am. And Dad. Baxter's simple little life has also been overturned.

Push it down, push it all down, I remind myself. It's the only way to get through this.

Grandma Amanda opens the front door. Paula and Craig are in a large living room with a small girl next to them. She has Paula's heart-shaped face with sandy-brown hair. Her arms are crossed, and her face has the complete opposite expression of Paula's. She clearly does not want to be here. Or is it me she doesn't want here?

"Welcome home," Paula says as she gives me another hug. "I'm so glad you made it home safe."

My stomach drops every time she mentions the word "home."

"And this," Craig says as he pulls the girl in front of him, "is Sarah. Your sister."

"Half sister," Sarah clarifies.

Craig bends down and whispers in her ear, but I can still hear. "What did we talk about?"

Sarah grimaces at me and then extends her hand in a formal manner. "Welcome to our home," she repeats in a robotic voice with the slightest inflection on the word "our."

"It's your home now," Craig says to me.

There's a moment of awkward silence between us. I'm sure this isn't the grand homecoming they were expecting.

"We want to give you a little tour before we go out to the back and have the family descend upon you." Paula gestures to the large living room with cozy couches and a huge flat-screen TV. I follow her into a kitchen with shiny stainless steel appliances and a refrigerator that's at least twice the size of the one we had back home. The kitchen leads into a dining room with a long rectangular table that seats six. On the other side are two French doors that open to a screened-in backyard with a pool, patio, and, oh, about a few dozen pairs of eyes staring at me.

"Shoo!" Paula waves away the crowd that has gathered to gape at me. I feel like an animal in a zoo. Same concept, really. Those animals are also trapped in an artificial habitat that will never be their real home. "They are all so excited to see you," she explains.

Craig claps his hands together. "Why don't we go upstairs so you can see your room?"

The four of us head upstairs on plush carpeting to a long hall-way with four doors.

"This is Sarah's room." Craig gestures to a closed door. Sarah stands in front of it with her arms crossed, not making any movement to let me see it. "Well, let's move on to our bedroom."

We walk to the end of the hallway where Craig and Paula sleep. The room's huge. In addition to the biggest bed I've ever seen, there's a chaise lounge in the corner next to a door that opens to a deck that overlooks the backyard.

"Now, let's get to the best part," Craig says as we walk down to the room across from Sarah's. He opens the door to another bedroom. There's a large bed with a fluffy floral duvet. The dark wood and silver bed frame match the two nightstands and large chest of drawers. It opens into a bathroom that looks like it belongs in a hotel: all white marble and stainless steel fixtures. I'm so afraid I'm going to break or mess up something. I look down at my beat-up All Stars and hope I'm not tracking any dirt on the off-white carpeting.

"We can make any changes you want," Paula adds. "I also have a couple boxes from your old room for you to go through. Obviously, it's all from when you were a baby, but I thought you might want a few things."

Craig puts his arm around her. "We've only been in this house for two years because your mother didn't want to leave the house you grew up in."

"I was convinced you'd show up one day and I wouldn't be there," Paula says.

"The new owner has a file for what to do if a girl knocks on the door and starts asking questions. A very large file."

Wow. Since I have no recollection of living in Florida, I wouldn't even know where that old house was, but I'm not about to inform Paula of that.

Sarah remains in the doorway, a neutral expression on her face.

Actually, it's not neutral at all. There are quick flashes of boredom, then anger, but most of all it's clear she is not having any of this.

Me too, I want to say to her. We have more in common than she realizes.

"This is great," I say, because it is a really nice room. It's just another thing I'm accepting: this is my new room. "I don't need anything." Plus, I don't have enough clothes to fill half the drawers, let alone the walk-in closet.

"Well, we can go down to the party whenever you're ready," Paula says.

I don't think I'll ever be ready for what waits for me downstairs.

I guess there's no point stalling. It would also be nice to get away from the hateful glare Sarah is currently giving me.

"I'm ready," I lie.

We walk downstairs. Sarah breaks off from the group and opens the door to the patio. Noise that was floating from a bunch of different conversations stops as everybody turns around. I freeze.

"Here she is!" Paula says with a beam. "Our baby has returned home."

A round of cheers erupts, and I'm enveloped in a flurry of hugs, introductions, and a few tears.

This is my family, I keep reminding myself.

This isn't real life, my head screams back.

But I stuff that thought into the recesses of my mind. I allow a numbness to come over me. I try to play the part, as if I've been beamed into someone else's life and I'm supposed to simply go along. So I smile and say hello. The new faces are never-ending. I'm inundated with questions. I answer how I'm doing a bunch of times—*fine, thank you*—and decline the plates of food that keep appearing in front of me.

Paula stays by my side and keeps telling me how I know everybody. All these faces and names that I'm trying to keep straight offer their claim to me: this one was my first babysitter, that one would give me piggyback rides. I try to hold on to the stories, but they float out of my grasp a moment later.

It's like there is a black hole in my memories. I wish I could have one moment, even a flash of recognition. How could being around all these family members not click something in my brain?

"Are you sure I can't get you anything to eat?" Paula asks.

"Yeah, I'm okay." Maybe later, when the house is quiet and I'm . . .

What?

What exactly do I think is going to happen when it's just Paula, Craig, Sarah, and me? Do I really believe that it's possible to wake up one day and feel as if everything has righted in my life? Do I even want that? What would that say about everybody back home, my real home?

I step away from the group to get some air and distance from the questions that keep spiraling in my head. A guy in his twenties with a beard and receding hairline comes over to me. He's wearing a Buccaneers jersey and cargo pants. A beer is in his hand. "Hey there."

"Hi," I reply, trying to search for his name.

"It's good to have you home."

"Thanks." It's the same conversation I've had with everybody. I think it's the only thing we know to say to each other.

"I get that Paula said you aren't interested in media, but, man, you could go on like the *Today* show and probably meet a bunch of celebrities. You should enjoy your fifteen minutes of fame."

I don't want fame. I don't want any of this. Besides, I'm not famous. "Amanda Linsley" is having a bit of a moment, but Ally would like it to be over.

He shakes his head at me. "You're not thinking about all that money you can bank on this. Get a book deal or something. Milk it. That's what I'd do."

I stare blankly at him, not even remotely interested in what he's suggesting.

"I got some buddies who could help you."

"It's okay." I look around for Paula. The one time I need her hovering, she's disappeared.

"Hey." He takes out his phone. "Let's get a selfie." He positions himself next to me and holds out his phone. He's smiling, while a horrified and uncomfortable me appears on his screen.

I put my head down and step out of the shot. "I'd really prefer—"

"Randy!" Craig comes over, an annoyed expression on his face. "We made it very clear we do not want any pictures of Ally taken today. Okay? Now, leave her in peace. You and I need to have a little conversation later."

"So she's going to keep her name?" he asks as if I'm not standing right there.

Craig drags him by the elbow. I can't hear what he's saying, but it's clear there's a heated exchange between the two.

Randy. That name's familiar. I search the plane ride conversation to figure out what Paula had to say about Randy. Is he an uncle or cousin?

Randy stomps out of the backyard. Craig comes over. "I'm really sorry about that. Randy is a bit of a—What's the polite way to say he's a little obsessed with celebrities? I didn't want to invite him, because I knew he'd be trouble, but your mother insisted that everybody be included." Craig clenches his jaw.

Oh, that's right. Randy's the one they think alerted the media. I make a mental note to stay as far away from him as possible. I can't believe Paula knows this about him but still insisted he be invited. The Gleasons would never tolerate that kind of behavior from a family member.

But you're no longer with the Gleasons.

"You can't choose your family," Craig says as he throws his arms up in the air.

Like I need to be reminded of that.

"How are you holding up?" he asks. "I'm sure this is a lot. I was overwhelmed the first time Paula introduced me to her family, so I get it."

I give Craig a small smile. "It is a lot. Would it . . ." I feel bad abandoning everybody, but I need to get away from this.

"Do you need a break?" Craig has read my mind. He seems to get me more than Paula does.

"Yeah. Would it be okay if I went to my room for a bit?"

"Of course. Whatever you need. Do you want to take some food up?"

Looking over at the table full of food does make my stomach rumble, but I'm too terrified of spilling in the pristine bedroom. "Maybe later."

I look down to avoid eye contact and more awkward conversations as I head upstairs to the room where I'm staying. I get a little excited that there's a TV in there. Part of me wants to shut the door, turn on the TV, and pretend I'm on vacation, since I don't know what else to do. It takes all of fifteen minutes to put my clothes in the closet and toiletries in the bathroom.

Now what?

I sit down on the bed and stare at the Monet print that's near the door. I read through the dozen or so "How are you?" texts from various Gleasons checking in. I smile at the thought of my extended family worrying about me, but I don't know how to reply. Besides, it's too hard to think about what they're doing now. While I know their lives have changed with me leaving, they'll eventually go back to their routines and lives. It'll be like I was never there at all.

I startle as I look up and see Sarah studying me from the doorway.

"Oh, hey."

She gives me a blank stare in reply.

"Ah, do you want to come in?" I offer. I want to take a sledgehammer to the wall she seems to have built around us. Part of me doesn't blame her. I'm this stranger who has come into her house to live with her. Her life has changed as well. Since she stays in the doorway, I extend an olive branch. "I know this is weird."

"You think?" Her eyes narrow as she pushes off the door frame. I think she's going to leave, but she takes one step into the bedroom and tilts forward. I find myself leaning toward her as well, waiting to hear what she's going to tell me. Maybe she'll give me the inside scoop on living with Craig and Paula.

She shakes her head back and forth as she examines me up and down. "I wish you were never found."

And with that, she turns on her heels. I jump as she slams her bedroom door shut.

Chapter
TWENTY-NINE

Sarah's words echo in my head as I lie in bed. It's not even ten o'clock, but after everybody left, I claimed exhaustion and got into bed. I had at first turned the TV on and was overwhelmed by how many channels they have. I came across *The Empire Strikes Back*, one of the Star Wars movies Dad and I always watched on my birthday, and had to shut off the TV.

I've been staring at the darkened ceiling ever since.

I have no idea what to do about Sarah, because I agree with her 100 percent. If I hadn't been discovered, I would be in Valley Falls right now, having Thursday game night with Dad. Instead I'm in a strange house in an unfamiliar bed.

I turn over on my side and see the glow of the hallway light outlining the bedroom door. On the other side: a half sister who resents me and a mother I don't know.

I grab my cell phone from my bedside table and turn it on.

I need my best friend right now. It's been a little over twelve hours since I last saw her, but it feels like months.

Greetings from Florida, I type.

My phone rings a few seconds later, and Marian's name appears on my small screen.

"Hey," I say.

"Are you okay? We are so worried about you. How are things? How is the home? How is everybody? We miss you so much." She's speaking so fast I don't have a chance to answer. Which is good, since I don't know if I can even speak. I wipe away the tears that have plopped onto my pillow.

"It's been hard," I admit. "Really hard."

"Oh, Ally." There's a tremor in her voice. "I'm so sorry. I don't know what to say. I want you here."

"I want to be there. I don't belong here." I know how much it means to the people I met today to have me here, but I'm not one of them. You can slap whatever name you want on me—Cardiff, McMullen—but it doesn't automatically make us a family. I'm the person Dad raised me to be. I can't change because I now live somewhere else. Sharing DNA doesn't automatically make you a family.

I hear voices in the background asking about me. Marian shushes them, and then I hear her walking up the stairs. There's an excited bark.

"How's Baxter?" I ask, and the injustice of it all breaks me. Sure, Paula now gets her daughter, but what do I get?

Nothing.

I get nothing.

"Baxter is good. No surprise that we can't help but spoil him rotten. Next time you see him, he's going to be so fat. Right, Baxter?" Baxter barks in response.

"I'm getting an iPhone tomorrow, so we can FaceTime."

"I hope you get a good package, because we are going to have to FaceTime every day."

"Every second."

"It's so good to hear your voice. We were all freaking out when we saw the news reports from the airport. Uncle Brian was beyond angry someone tipped the media off."

"Oh." I hadn't watched the news or googled "Amanda Linsley" since I arrived. I don't want to know what's being said. I hope that the press will eventually move on to a different target. Paula and the sheriff here talked about releasing yet another statement asking for my privacy. All I know is that I don't feel comfortable being out in public with the media vultures circling. Not like I see myself feeling okay about anything ever again.

"How did you end up leaving the airport without being discovered?"

I tell her about my grandmother and then about the party. And Sarah.

"Oh, no. I'm so sorry." Marian's voice, which is usually full of life and bubbly, is strained. "I'm sure she just needs time."

"I know." I think that's what we all need. But will I really wake up one day and be okay with everything? Or will it happen little by little? All I know is that when I have woken up every morning since this all began, I have a few seconds when I don't realize what's happened. For a few precious seconds I can convince myself that it was a horrendous nightmare. When I finally remember that no, it's real, I feel even worse. Every day it gets worse. Every day there's a new revelation.

It was harder and harder to get out of bed at Marian's house—there was that one day I didn't leave the bed. That was when I was in a familiar house with familiar people. Am I even going to have the strength to get up tomorrow and face the day?

And the day after that.

An idea hits me. "Hey, you remember that calendar system with my dad?"

"Yes! You were the gold star queen!"

"Maybe that's what I need to do: get a calendar and get a star for every day I survive here. Your uncle said I just had to graduate from high school. So for every ten, no, make it every five days I get through, I can get an ice cream or Frappuccino or something. Baxter won't be the only one packing on the pounds."

"Whatever it takes to get you through."

I nod, even though Marian can't see me.

Whatever it takes to get me through.

"So, how was school?" I ask, desperate to get my mind off me for a few minutes.

"It's school. Reporters have stopped stalking it. So I guess that's good."

"Yeah. What else is going on there?"

"Nothing. We're mostly just missing you. Umm . . . I know

you have a lot going on, but can you please text Neil back? He's about to have an aneurysm."

"Yeah. I wasn't in a very chatty mood today."

"So . . . ," Marian starts, and right then I know she knows.

Of course she knows.

"Oh God, he told you."

There's a slight pause. "YES!" she screams. "I can't believe you didn't tell me you were macking down with my cousin."

"You didn't just refer to it as 'macking down,' did you?"

"What would *you* call it?"

Mauling, but I keep that thought to myself.

Marian continues, "You always had your act together with everything else, but it took you forever with him. I've wanted you two to get together for forever. We all have! You guys were the will-they-or-won't-they of the group!"

"What? You guys have talked about Neil and me?"

"All the time!"

"And why didn't you tell me this?"

"Because I knew you'd be horrified and I didn't want to force you to do anything you didn't want. I mean, it's my dream for you to be like my cousin-in-law or whatever. And you should've seen the look on his face when he told me. His face, no lie, was the color of his hair. It was hilarious and pretty adorable because he was both confused about what happened, but also, like, totally turned on by it."

"Marian!" I scold her, even though I'm laughing. I have to

admit, Neil is a nice distraction. I can think about him and think about possibilities, and it won't really matter because I'm hundreds of miles away from him.

"Believe me, I don't want to think about my cousin being all hot and bothered—"

"Oh my God! Stop!" Although I'll be honest: I keep thinking about that kiss as well. And it does leave me with some feelings of the warm and tingly variety.

There's a knock on my door, and Paula cracks it open. "Everything okay in here? I heard a scream."

I put my hand over my phone. "Sorry. I'm talking to Marian."

Paula looks blankly back at me.

"She's my best friend from home."

No recognition.

"Her uncle's the sheriff."

Nada.

"You picked me up from their house. She's coming here for winter break."

Did she take a pill to completely wipe her mind clear of her time in Wisconsin? Seriously.

"Um, she has my dog."

There it is. Paula winces at the mention of Baxter. "Oh, that's nice. Let me know if you need anything."

"I will." She gives me one more glance before closing the door.

"Sorry, that was Paula checking in on me," I say to Marian.

"Do you call her Paula or Mom?"

"I try to avoid calling her by any name."

There's a pause for a slight moment. "Do you think you'll be happy there?"

I weigh the options in my head. It doesn't take long since I don't have many of them. I'm stuck here, so I either have to suck it up and get used to it . . . or I guess I could just have a horrible attitude and make everybody's lives, including mine, miserable.

"I'm going to try."

"Oh God, Ally, I can smell the bullshit from here."

This is the thing about Marian. She can sense the lie on me even when we're on the phone.

"I don't know what to do," I confess.

"I can't even imagine what you're thinking. And my parents told me that I'm supposed to be positive and everything and that you have this family that has missed you, but it's not fair. And I'm so pissed. I'm pissed that you've been taken away from us. I know I should be only thinking about you, and I am, it's just this sucks."

"It does!" It's nice to say it aloud and stop burying it inside.

"I wonder if I can kidnap you when I visit. Or is a kidnapping reference too soon?"

"It's not." I know my father did this horrible thing, but I still don't understand: how can someone kidnap their own child? I'm pretty sure if Paula and Dad would've gotten a proper divorce and I had to go to court and choose between them when I was little, I would've chosen Dad. So what's the difference?

Wait a second. How can Paula and Craig be married if Paula and Dad never got a divorce? Or did they? Can you divorce someone who has disappeared? There's really so much I don't know about what happened. Or about Paula and what she did when she figured out I was gone.

I realize, I really do, that I should have more compassion for this woman who is my mother. I don't know her. So maybe I should try to understand her. To find out about my life before. So far she's stayed with safe subjects: pictures and stories about family members. Knowing the good is fine and all, but I also need to understand the bad. How things between my parents could go so wrong that they were living apart. That Dad was convinced she was going to take me away from him.

But would I believe her? Is she a trustworthy source?

Dad is in jail now. Whatever happened between them had to have been bad for him to risk everything to get me away.

"I don't feel safe here," I say, so quietly Marian doesn't hear me.

Is that really true, though? There's nothing Paula or Craig has done to make me think they're going to do something bad to me. It's more that I don't feel like myself here. Then there's Sarah. I'm tempted to lock the bedroom door because who knows what she might do to me in the middle of the night.

I kick the duvet off me and go over to the door and lock it, just in case.

"My parents keep saying your mom should be given a chance," Marian says, her voice also low.

"I know. And I'm horrible for wanting to leave."

"No, you're not," Marian assures me. "Yeah, it sucks for Paula, and my mom feels bad for her, but what about you?"

"Exactly. Am I being selfish for only thinking of me in all of this?"

"Ally." Marian uses the voice she reserves for whenever she needs to be blunt with Rob because he's being an idiot. So she uses it a lot. "This is your life. And none of this is your fault. You shouldn't be punished because of it."

"Thanks."

"Besides, it's only six months until you graduate. Then you can come up to school here. And we now have a sweet place to go to during winter break to de-ice ourselves. You can survive six months there, right?"

"I guess." She's right. That is a lot of ice cream rewards, but I can do it. I finish out my senior year here and then go to Wisconsin for school. I can get a summer job and stay with the Gleasons.

"But poor Neil. Forcing that dude to wait that long to be reunited with his one true love will be torture."

"Marian!" I say before burying my head into a pillow.

Although this is the first time in a week that I don't completely dread the future.

Chapter
THIRTY

Florida is weird.

Not only am I sweltering in December, but this is an outdoor mall, too. And not any outdoor mall, but one over an hour away from Paula's house, just in case anybody might recognize her. Because it's her face that has been plastered on the news, not mine.

So far.

This is my new life now. Taking precautions simply to go outside.

Not sure what's stranger: being overly cautious of every person we cross paths with or shopping outside in December.

Every mall I've ever been to has been enclosed. The thought of walking around outside in the winter to shop doesn't make sense. It would probably be the worst business decision to have one of these malls in northern Wisconsin. There are times in the winter when it's so cold, you can't be outside for more than five minutes without the risk of frostbite.

But I love those days. We don't have school, so we hang out at home, watch TV, and eat junk food. It's a little vacation from real life.

As I enter the cell phone store with Paula and a continually scowling Sarah in tow, I feel like this is a vacation from my life. None of this feels permanent.

Or I at least won't let my mind realize that this is my life now. It's Ally McMullen's. Whoever she is.

When I woke up this morning in a new bed and foreign room, I had a moment of confusion, followed by panic. When I finally remembered where I was and why I was there, I felt even worse.

At breakfast Paula tried to act like everything was normal. Just a regular morning as we sat down for breakfast at a diner on the way to the mall. There were eggs and bacon served with a side of stilted conversation.

Sarah has refused to utter a single word to me or even look in my direction. I thought she might be happy that Paula kept her out of school on a Friday. But, nope.

I wish I had school to distract me. We're looking at my new school on Monday, and I'll begin classes there on Tuesday. It's silly for me to start so close to Christmas break, but I need something to do with my time. Staring numbly at the wall is getting tiring.

"Hello!" Paula says brightly to one of the store associates. She gestures at the bags we're carrying. "It's been a day."

Yes, it has.

I've never been that kind of girl who loved going into stores and trying on a bunch of outfits and not solely because we didn't have the money. When there were sales, I'd go and stock up on the basics: jeans, long-sleeved shirts, sweaters for winter, and a good pair of sneakers and boots. I didn't need much. That doesn't change simply because I'm in a new state.

Paula, however, disagreed with my logic. It shouldn't surprise me since for a trip to the mall she's dressed in black skinny capris, a silk tunic and light cardigan, layers of four different necklaces, and black wedge sandals. Her long hair is curled, and she has on more makeup than I wore to Homecoming. I, however, am in basic jean shorts and a nondescript green T-shirt with Marian's plastic flip-flops.

Paula wanted me to get a whole new wardrobe since I only have one other pair of shorts and a half-dozen short-sleeved shirts. I felt uncomfortable having her spend money on me, but it seemed to make her happy. So I, once again, was forced to play the role of agreeable daughter and tried on what she pulled for me and ignored Sarah's glare when I'd come out of the changing room in a new outfit that was a bit more girly (lace tank tops and short skirts) than I would normally pick out for myself.

"Oh, so *she* gets the new iPhone," Sarah complains when Paula picks up a phone for me. I shudder when I see the price.

"I really don't need anything fancy," I say for what feels like the four-hundredth time today.

Maybe Paula's making up for lost time, but with every swipe of the credit card my guilt deepens.

"Well, we might as well get you the newest one," Paula reasons.

"Can I go to Starbucks?" Sarah asks.

"I think we should stay together," Paula replies.

"She's here, okay?" Sarah points at me like she's accusing me of something. "Everything is fine, just perfect. You have what you wanted. What you always wanted."

"Sarah, sweetheart." Paula reaches out to her, but Sarah backs away.

"I can be on my own for a few minutes. I'm eleven. My friends are allowed to go to places by themselves."

"Come here," Paula says sternly as she takes Sarah by the arm. She leads her to a corner for some privacy. I try to ignore their not-so-quiet argument.

"Here we are," a guy with brown skin and long locs says to me as he brings out my new phone. "Do you want to keep your number and plan, or do you need a new one?"

"Ah." I have no idea what I need. "I think I need a new plan?"

"Is that your mom?" He gestures over at Paula, who attempts to give Sarah a kiss on the forehead, but Sarah storms out of the store, stomping with every footfall.

"Ah . . ." I mean, yeah, Paula is technically my mom. The guy looks confused, for which I don't blame him. "Is that your mom?" is a pretty simple question. For most people.

"Um, Paul—" I stop myself. "Mom?" I call out to Paula. She

freezes, and there's a weird look on her face. I guess it's a combination of shock and joy. I don't really know how to describe it.

Paula walks toward us. Her hands are on her heart while her eyes are filling with tears. "That's the first time you've called me Mom. Well, in at least fifteen years."

The sales guy looks between us like he's trying to figure out an equation. He's also probably wishing he were waiting on anyone else.

"Um, yeah, so." I gesture at the phone and focus my attention on it. It's too difficult to see the look Paula is giving me. How much she wants me to fit into her world. And how I simply can't. "Ah, I think I need a new plan."

"What? Oh, yes. Yes, the phone." Paula shifts back to her hyper shopping mode. "We want all the accessories, and Aman— Allison needs to join our family plan."

The guy looks between us again, but he gets to business once Paula pulls out her platinum card.

I zone out while they go over my contract and new number. I come back as Paula asks him about his orange-and-blue lanyard with alligators on it. "Oh, I see you went to Florida."

"Go, Gators!" he replies.

"My daughter"—and she says those words with so much pride—"is a senior, and we need to start looking at schools."

"Can't go wrong with Florida."

I nod along since I'm certainly not going to bring up in front of a stranger that I have no intention of going to college in Florida.

"And the weather here is way better than Wisconsin," Paula says as she tucks a strand of my hair behind my ear.

"Wisconsin?" the guys says with a laugh. "It is *cold* there. Wait a second, do not tell me you're a Badgers fan."

"Sure am. And a Packers fan," I reply.

The guy shakes his head as he takes my phone out of Paula's hands. "Well, I wish you would've told me that up front. We don't sell phones to Packers fans."

He and Paula have a good laugh at my expense.

"I have a question," I state with a bit of a smile, a bat of the old eyelashes. Luring this dude in.

"What can I do for you?" He folds his arms. "Besides educate you on real football?"

"Yes. When was the last time the Buccaneers were even *in* a Super Bowl, let alone won one?"

"Ow!" The guy puts his hand to his mouth. "Okay, okay. Fair enough. Well, I guess I can set this phone up for you."

"Thanks."

I'm smiling a genuine smile until I turn around and see Paula studying me.

For the brief moment I was bantering and trash-talking with the sales guy, I had felt normal.

One look at Paula and I'm reminded of why I'm here.

"We really need to start talking about schools," Paula says. "We have some time but best to start looking now. I'll come up with a list, but University of Florida should be at the top—Florida State, too."

And then things get even worse.

"I've already applied to the University of Wisconsin at Green Bay—my top choice," I state. Although I don't add it's all in limbo until everything gets straightened out with my social security number. Not to mention how I'm going to pay for it.

Paula ignores my comment. "I'll make up a map and we can road-trip! Florida State is where I went to college. You'd love it there."

She conveniently leaves out that's where Dad also went.

She continues, "It would be good for me to know what you want to major in so we can really focus on the places with the best programs."

The guy raises his eyebrow knowing this is a really weird conversation for a mother and daughter to have. I wonder if he'll figure it out. Amanda Linsley is coming back to Tampa. I mentioned I'm from Wisconsin. And the biggest red flag, Paula and I do not act like a mother and daughter.

"A road trip sounds fun," I say only to change the topic so we don't give the sales guy any other reason to alert the press.

I'm given a demo of all the bells and whistles of my new phone. Even though I've never owned a smartphone, all my friends have them, so I know the basics. I plan to FaceTime with Marian as soon as I get back to the house. It would also be nice to see Neil's face.

"Want a coffee or treat?" Paula asks as we walk out of the store. "We're going to meet Sarah at Starbucks."

"Sure." It's crazy that they can get Starbucks whenever. I saw like four of them on the drive over.

Sarah is sitting outside, sunglasses on, as she's drinking one of those delicious frozen drinks.

"Want anything else?" Paula asks her.

"I'm going to head over to Forever 21," she states coldly as she gets up and starts walking, not bothering to wait for a response.

"We'll meet you there. Stay in the store," Paula calls out after her.

I save a table as Paula gets our drinks. I look around at all the people milling about. I'm the only one wearing shorts. I guess temperatures in the upper seventies aren't hot for people who live here. I, on the other hand, have to wipe sweat off my forehead. And if I'm being honest, I keep having to lift my arms to give my armpits some air.

Paula comes out with our two iced drinks and sits down.

"Thanks for the coffee. And phone. And clothes," I say, rattling off all she's bought me in the past two hours. "It's really nice of you."

Paula pushes up her ginormous sunglasses. Now I can see her eyes, *my eyes*. "I'm thrilled to be able to do it. I'm so happy you're here." Paula gives me a warm smile as she reaches across to hold my hand.

It's the first time we've been alone, just the two of us, since . . . well, for as long as I can honestly remember.

Paula looks around before leaning in. "How are you finding everything? Truly?"

Does she really mean "truly"? Does she want to know the truth? That I feel like I'm living my life in a fog. Everything is hazy. It feels surreal. That I wish I were back home. That she's really nice and all, but this isn't my life.

Instead, I go for a version of the truth. "It's different."

"I know." She leans back in her chair. "It's different for me, too."

Of course it is. How can it not be for her? She now has two daughters.

Paula continues, "It's going to be an adjustment for us all, but a wonderful adjustment. Just give us some time to get into a flow. You'll soon understand the beauty of living in Florida. You were born here, after all."

I look around at the palm trees, sun, and fountain that isn't frozen over in December. It's all so foreign. Yeah, I'm a native Floridian, but I've always had the kind of skin that burned in the sun. I could never get a tan like Dad. So I must get that from Paula. She's sitting under an umbrella and wearing long sleeves.

You are a part of her, I remind myself.

"Can I ask you something?"

She smiles at me. "Of course."

"What happened?"

"With what, dear?" She looks back at me, and I can tell she has no idea what I'm really asking.

"Between you and Dad. What happened?"

The smile she's had plastered on her face all day quickly dissolves. She begins shaking her head as if there's a memory she doesn't want flooding back. "Oh, Mandy, that was such a horrible time. I don't think I can talk about it. It's just . . . Your father and I loved you very much, but things weren't working out for us. We separated. Your father was supposed to drop you off one day, and he was late." She stares off into the distance. "I didn't think anything of it at first. I went about doing laundry and making dinner. I called Dan on his cell, but he didn't pick up. By dinnertime I kept calling and calling, and he wouldn't answer. I didn't know what to do. I called the police. They weren't concerned at first since you were with one of your parents. But I knew he took you. I knew." Tears begin running down her face.

I hate that I had to bring this memory back, but I need to hear it from her. This is part of my history. The history that had been taken from me, and I need to know about it all, even the most devastating parts.

"Were things that bad between you?" I press.

"What did your father say?" Paula asks, her voice hard. "Didn't you talk to him?"

The options of how much to share weigh in my head. I don't think I need to remind her of how I had thought she was dead until a week ago and that I apparently preferred my dad when I was younger. "I only got to see him once while he was in custody. He said you guys were separated. Did you end up getting a divorce?"

She laughs bitterly. "You bet I got a divorce from that son of a bitch." I flinch when she curses Dad, but Paula doesn't notice. "Since he was missing, I had to get something called a divorce by publication, which meant I had to put an ad in the paper. Because he hadn't humiliated me enough. I want to make something clear to you: I had every intention of splitting custody with your father before he took you. Unlike him, I'm not a selfish asshole."

I suck in air. Of course Paula was going to hate Dad for what he did. But still . . . My dad may be many things, but I lived with him my entire life until a week ago. He is not selfish. "Dad did everything for me," I say.

"Oh, please."

"No, he—"

"I don't want to hear it, Mandy."

"It's Ally," I remind her. "And I really need you to hear this. Please."

She lets out an annoyed breath but doesn't argue with me.

"I'm mad at him, too," I admit. The joyful look on Paula's face was the reason I didn't want to confess my true feelings about what happened. I didn't want her to use it against Dad. But she does deserve the truth. "I don't know what to think or feel about my life since he lied to me for so long."

"See? Selfish bastard," Paula hisses.

"No, please. No." Yes, he did something awful. Yes, I am horrified that my life has been one big sham. But . . .

And there it is again, the "but" of it all. Paula needs to understand why I have such a hard time being on Team Dad's a Selfish Asshole. "Listen, I am angry at what he did. To me, to you, to your family. To us all. But I also love him. You need to know that he was a really great parent. He worked overtime so we always had enough money. He made sure I did my homework. He read to me as a kid. He listened to me. He was my best friend. He gave me a good life." Now I'm the one with tears cascading down my cheeks. "I was never in any danger. I always felt safe around him.

I was safe. And I'm sorry for what he did to both of us. What he did was wrong. SO wrong. But at the end of the day he is not this horrible villain you've built up in your mind. He's not."

Paula stands abruptly. "You may think you know your father, but he took you away from me. For fifteen years, I had to wake up with the thought that I had no idea where my daughter was or if she was even alive. He did that to me. He took you away from your family. He did it for himself. You may think you know your father, but I know him. He is no saint." She angrily wipes the tears off her face. "End of discussion."

She takes her coffee and starts walking toward Forever 21 while I remain frozen in my seat.

Chapter

THIRTY-ONE

It has become very clear that I'm swimming in a vast ocean of ignorance without a life preserver.

So let's look at what I do know: I lived with my dad as my sole parent for fifteen years. I have a good work ethic, I'm the top student in my class, and I've never gotten in major trouble, or any trouble, really. I've had the occasional beer at a party, but always with Dad's knowledge. He didn't want me hiding anything from him. (Pretty ironic, I'm aware.)

So what would've happened if Dad never left and Paula was my primary caregiver?

What would that reality look like?

I would've spent the past fifteen years being shuttled back and forth between two parents. My relationship with Dad would probably have lessened over the years, and we would at least not have been as close as we were. Or are. I don't know how to reference our relationship anymore. I'd be living a Floridian lifestyle with outdoor malls and flip-flops. I'd have completely different friends, maybe even a boyfriend. I wouldn't even know the Gleasons existed, let alone the wonders of Wisconsin food: frozen custard, fried cheese curds, Friday night fish fries, and butter burgers. I'd be someone with different wants, needs, desires than I am now.

I'd be a completely altered person.

I guess the person I'd be most like is Sarah.

I decide to knock on her door. Paula didn't talk to either of us on the drive home. Instead she turned the radio on loudly and sang along to the songs as we all ignored one another. Once we got inside the house, Sarah went straight upstairs and slammed her bedroom door shut, while Paula went outside to talk to Craig, who was doing some yard work. I'm sure she's discussing what an ungrateful child I am.

That left me to hang up my new clothes and decide that enough was enough. It's time my sister and I had a talk.

I knock, and Sarah doesn't answer, but I can hear her stirring inside with her television on.

"Sarah?" I say to the door. "Can we talk? Please. I only need five minutes."

I wait a few beats, feeling foolish standing outside her door, begging her to talk to me. It isn't like I want to talk to her, either, but if I'm going to live here—and I am going to live here whether we both like it or not—we need to at least be civil. I don't have anything against her. Hell, I don't even know her. I do know she hates me.

The door opens, and Sarah is wearing her usual scowl. She holds up her phone, which despite her complaining looks exactly like mine. There's a clock displayed on the screen, and it's counting down from five minutes.

"Speak."

"Can I come in?" I ask, wanting some privacy.

Sarah sighs as she steps away from the door and plops onto her bed. I take a few cautious steps inside her bright room, the complete opposite from her disposition. She has giant sunflowers painted on her wall. It takes me a second to recognize her in the numerous photos on her bookcase because she's smiling. She looks much younger when she's smiling. I have yet to experience that in person.

"Clock is ticking," she states.

I sit down next to her on the bed, which instantly I know is a mistake. She shifts uncomfortably.

"Look, I don't even know what to say or where to start, to be honest. I know this must suck for you. To have this sister pop up out of nowhere. And I'm really sorry. This has been really hard for me, too. I didn't even know you guys existed a week ago, and now I'm living here. I just, I want you to know that I'm aware this must be difficult for you."

She is staring me down and not moving a muscle. I don't think she's going to respond, so I start to stand.

"You don't get it," she finally says.

"No, I don't," I admit. "Not at all."

"Do you have any idea what my life has been because of you?"
I shake my head. "Please tell me."

"I couldn't go outside and play. Mom was so terrified I'd get snatched up. So I had to sit inside while I listened to my friends having a great time outside. When we finally left the old house, I thought maybe she was starting to move on. Maybe I'd get some freedom. But no. We not only live in a gated community, she chose this house because of the back. Did you not notice the ten-foot fence around our entire backyard? Do you think that's normal?"

Honestly, I thought the fence was there to prevent people from coming into the pool. I didn't realize it was because Paula didn't want her daughter going out.

"I've been a prisoner. I couldn't go to sleepovers until I was ten. By then people stopped asking me because I couldn't go anywhere without one of my parents. The fact that she let me walk fifty feet today in a public space without her was a miracle. I have lived this sheltered, suffocating life because of you. Because you were taken, I had to suffer."

"I'm so sorry," I say. "I really am. I had no idea. And—"

"Saying sorry doesn't change anything." Her voice cracks. "Now you're back, and I should be happy because maybe she'll loosen her grip. Maybe I can go to the movies with friends and not have her sit *right* behind me."

"Oh God," slips out of my mouth but causes the corners of Sarah's lips to curl ever so slightly. "That sounds like the worst."

"Right? She drops me off at the front *office* at school every day, and that's where I meet her after school. I can't do any after-school activities if they're outside. If I want to do something, she has to be able to come."

Poor Sarah.

"Did you know that Mom is on medication for anxiety?" She notices my shocked expression. "No, of course not."

Seriously, I could fill an entire library with all the things I don't know about Paula and her family.

Sarah sighs. "Okay, like, I get that you were taken from her, but she has a kid who's right here. I never seemed to be good enough. Not like I could fill a void or whatever, but I had to live in your shadow all my life. There are yearly marches on the date you were taken to remind people that you were still out there somewhere. Ever since I could remember, I've been that girl whose sister was kidnapped. I just want to be Sarah."

There were marches? I hadn't really considered what everybody else had been going through here while I was away.

Fifteen years.

Fifteen years is a really long time. I should be happy Paula never gave up on me. That she fought to keep my memory alive while I was living a perfectly happy life completely unaware of her existence.

"I didn't realize . . . all of that . . . stuff happened." It's even hard to process. "All I can say is that I'm sorry. And I want us to be . . ." Friends? Are sisters friends? I think about the close relationship between Jan and Julia. They're more than sisters. They're a little unit. Then I think about Rob, who couldn't stand to be in the same room as his brother and had a party when his brother went to college. I wish Sarah and I could be somewhere in the middle, although it seems as if we're tilting toward estrangement.

Sarah's cell phone starts to chirp. "Time's up," she states.

I look at her. Her demeanor had intimidated me a little, but she's only eleven. She's had to live with this burden for her entire life. All because of what our parents have done. Neither of us should be punished for our actions.

She seems so small, so young—sitting on her bed with her arms around her legs and wearing a shirt with an owl on it and rainbow socks. There are three stuffed animals on her bed, which I would wager she sleeps with. She probably needs the comfort. Maybe she's never felt safe.

Before I can second-guess myself, I reach over and hug her. She tenses at my touch for a second, before she puts her arms around me. "I'm so sorry," I repeat. "I'm here now, and maybe things will get better for you."

I feel this tug toward her that I hadn't before. I want to protect her. I want to make up for my absence in her life. The absence that has caused her so many problems. I want to make it right. I want to make her life better.

Sarah and I remain there for a few more moments, comforting each other.

Like sisters do.

⌒

The rest of the afternoon I spend in the bedroom thinking about everything Sarah told me. Then I do perhaps the scariest thing of all and put myself in Paula's shoes. And it's even worse than I could possibly imagine.

I approach Paula and Craig's bedroom after dinner. Paula is on the deck, staring out into the distance with a glass of wine in her hand. I loudly knock on the door so she can hear me.

When she sees it's me, a sad smile creeps on her face. "Come in. You can always come in. This is your home now."

I sit down on the chair next to her. We haven't really spoken since the disaster that was this morning.

"I was going to bring you this." She gestures to an open box at her feet.

I pull it over to me. As I look inside, I see several small teddy bears, a night-light with balloons, and some other trinkets. I pick up a silver frame that has a picture of a baby fast asleep on a cozy white rug. Her chin is resting on her hands; she's wearing nothing but a diaper and a tiny pink headband with a giant flower attached.

"You slept through the entire photo shoot," Paula comments before taking a large sip of wine. "The photographer said he'd never seen such a peaceful baby."

I stare at this baby, searching for clues in her face that it's me. Truthfully, I've always thought all babies look somewhat alike.

One by one, I take out each teddy bear. They're smaller than Snuggles, who remains on a shelf in the closet. At first, I was going to place him on the dresser, but he's a reminder of a past that I can't seem to grasp.

This whole box is one giant blank space for me.

"Your room was decorated with teddy bears," Paula says in a small voice. "I have a picture somewhere of you even dressed up as one for your first Halloween."

But to Paula, this box is yet another giant reminder of all that was left behind.

I close the box. "I wanted to say I'm sorry."

"You shouldn't have to apologize for your father," she says as she rubs her tired eyes.

That's true, but all I seem to be doing lately is apologizing. It's not my fault, but somehow I feel it is. Not the disappearing, but the reappearing and not being grateful for it.

"It's not about what he did, it's just—I didn't know."

"About the box?" Paula asks, confused.

"No, about any of this." I gesture around, trying to not focus my attention solely on Paula.

"Of course you didn't know. This wasn't your fault."

"I understand that, but I had no idea about everything you did to find me. Sarah told me about the marches. I went online and saw the news conference from when I first went missing." There was an old video from a press conference that was held a week after I'd disappeared. Paula was in front of a microphone, sobbing uncontrollably, begging for me to be returned. It broke my heart to see her in so much pain.

And now I've been returned all these years later and we're both uncomfortable around each other. We're strangers. She wants that daughter back, but I don't think either of us knows who that person is.

She leans back on her chair and closes her eyes. "It was an awful time. I couldn't look at the news for years after. I once started crying in the grocery store when I picked up a carton of milk, even though there wasn't an ad for a missing child. I couldn't escape it, and I didn't want to. Because I didn't want to give up on finding you."

I reach out now and put my hand on hers. "I'm not really sure how I can make up for the time I was away or what you went through. Or even how I can comprehend it." While Paula was in the grocery aisle having a breakdown, I was at school under the impression I was leading a normal life.

"You're here now, and that's all that matters." She brushes away her tears. "I think it would be best for everybody if we move on. I don't want to talk about it anymore. It's simply too painful. The fact is your father had you all these years, and now it's my turn. You're my daughter. So we are going to be a family."

If only it were that simple. I can't erase my past. As much as Paula wants me to, I can't snap my fingers and forget about the plans I had for my life.

Chapter

THIRTY-TWO

It's not getting easier.

Of course it isn't.

I can't sleep. Every time I feel myself drifting away, a random memory jolts me awake.

Dad and I watching TV.

Him putting another star on the calendar after I've finished all my homework.

Me laughing at his attempts to sing along to any song in a Disney movie.

Us cheering on the Packers.

Nothing big, just the life we had built together. Isn't that what a life is? It's made up of little moments that make you *you*. Relationships are built over time, not forced.

I turn in the bed and pull the covers over my head. I close

my eyes, take deep breaths as I begin to count sheep. Something, anything that will get me to sleep away part of my time here.

I printed out a calendar of December and already have two stars to mark the two days I've been here. I could technically give myself a third since it's well after midnight. But I can only give myself a star in the evenings. I have to survive the day.

Even though the month is halfway through, all the little squares that still need to be filled make me think getting through the next twelve days until Marian arrives will be impossible.

I can't even bear to think about next year.

Yeah . . . So much for counting sheep.

My mind wanders to an image of a young, crying Paula.

If Dad had been caught when he first took me, she would've had time to mold me into the image she's had in her head this entire time. I'd be a younger version of her with my hair and makeup always done. Stylish, or at least caring about style. Maybe we'd spend our weekends at the mall. Maybe I'd be a Buccaneers fan with Craig.

It's easier to picture the person I'd be on the outside. It's difficult to grasp the person I'd be inside. Would I really be that different?

How could I not?

But I like the person I am. Or I was.

I flip over yet again. I move my pillows around and try to get comfortable.

Even as I toss around some more, I know that becoming comfortable is never going to happen.

⟿

I'm still awake hours later as Paula calls down the hallway, "Breakfast! Come and get it while it's hot!"

I open the bedroom door right as Sarah opens hers.

"Morning," I say with a hesitant smile.

"Morning," she says, returning the smile. It's a small gesture, but I'll take it. "Just know this is all for you. We usually fend for ourselves for breakfast."

"That's not true," Paula yells out.

Sarah rolls her eyes, and I can't help but laugh. The one thing that I always envied about people who had sisters was not just the sibling bond but that you had someone in the battle against parental embarrassments.

The dining room table is set like in a magazine. There are place mats, and fancy cloth napkins set on top of blue-and-yellow plates. Everything is color coordinated. There's a large bowl of fruit placed in the middle of the table, surrounded by pancakes, an assortment of bagels and cream cheese, and hash browns.

"We're eating in the dining room?" Sarah asks. She turns to me. "Usually we eat at the kitchen counter."

"Stop making us sound like barbarians," Paula playfully scolds Sarah.

"I'm telling it like it is." Sarah sits down and immediately dives into the bagels.

Craig walks in carrying a tray of sausage. "Since we're telling it like it is, you should know we don't always eat like this, or I'd need much bigger pants." He pats his nonexistent stomach.

I follow Sarah's lead and take a bagel.

"Is Jen still coming over tomorrow night, or is Ally my new babysitter?" Sarah asks.

"Oh, no, we're canceling," Paula replies.

"Canceling what?" I ask.

"Well, every Sunday Craig and I have dinner with a group of friends, but we aren't going to go this week."

"I'll watch Sarah," I offer. "I don't mind." Plus, you know, I'll be here anyway.

"Also, I'm eleven and I don't need a babysitter," Sarah adds.

I didn't have a babysitter when I was eleven. Or ever, really. I'd usually get home from school, make myself a snack, and do homework. Dad spent most nights and weekends with me. If he had something, I'd go over to Marian's.

"I babysit all the time back home. I have a lot of regular customers and can get references if you need them."

Did I just offer up references to babysit my half sister?

I sure did.

"You know, in case you know of anybody looking for a babysitter," I add to try to cover up my blunder. Honestly, I wouldn't fault them for asking for references because *they don't know me.*

I had spent more time over at the Dorns before I was allowed to be alone with their kids than I've been here (tomorrow will be four stars, which is how I've decided to look at it instead of days). "Anyway, I'd like to get a job."

I can't have Craig and Paula keep paying for things. Plus, I need to save up for that out-of-state tuition.

"I think your focus should be on settling in here and your schoolwork," Paula states with a nod like the matter is settled.

"You know," Craig begins, "I think it would be nice to give the sisters some time alone. Family bonding and all that."

"Yeah," Sarah agrees. "Let me and Ally have some pizza-eating and movie-watching sister time."

Craig and Paula aren't the only ones taken aback that Sarah seems to want to hang out with me.

"That sounds great," I add. Even the idea of babysitting gives me a jolt of my past life. The old Ally. She's still in here somewhere.

"Fantastic!" Craig claps his hands together. "I'll call Charlie and let him know we're in."

Paula only nods in response, like she doesn't trust us to be left alone.

"I was thinking tomorrow for lunch that I'd do some grilling for the big game. Isn't that what you usually do when you watch Packers games, Ally?" Craig asks.

"Yes." I'm touched he remembers and wants to help keep whatever traditions I can.

"Requests?" He points around the table.

"Turkey burger," Sarah pipes up.

"What time is this game?" Paula asks.

"Noon," I reply.

"One o'clock here—you're on East Coast time now," Craig reminds me.

"So we'll eat before the game. Twelve thirty," Paula states.

"Oh, um." I close my mouth. The Packers aren't going to lose because I eat a burger before kickoff. Although it's the Bears, and do I really want to risk it? Thank Lombardi I brought my Donald Driver jersey with me.

"Wait a second, don't you usually do it at halftime?" Craig pipes in.

"Yes, it's tradition."

"When is halftime?" Paula asks.

"Probably around two thirty or three."

"No, that's far too late to eat lunch."

"Dinner isn't until seven, and we'll have a late breakfast," Craig argues. "Can't mess with very important and time-honored football traditions."

See, Craig totally gets it.

"What do you want me to grill up for tomorrow, Ally? Burger? Cheeseburger? Brat? I can go to Whole Foods and get some of those fancy salmon burgers or veggie burgers."

"Just a cheeseburger would be nice, thanks," I reply. I don't want him to make a fuss, but it does warm my heart that he's going through all this effort to give me a small sense of my life before.

"Come on! This is a big game. You got to keep up your strength! You know, I think you should come with me to the grocery store to make sure I don't get something offensive, like Vermont cheddar."

I laugh. It echoes loudly in the dining room. Sarah giggles along, and Craig is pretty pleased with himself.

"Okay, then, we'll head over to Whole Foods later. We'll get some meat and cheese. Maybe some dips. Oh, and I can grab some sushi for dinner later."

I wrinkle my nose at the mention of sushi.

"Have you never had sushi?" Craig asks.

I shake my head. I've seen it on TV, but could never imagine eating raw fish. I've watched Dad cut open fish all the time, and it's hard enough to eat that stuff after it's been cooked.

"It's delicious," Sarah replies. "Shrimp tempura roll for me."

"Got it! It's in the vault." Craig taps his head. "We'll start you off with something easy, Ally. Like a California roll and work our way up to sashimi."

"Okay."

Paula clears her throat loudly. Her face is sad. "You used to eat only grilled cheese."

"What's that, sweetie?" Craig asks.

"Mandy would eat only grilled cheese sandwiches when she was little. For dinner. For lunch. Once I had to make her one for breakfast. I couldn't look at a grilled cheese for years."

Way to bring down the room, Paula.

Besides, wasn't she the one who said we had to stop thinking about the past?

After yesterday, I'm slowly coming to realize how much damage my disappearance did to Paula. She's right: the only way we're going to move forward is to focus on the future. The past carries too many painful memories for us both. For her, it's all she missed in my life. For me, it's the people and plans I've had to leave behind. We've both been devastated by Dad's actions. Perhaps even beyond repair.

Craig seems to understand what we need. He's the one talking about the future. What we'll do tomorrow. Things I might want to try, while Paula refuses to leave the past. Maybe it's because it's the only thing she and I share? Although there's a part of me that is starting to get the feeling that maybe it's because I'm not that little girl who's been living in her memory all this time.

I've changed. She's changed.

And sometimes you can't force something to happen that's not there.

Chapter

THIRTY-THREE

Once again, I find myself in the guest bedroom I'm living in now. It's become my safe space. Craig, Sarah, and I are going to the grocery store in a little bit, so for now I . . . I'm not sure what.

I turn on the TV. I haven't watched the news since I got here. I decide to google my birth name. The main article on the *Tampa Bay Times* home page reads, Homecoming for Missing Teen. It states that I'm back in Tampa and getting to know my family, but a spokesperson for the family (they have a spokesperson?) has requested privacy. So, of course, that one age-progressed photo fills half the screen. "A source close to the family says she'll be attending a local public school."

Who's this source? Randy? Paula's right, Randy's a jackass.

There was not one word, except for Dana's ill-fated attempt at fame, from anybody in Valley Falls. Here in Florida, we have a spokesperson, and someone "close to the family" is blabbing my school plans. Why can't people shut their mouths and mind their own business?

I close out the news app and look at the other options, something to entertain me for a while.

I click on a few apps to see what the Gleasons have been up to, but none of their accounts have been active in days. The last post from Marian (or "Ariel Jasmine" as she named her profile after we spent a weekend binge-watching Disney cartoons) was from my birthday. A selfie of all of us with cake on our forks at lunch.

Nothing since. From any of them.

I'm a little relieved to see that I haven't been left out of anything big since I got here, but it also makes me miss them even more.

I close the app and see the FaceTime button, and before I can talk myself out of it, I hit one of the ten numbers I have saved on my new phone. I lean against my headboard and hold up the phone to get a good angle.

The screen comes to life, and there's some shuffling around, a hilarious "Dammit!" as the phone drops before the screen finally fills with Neil's face. "Hey!" He tries to sound cool, but I can tell how happy he is to hear from me.

Okay, okay, I'll admit that makes me excited.

"Hey!" I reply with the same silly grin on my face.

"How are things? How are you? How is your new family? And Florida?"

"The truth?" I ask.

"Always," he replies. Seeing his face and knowing he's in his messy bedroom at home while I'm over a thousand miles away makes me long to be back on familiar ground.

"On a scale from one to ten, negative forty-four billion."

Neil winces. "I'm so sorry. It's only been three days; maybe you'll get used to it?"

Three days/stars. It feels so much longer than that. The hours are stretching out and making six months until graduation feel like an entire lifetime.

"Plus, home is just a press of a button." He points at the screen.

That will never be enough.

"How are things back in the sprawling metropolis of Valley Falls?"

"The truth?"

"Always," I reply with a wink.

"They completely blow. We're all just angry and sad. Even Rob hardly talks at lunch, so you know things are bad. We all stare at the seat where you should be sitting. It's not fair that you can just be taken from us. Like, I know she's your birth mom and everything, but you're not a piece of property to be passed around."

I lower the volume on the speaker so Paula doesn't overhear. "I know you don't want this, either. We miss you."

"I miss you guys, too. Even Rob," I admit.

Neil's eyes get wide. "It's even worse than I thought!"

We share a laugh, but then Neil's face creases with worry. "Are they at least treating you well?"

"Yeah," I begrudgingly admit. "I guess. Paula got me this phone and all these new clothes yesterday. I have everything I could need: clothes, food, shelter, you know, whatever that hier-archy thing is we learned last year in Ms. Fogelman's class. But it's too forced. They don't feel like family."

Neil snorts. "Sorry! But you do realize that your family dynamic here wasn't normal, right?"

I give him a look. *Yeah, clearly my life was anything but normal.*

"No!" Neil hits his forehead. "That's not what I mean. It's just you and your dad are so close. It was cool to see and all. It's like you shared the same brain."

I can't reply. It's nearly impossible even to think about Dad and my situation without breaking down. Especially since this hurt, this pain, is all his fault.

"I didn't mean to upset you."

I shake my head to rid myself of the devastating thoughts. "I get that I'll never be able to have what I had with my dad with them. It's . . . I don't feel at home here. It's like I'm biding my time until I can leave, but Paula is insisting I look at colleges here."

"You can't stay in Florida." Neil clenches his jaw.

"There is zero chance of that happening. When we were at the mall yesterday, Paula wanted me to get all this new stuff for this bedroom so I could make it my own." I gesture to the pristine guest room. That's how I look at it: I'm a guest. "I didn't even want to get a throw pillow."

It makes me uncomfortable to keep spending her money, especially on something as frivolous as a forty-dollar pillow to decorate a bed. I should've said yes to make Paula happy, but I got on a plane and left my life behind to make her happy.

"Ah, what's a throw pillow?" Neil asks. "Is that a Florida thing?"

"Probably. It's a fancy pillow used solely to decorate a bed, but then you just toss it aside when you want to actually sleep."

"So it's useless." He laughs.

"Pretty much."

"They seem to have a lot of money. What do they even do for a living? So, you know, when I grow up I can have enough money to buy throw pillows."

There's admittedly a lot I don't know about Paula and Craig, but this question I can answer. "Paula works in marketing for a hospital, and Craig's a CFO—that stands for chief financial officer, so, the dude who handles all the money—for a tech company."

Neil's eyes get wide. "So, yeah, they have money. Do you have to refer to Craig as Chief?"

"No, Craig's pretty cool, but the money thing is weird. They don't worry about it at all here. I've had Starbucks every day so far."

"Now you're just bragging. I should remind you that we have fried cheese curds and frozen custard."

The smile on my face vanishes. "You know I'd rather be there."

"I do."

There's an awkward pause in our conversation. I look away from the screen.

"I wish you were coming with Marian for Christmas break," I admit. I can't look at Neil's reaction. The distance has made it easier for me to be bold with him. Right now all I want is to be in the same room as Neil. To not have to rely on a phone screen to see him.

And let me put it out there. I don't just want to see him. I want to touch him. To hug him; Neil always gives the best hugs. And, yeah, kiss him.

When I finally do glance at the phone, I see a beaming Neil. "Really? You know I'd love to. I heard you're going to Disney World."

"Oh, so you're more interested in visiting Cinderella than me? Okay, I get it. I see your priorities," I tease.

"Hey, there's only one princess in my heart."

Oh my God, that is the cheesiest thing ever, but I love it.

I shake my head, even though I'm blushing from his comment. "I mean, it's Disney World. So we should have fun."

What kid hasn't begged their parents to take them? I used to ask Dad all the time.

Oh. It just hits me. When I used to ask Dad, he'd say no because we couldn't afford it. While, yeah, we didn't have the money for a vacation to Florida, he also couldn't risk coming here again. Orlando is less than a two-hour drive from Tampa.

"I wish I could be there. I miss you." Two dimples appear as Neil frowns.

"I miss you, too."

It's nice being with someone I can not only be myself with but who I can tell the truth to. With every "fine" and "good" that I tell this new family, I feel like I'm losing a part of myself. Burying the true me.

What if she disappears completely?

"Ally?" Neil touches the screen.

I touch it back. "Yeah?"

"We are going to work this out, okay? None of us are giving up on you, especially me. We are going to get you back, I promise."

I've had a lot of promises made to me over the years, namely Dad telling me things would be okay.

I've never wanted a promise to hold up as much as this one.

"Well, you've done it!" Craig throws his hands up in the air at the end of the Packers–Bears game. "You've turned me into a Packers fan."

We're in Craig's man cave, which is on the second floor of the garage. I thought the TV in the living room was huge, but it is nothing compared to the monstrosity in front of us. The room—the size of my old home—has an oversized U-shaped couch, a mini-kitchen with a refrigerator filled with soda and beer (which Craig made sure to tell me with a wink that he keeps tabs on), and every kind of chip you can imagine in the cupboards.

Sarah came up to watch the kickoff but quickly got bored, while Paula kept coming in to check on us but wouldn't sit down. I couldn't tell if she was curious how Craig and I were getting along or if she wanted to make sure I was still there.

"You're welcome," I reply to Craig before I put another piece of cheese in my mouth.

"And this stuff." He picks up a piece of Wisconsin white cheddar that was like thirty dollars a pound at Whole Foods. "Amazing. You've taught me so much. Aren't I supposed to be the one to instill life-changing knowledge?"

"You can show me how to avoid a sunburn," I offer. My right arm had gotten scorched from the car ride to the grocery store yesterday. I never had to think about putting sunscreen on in the winter. And despite the blazing sun outside, it is winter.

"Hey, so I wanted to talk to you about a few things." Craig presses mute on the TV remote.

"Okay," I say as a pit forms in my stomach. There hasn't been a single "talk" by an adult in the past several days that has made me feel anything but worse.

"I know things are difficult for you. They have been for Paula. She's been so focused on finding you I don't think she realized all that comes with you being here."

He continues, "The most important thing right now is your safety and privacy. It's probably best for you to have an alias for school. Paula's name has been in the news a lot lately, so having you go to school as Allison McMullen might set off a few alarm bells."

He's right. Paula McMullen has been mentioned several times in every article; the photo of her tearstained at the first press conference when I went missing has been plastered all over the media as well.

"Do you want to think about a last name before you visit the school tomorrow?" Craig asks.

I nod, although Gleason automatically pops into my head. Allison Gleason.

"Or may I suggest Johnson, since it's the second-most-common last name in the US behind Smith. I googled," Craig says with a laugh.

Allison Johnson.

It doesn't feel like me. But neither does Allison McMullen. Or even Amanda Linsley.

"Sure." I relent.

"Great!" Craig says with a thumbs-up before his face turns serious again. "Has your mom talked to you about the social worker?"

I shake my head.

He sighs. "It's probably another thing she doesn't want to think about, but you have to meet with a social worker. She's doing a home visit tomorrow, just to make sure everything is okay here. And also, I don't know how you feel about this, but maybe it wouldn't be the worst idea for you to talk to a therapist. Is that something you'd like?"

"I don't know." I shrug. No shock that my only experience with therapists is from TV. "What would we talk about?"

"Anything you'd like. Same as with the social worker. I know this has been a lot for you and, I really hate to use this word, but you are a victim. You were kidnapped."

"By my own dad," I clarify. I know people always hear the

word "kidnap" and have these horrible visions. Rightfully so. But that's not what happened with me. "I really liked living with him. Plus, I didn't know anything was wrong. At all."

Craig nods thoughtfully. "I know. But this is a lot for anybody to handle. You have to reconcile a great deal about your past and your father. I've got to be honest: when we heard you were found, I didn't know what to think. I'd been living with this idea of you for so long I almost didn't believe you were real. But here you are."

No surprise that I hadn't spent any time thinking about how this all affected Craig. "I'm sorry." Will I ever be able to apologize enough to them?

Although it would be nice if someone here would apologize to me, or at least acknowledge how unfair all this has been. Or not pretend that the past fifteen years didn't exist for me. And they were good years.

"Oh, Ally, you have nothing to be sorry for." Again, Craig gets it! "This has been hanging around Paula since I've known her. Even when Sarah was born—which was the happiest day of my life—there was a sadness in Paula. I've known about you for years, while you're just finding out about me and Sarah and, well, your mother. So as far as I'm concerned, you're handling everything really well. Your mom doesn't think you need therapy. She'd be mad at me for even mentioning it. She really wants to get on with our lives, but I know this is going to be an adjustment for you. A tough one. So anything you need, you can come to me."

"Thanks, Craig. Really."

I weigh the idea of a therapist in my head. Do I really need to talk or think about what happened to me any more than I already do?

There is something I want to talk to Craig about. It's been nagging me since the plane ride, and I figure he's my best shot to get some answers. "I have a question for you."

"Of course!"

"Do you know anything about my dad's family? I know my grandfather died."

Craig's friendly expression falters for a minute. "Yes. They live outside Atlanta. Your father's mother is in an assisted living facility near where your aunt lives. They've been in touch, but your mother doesn't think it's a good idea for you to talk to them right now."

"Wait, they've spoken to her?"

"Yes. And I'm sure you want to talk to them; it's your right. But we need to give us all time to adjust. I hate to admit it, but Paula blames them."

"He took me away from them, too," I protest. Not to mention that Paula keeping me away from them is the same thing Dad had done to us.

"I know, believe me, I know." Craig rubs his forehead. "Please give your mother some more time. I don't think she realizes how immovable she's been. So I'll work on her and get you to at least be able to talk to them soon."

"Okay," I concede, because this is just another thing I have absolutely zero control over.

He slaps his hands on his legs. "Well, I want to make sure that you mention to the social worker how kind and giving your stepfather is. Remember: burgers, cheese, so much food."

I look at the giant coffee table filled with food in the center of the sectional.

Craig is right. Paula isn't the only one who needs time to adjust. Once I get this family under my feet, I can work on getting to know Dad's. I, unfortunately, have nothing but time here.

Craig continues, "Plus, I got you not one, not two, but three, count them, three dips!"

"And they were all delicious."

"I'm going to be too full for dinner tonight, but don't tell your mom that."

I pretend to zip my lips.

"But, seriously, I hope you give us a chance."

I nod, but feel torn. I like Craig. I like Sarah. But I love the people back home. I know a lot can change with time, but *a lot can change with time*. That includes things back home. What if by the time I get there, they've all moved on? Marian has a new best friend, Neil has a girlfriend . . .

The door to the first-floor entrance opens, and we hear Paula coming up the stairs. "Did your team win?"

"Yes," I reply.

She stands over Craig and me with her arms folded. "Good."

"Yeah."

Pause.

More silence.

More awkwardness.

There's this rhythm that I have with Craig and Sarah, even with the cell phone guy, that I can't seem to find with Paula.

I'm trying, but we got nothing.

Chapter
THIRTY-FIVE

"I don't like this."

Paula is rubbing her hands as Craig waits for her by the front door. She keeps looking between Sarah and me—her two daughters. She glances back at Craig. "I think it's too soon to leave them alone. We should cancel dinner."

"*Mooooom*," Sarah protests. "We aren't going anywhere. We're going to watch a movie and order food. And, no, we will not let the delivery guy into the house. Relax." She stomps off while Paula looks me up and down. Every time she does this, I wonder what she's looking for. The baby she used to bathe? The toddler who clung to her leg? Who?

"It's going to be fine. I have my phone if you need to reach me." I use the soothing voice I reserve for when I'm babysitting for a family for the first time. "I can text you every so often to give you an update if that will help." There was one family who I had to send a photo of their newborn to—aka proof of life—every half hour.

Paula bites her lip. "I guess. Just so I know everything is okay."

To be honest, I'm excited for a little break from Paula's hovering and the feeling I can't seem to shake that I am not the daughter she was looking for.

"That's a nice dress." I compliment Paula's baby blue maxi dress. Her hair is up in a high ponytail, and she looks younger.

"Thanks." She fiddles with her bracelet. "And you know where the emergency numbers are?"

"Yes. I also programmed them into my phone, just in case."

"Smart girl," Craig says as he opens the door, hoping it will get Paula to move.

It doesn't.

"Do you want Chinese or pizza?" Sarah comes back into the living room with menus. When she sees her parents, she stops. "You guys are *still* here?"

Craig starts walking out the door. "We're going! We're going!"

Paula pauses before she follows him.

Once the door clicks and we hear the garage door open, Sarah throws her head back. "Finally! So, pizza?"

Even though I'm still full from watching the game, I nod. Pizza and Movie Sister Sundays.

It's a tradition I wouldn't mind starting.

⌒

"Is Neil your boyfriend?" Sarah asks when she notices me texting with a smile on my face.

"Um, no," I reply.

She stretches her legs out on the couch, a half-eaten piece of pizza in front of her. "You sound like you don't know."

"Well, technically we're friends."

"But?" she prods me. She takes a bite of pizza as she wiggles her eyebrows.

"But . . . I live here now," I state bluntly.

"Oh." Her mouth hangs open a little. Her playful demeanor shifts. "Do you like it here?"

"It's nice." I don't want to upset her by telling her how much I want to go back home. "I'm happy we're hanging out. And I like hearing about all your friends."

She smiles at this. I want to brush back the strand of her long hair that is hanging in front of her face, but I don't feel we're at that level of closeness yet.

We spent the half hour waiting for the pizza by telling each other about our friends. Sarah wanted a couple of them to come over today, but Paula thought it was too soon. She was worried they'd take pictures of me or something.

"Have you and Neil kissed?" Sarah takes her two index fingers and moves them around while making smooching noises.

Kids.

Although it was the exact same gesture I'd done to Neil when I asked him about Dana.

Like big sister, like little sister, I guess.

"None of your business," I state with a flip of my hair. I then take a big bite of pizza so I can't talk for a while.

"Oooh!" Sarah coos. Her phone beeps. She picks it up, laughs, and then frowns again. "I don't know how I'd feel if we had to move. I was angry when we moved two miles from our old house. I used to live only a block away from my best friend."

"Stacey?" I confirm.

"Yeah, Stacey. I'd be, like, really upset if I couldn't see her again."

"Well, I'll see Neil again." I hope. "And Marian is coming next week. I can't wait for you to meet her."

Sarah nods. "Me too. But then she has to leave."

I try to not let her see how much that's ripping me up inside. "Yes, then she has to leave. But I'll see her again."

"But it's not the same."

"No, it's not the same."

"But you're staying here until at least graduation, right?"

"Right," I reply.

"Promise?" She holds out her pinkie.

This is not a hard thing to pinkie swear, since, you know, I don't have a choice. "Promise."

"Good!" She beams. "I overheard Mom and Dad talking, and they didn't think you'd stay. That's why they were so quick to come get you. I guess they wanted to start the bribing as soon as they could."

My face scrunches as I try to understand what she's saying. So were the iPhone and clothes and Packers watching some sort of bribe? But for what?

"I'm sorry." Sarah looks down at the floor. "I'm sorry I was so mean to you when you came here. I just . . ." A tear starts to fall down her cheek.

"Oh, Sarah." I sit next to her and wrap my arms around her. "I don't blame you for being upset. This has changed a lot for you, too."

"I know. It's just . . . It's not fair. I'm glad you're here, but it's just not fair."

No, it's not.

Chapter
THIRTY-SIX

"Come in! Come in!" Paula brightly greets a young woman in a navy suit on Monday morning.

I stand uncomfortably near the door in a floral dress that Paula had insisted she buy on Friday and that I wear now to meet the social worker.

Ms. Martinez gives me a warm smile as we're introduced. I feel my nerves creep up. I have zero power over what's happening to me, but this woman does.

"How are you doing?" Ms. Martinez asks me.

"I'm good," I reply flatly.

Paula laughs nervously. "Would you like another tour of the house?"

"Another?" I ask.

Ms. Martinez turns to me. "I came here before you were allowed to move in."

But I came right from Wisconsin with Paula and Craig; when did she come?

Ms. Martinez can sense my confusion. "I was here the day before your mother and Mr. McMullen flew to get you." She turns to Paula. "I'd like to speak to Amanda alone." Ms. Martinez gives Paula a tight smile. There's something in her smile, a don't-challenge-me look that brings my hopes up.

"Of course, of course," Paula says as she gestures for us to sit down on the couch. "I'll go upstairs to give you some privacy."

Ms. Martinez studies the staircase that leads to the second floor, which looks over the living room. "We'll be in the kitchen."

I follow her into the kitchen, where we sit down at the counter as Paula heads upstairs. Ms. Martinez opens her briefcase and pulls out over a dozen manila file folders. She scans them until she selects one and then crams the rest back in.

All the hope I had felt simmers out. I'm one of many. When you come from a small town, you're used to having people look out for you. But for Ms. Martinez, I'm simply another case number.

"How are things going here?" she asks as she flips open the file and starts jotting down notes before I even speak.

"Fine."

"Are you adjusting to your new family well?"

"I am, but—"

Ms. Martinez cuts me off and continues checking off items on her list. "And it says you're going to start school tomorrow?"

"We're going over this afternoon so I can get a tour, but yes.

I want to start as soon as possible. I haven't been to school in weeks." It feels like months, but when I count back, I've only missed one entire week of school. "I really want some normalcy. Get back to a regular schedule," I explain. Plus, I'm bored. I don't feel comfortable enough to really feel at home. But I can't tell her any of that. Or can I?

"Is the family treating you well?"

"Can I ask you a question?"

She looks up from her notes. "Yes."

"What are my options? No one has ever explained what my options are. I've been told I'm a minor so I have to go with my parent. Everybody keeps saying I have to stay until graduation. But do I have any choices?"

"What's the problem?" She looks around the pristine kitchen. I see how it appears to her. She probably has lots of clients in houses that aren't this nice. Kids with abusive parents. I know I have it easy compared to others.

"There isn't a problem, per se. But I've had my entire life turned upside down and I really want to go back to Wisconsin."

"Your family is here," she states bluntly. "Have you been touched in an inappropriate way?"

"No!"

"Are they not providing for you?"

"They are."

"So what's the issue? They're your family. They've given you a lovely home to live in. From what I understand it's a vast improvement over your past living situation."

Okay, now that pisses me off. I don't need stainless steel appliances or down pillows or organic chicken to make me happy. Maybe I'm super messed up or maybe I do have Stockholm syndrome, but I miss the life I had with my dad.

At first, I felt obliged to right Dad's wrong when it came to Paula. I should get to know my mother. Just not in a move-to-Florida-forever sense. I was in such a haze when everything happened that I went along with what the grown-ups told me. Sheriff Gleason said I had to stay until graduation. Now I'm starting to see more clearly. There's been something nagging at the back of my mind after what Sarah said yesterday about Paula and Craig thinking I was going to leave. "What happens when I turn eighteen?"

She raises her eyebrow at me. "You're an adult."

"So that means I can decide what happens to me."

She sighs. "Being an adult is more than an age. If you leave here, how are you going to provide for yourself? I believe your father's assets have been frozen. You only have"—she looks at my file—"less than twelve hundred dollars in savings. Where are you going to live? How are you going to pay for food or shelter? What will your transcripts look like with you bouncing around from school to school?"

As I absorb her words, I realize turning eighteen doesn't automatically make you an adult in the real sense. Yes, I'd be allowed to leave Paula's, but then what? I can't be more of a burden to the Gleasons—financially or otherwise. That's probably why Sheriff Gleason told me I had to stay until graduation.

Ms. Martinez glances at her phone. "Anything else you'd like to tell me?"

So, basically, I need to just shut up and deal.

Six months.

I can do this.

"Yeah," I reply. She looks up from her notes. "Can you not tell Paula about this?"

"Everything between us is confidential. I'll give you my card, and call if you need anything. I'll come again in two weeks to check in on you."

Two weeks. I've been here for five days, and it already feels like an eternity.

She stands up. "I know this is an adjustment for you, but you should realize how lucky you are."

Funny, I don't feel the slightest bit lucky. I feel cursed. Doomed to a life that belongs to someone else.

Amanda Linsley would have—*no doubt*—been happy here. She would've lived with a life intact. She would've been happy shuffling back and forth between her two parents. Or maybe she would've eventually lived with her dad. I have no idea.

What I do know is that I am not Amanda Linsley. Or Allison McMullen. Or Allison Johnson.

I'm Ally Smith. And Ally Smith has to wait six months to go home.

Chapter
THIRTY-SEVEN

Because I'm one of those nerds who like school, the first day of school was always fun for me. Maybe that's why I'm so drawn to a future in education. I'd pack my book bag with brand-new notebooks and pens. I couldn't wait to fill them, and my brain, with new information.

I can say with absolute certainty I've never had a first day like this before.

When Paula took me to visit John F. Kennedy High School, I didn't want to get out of the car. It's the size of two city blocks. There are nearly two thousand students—the population of Valley Falls. As I was given the tour, which included a map, I knew I was going to get lost. Not just physically lost, but lost in a sea of students.

Back home, I was top of the class. Here, I'm one of many. I'm not even qualified to be in their AP classes.

Paula, of course, was excited. "Look on the bright side: new friends!" she remarked cheerily. Yet another thing to make me a new person. A different person. Not me.

I walk downstairs to an empty kitchen. I forgot to ask what the morning routine is around here during the week. Craig and Sarah were gone by the time I got downstairs yesterday.

I open the refrigerator and pull out items to make myself lunch. I feel like an intruder opening drawers trying to find sandwich bags and utensils. I was told to make myself at home, so I make a turkey sandwich and grab an apple, and some leftover chips from Sunday.

"Good morning." Paula's dressed in a nice blue-and-green wrap dress. She's going back to work today at the hospital. Everybody is getting back to their normal lives. "I was going to give you money for lunch."

"I like to bring my lunch," I state, although I did get to see the cafeteria during the tour. It was—no surprise—huge. I already planned on taking my lunch outside to sit under a tree and read.

"I can make eggs for breakfast." Paula opens the fridge. "Or do you want cereal?"

"What do you usually do?"

"We usually watch TV and do our own thing," Sarah says as she walks into the kitchen wearing her middle-school uniform. I'm a tad jealous she doesn't have to think about her school outfits in the morning. I didn't know what to wear today. The students I did see yesterday were all stylish: colorful dresses, fitted tops, tight jeans, heels. It was all jeans and sweaters back home. I settled on a new outfit from the other day: a pair of dark skinny jeans and a short-sleeved cotton-and-lace T-shirt.

Sarah opens a drawer and pulls out a box of Honey Nut Cheerios. "You want some?" she offers.

"Yeah. That would be great." I go into the fridge and get the milk. Sarah pulls out the bowls while I find the spoons.

We're so busying pouring ourselves cereal, milk, and juice that it takes us both a few minutes to realize that tears are sliding down Paula's cheeks.

"What's wrong?" I ask.

"It's something I never thought I'd ever see. The two of you. Together. In my home."

I give her an awkward pat on the hand. Will there ever be a time when she can look at me and not be sad? I inadvertently hurt her by going missing for years, and I sometimes feel that maybe having a walking reminder of what happened hurts her just as much.

"I'm making toast," Sarah states as she ignores her mother. "You want some?"

"Yes, please."

Sarah puts four pieces of bread into a big toaster. "Butter's over there." Sarah gestures at the counter, where I find a ceramic butter dish that matches every other item in the kitchen.

Sarah pulls out the plates while I put our bowls of cereal on the counter.

I could get used to this kind of relationship with Sarah. Just two sisters having breakfast before school.

Dad was usually gone by the time I got up during the week, but I'd often wake up to him making breakfast on Sunday mornings. Pancakes were his specialty. When I was younger, he'd make them look like Mickey Mouse, complete with berries to dot Mickey's nose and eyes and a banana for a smile. If he'd had a good week at work, there would be chocolate chip pancakes. Even as I got older, the pancakes continued. In the winter, he'd drink coffee, while I had hot chocolate. In the summer, we'd sit out in the backyard. Iced coffee for him, chocolate milk for me.

I miss those breakfasts. I miss our routine. I miss him.

Craig comes down and helps himself to a cup of coffee. "How are you feeling about your first day of school?"

Like a hammer, I'm brought back to my new reality.

"I'm a little nervous," I admit.

"You know you can call me if you need anything," Paula offers. "And I will leave work if you need me to get you."

"She's going to be fine, Paula," Craig assures her. I wish I were as confident as he is.

"We should leave in about ten minutes," Paula says as she glances at her watch. "Will you be ready?"

"Yeah." I'm technically ready: book bag packed, lunch made, and map of the campus studied so I'll, hopefully, have a clue where I'm going.

Am I emotionally ready for this new adventure?

I have no idea.

When it comes to school, I'm an expert about devising a plan of attack and sticking to it.

The plan to survive this new school: study, keep my grades up and my head down, talk to Ms. Pieper about how this will affect my UW–Green Bay application, and try to blend in.

The students here aren't like back home. Everybody basically looked the same in Valley Falls. We were like 95 percent white and Christian. Julia started a gay-straight alliance when she found out there was a closeted member of the Student Council. But that was it for diversity.

Here the hallways are filled with so many different types of people. And there are clubs and organizations for everything and everyone. Part of me wants to embrace the opportunity to branch out of my small comfort zone. The other part wants to hide away from it all.

I felt good in my classes this morning. I'm probably the only one who was excited every time homework was assigned. It would be something to distract me.

As I walk to lunch, I realize that I haven't really had to make any friends since we moved to Valley Falls. It can't be that hard. I just need to find a familiar face from one of my classes and say hello.

"Oh, hey," a girl with bright red hair in braids calls out to me. "You're the new girl. We're in Calc together." I remember her not only from her bright hair but also from her black-and-white-striped leggings.

"Yes! Hi, I'm Ally . . . Johnson," I reply with my new name.

There are only three people in this school who know my true identity: the principal, the vice principal, and my assigned guidance counselor.

"I'm Jordis," she says. "I used to live in Chicago."

"Cool," I reply, since I was introduced as "recently moving here from Chicago" by all my teachers this morning.

"I do *not* miss the weather." Jordis wraps one of her braids around her finger as we walk in the direction of the cafeteria. "We were in Bucktown. What part did you live in?"

"Portage Park," I answer with where Dad and I once lived. I really hope she doesn't ask too many details, since I haven't been there in years.

"I don't think I've been there," she says while I relax slightly. "My stepdad has our entire basement decorated in Bears gear. You a fan?"

I may not have figured out much about Allison Johnson, but I can guarantee that no matter what name you call me, I will never, and I mean *never*, be a Chicago Bears fan.

"Not really," I reply evenly.

"Yeah, not a big sports fan. I'm more into poetry." She glances at me. "So what's your deal?"

"Um," I start.

"Yeah. Why'd you move? Who'd you move with? You know, all the boring get-to-know-you stuff I was asked when I moved here last year," she says with a laugh.

I freeze.

I had assumed that I'd make a couple of friends here, but

now . . . How can I possibly get to know people when I'd have to continually lie to their faces about anything from my past? What happens if they want to come over to the house? Will they recognize Paula? Could I ever trust anybody here with the truth?

I'm one person, one click of a phone, away from having my real face plastered on the news.

Everything is going to be harder here.

"So . . . ," Jordis says quizzically.

"Oh, I moved with my mom, dad, and sister," I lie. "Dad, ah, got a new job here."

The instant the fake story comes out of my mouth, I make a mental note to write it down. I have to keep everything straight. God, this must've been what it was like for Dad. He had to do the same thing.

"Cool," Jordis replies. Her face lights up as she waves to someone across the crowded cafeteria. "See ya later," she says before walking over to a table without another glance over her shoulder.

I'm left holding my lunch bag without anywhere to go. No matter who I talk to, I'm going to have to answer the same questions. I'm going to have to lie. So I keep my head down as I walk outside to the courtyard and find an empty spot underneath a tree in the far corner. I don't want anybody to wave me over or sit next to me. I don't want to have to keep making things up.

All I want is to be me.

I take a picture of my crossed legs with my lunch bag in the middle and send it to Marian. Lunchtime.

How's school? she texts back right away, even though I know

276

she's in Mr. Sulikowski's History class right now and would get in so much trouble if he knew what she was doing.

Meh.

Made any friends?

Not yet, I reply, even though I now think it's going to be really hard for that to happen.

How many stars is today?

Six. I've survived six days.

How many until I see you?

Too many, I reply, then quickly text her, 8.

I'm aware that I'm spending too much energy wishing the time would go faster instead of living it.

But what's a life worth when you don't want to be part of it.

Chapter

THIRTY-EIGHT

I somehow make it through the week.

Day nine in Tampa.

I see Marian in five days.

Despite Paula's offer to give me a makeup tutorial, I don't put in a lot of effort in the morning to do my hair and makeup before school. But I find myself putting on a coat of mascara and some lip gloss after dinner. I examine myself under the bright fluorescent lights in the bathroom and figure it's as good as it'll get.

It's Friday night, after all. And I have a date.

I tap on my phone. Before I have a chance to get a good angle, he picks up.

"Hey!" Neil greets me.

"Hey."

"Do you have everything we talked about?"

"Of course!" I show him my popcorn and soda. I've got my TV muted since the movie doesn't start for a half hour.

"Here's to winter break!" He gives me a cheers with his can of Coke.

"Cheers!" I take a sip of Diet Dr Pepper, since it's the only soda in the refrigerator downstairs.

"And you don't mind spending a Friday night like this?" he asks.

"Because you know how rockin' my Friday nights were back home."

"Hey, you were a hard girl to pin down, which is why I had to wait until you were a million miles away before I could get you to have a date with me. Now, remind me again, what was Friday night in the Smith household? Arm Wrestling and Hot Pockets Fridays?"

"Ha ha. We'd watch a movie or some TV on the weekends."

"Oh, so we're keeping up with tradition, nice! What are the McMullens up to?"

I shrug. "Every night has been all over the place. Craig has some meeting or Paula has to take Sarah to one of her activities." Whenever I'd sit down with any combination of people at this house, it's all boring family conversations. Like, "How was your day, dear?" Nothing of substance.

I'm partly to blame for any stilted dinnertime conversations, since I haven't been particularly forthcoming or chatty. I've started to shut off the part of my brain that feels. Every day this week, I've gone through ticking my boxes. Breakfast is done. Check! Up next, school. All so I can get to the end of the day, when I can add another star to my calendar.

I could put more effort into things. Join a club or make a friend, but that would just lead to more questions about "Allison Johnson." There's also a part of me that feels like I'd be betraying not only my friends back home but Dad, too. As if fitting in here would mean that he made a mistake for taking me away.

"Ally?" Neil asks, his brow furrowed.

"Sorry, zoned out for a second. I have something to show you," I say, changing the topic, shoving any negative thoughts away. This evening is about Neil and me.

I flip the phone camera around so he can see the room. I walk over to the large dresser to show him a photo of him, Marian, and me that's in a frame. Paula bought me some picture frames yesterday so I could make the room more "homey." I went through all the photos in my computer and printed out the one with Neil and Marian, another group photo from Homecoming this year, one of Marian's family in Door County, and one of Dad and me at Lambeau. When Paula came in later to see what I did, she was all smiles, but I could tell the photo with my dad upset her.

"I made the room!" Neil says with a fist pump. "So now you can look at all this anytime of day. I like it! Although I think a life-sized cardboard cutout might be even better."

"Don't make me turn the photo around," I tease.

"Well, I'm honored. So, tell me about this scary, big school."

"The senior class alone has over six hundred people."

"What?" Neil's eyes bulge. "That's insane."

"It is."

"Have you made any friends?"

"Not really." Four days in, there are a few people who say hi to me in class. Jordis will give me the occasional wave in the hallway, but that's it. Making small talk while I'm hiding this big secret makes me too anxious to build any kind of relationship.

A smile spreads on Neil's face.

"Oh, so you're happy I'm a lonely loser here?"

"No, no!" His cheeks redden. "I know I shouldn't feel like this or anything, but I sometimes get worried that you'll forget about us here with your new life."

"I could never forget you guys."

"But you have the beach and the sun there," he counters.

"The water in the Gulf is too cold to swim in." Craig did bring us by the beach the other day so I could dip my toes in. The bite of the cold water barely made it to my ankles before I ran back to the warmth of the sand. "So the score is still a gazillion to zero, advantage Wisconsin."

"Phew, good." Neil's face falls for a second. "But I want you to be happy. Maybe you should try to make a friend. But not a guy friend. Unless he doesn't have an ounce of charm and is hideous."

"I already have enough friends, including hideous guys."

"I'm going to tell Rob you said that about him!"

It feels so good to laugh. To talk to someone who I have inside jokes with. Someone I don't have to censor myself with.

"No guys, then. You don't have another FaceTime date this

weekend?" Neil bites his lip, like I'm honestly going to tell him that, yeah, I'm beating the guys away with a stick.

"No, none. You should see the girls I go to school with. They're tall, gorgeous, and somehow all seem to use the same shampoo that makes their hair glossy and perfect. I'm invisible to guys here. Nobody sees me."

Neil moves closer to the camera so his face takes up the entire screen. "I see you."

There's a beat between us. He does see me. He's always seen me.

I touch the screen, wishing there wasn't this distance between us.

"I see you, too."

Chapter

THIRTY-NINE

Day twelve. Christmas. I knew today was going to be hard.

I never fathomed how impossible it would be. Last night after Christmas Eve mass, I smiled along and played the part as Craig and Paula welcomed their family over for drinks and snacks. I answered questions, but mostly I stayed in a corner, trying to be invisible.

It's become my new go-to setting, at school and in this house: tuck myself away.

As the morning sun slowly started to lighten the room, I threw the duvet over my head, hoping I could delay the inevitable.

I turned on the TV, but "I'll Be Home for Christmas" greeted me, and it started my breakdown. It caused my entire body to shake. It unleashed an unsteady breathing until I got up and locked myself in the bathroom so I could have some privacy as I sobbed.

That's where I am now. Lying on the bathroom floor, I let the cool tiles soothe me as I ache for what I used to have. Memories burn into my head of Thanksgiving, merely four weeks ago, with the Gleasons and Dad. The laughter. The joy. The kind of peace you have when you truly belong with people.

As much as I try to bury certain thoughts deep in my mind, I can't forget about Dad. How we'd come home from Christmas Eve mass and immediately put on our Christmas-themed pajamas. Dad wore a Wisconsin Badgers sweatshirt with green-and-red-striped pajama bottoms. Mine were flannel with reindeer and Santas on them with Ho! Ho! Ho! printed throughout.

I forgot to pack them since they were in a holiday box in the garage that I never thought about going through. The image of that box—filled with ornaments we'd collected through the years along with all our holiday decorations—gathering dust brings more tears to my eyes.

I feel guilty that I turned my back on my father the last time I saw him. Even though he knows I'm sorry, I want to tell him. It's Christmas, and I can't talk to my father.

How can you be so angry with someone, be so devastated by their betrayal, yet still love them?

I pull the yellow-and-white bath towel from its hook near the shower and press it against my mouth as I let out a sob, trying to mute myself. I don't want anybody to know the condition I'm in. I want to stay in here all day.

There's a knock on the bedroom door. "It's present time!" Paula's voice calls out.

I reach up and lock the door to the bathroom.

"Hello?" she calls. Her voice is louder, so I assume she's in the bedroom now. "Sweetheart?"

"I'll be down in a minute," I manage to call out. "You can start without me."

"Nonsense." I can see her feet under the door. I hold my breath, not wanting to make a sound that would tip her off there's a problem.

She's hovering, so I flush the toilet.

"Okay, well. See you soon. Merry Christmas!"

I drag myself up from the floor and study my blotchy red face and bloodshot eyes in the mirror. My hair is a complete disaster. I pull out my ponytail and try to comb it into submission. I splash cold water on my face, but it doesn't help.

Maybe it's no use pretending. Maybe I need to stop pushing everything down and let Paula know how miserable I am. I don't want to hurt her anymore, but I can't keep pretending. It's eating me up inside. She wants us to be this big happy family, but I can't simply disregard the person I was before.

I take a deep breath and start heading downstairs. Laughter and music drift up the hallway. I pause when I realize "White Christmas" from *Holiday Inn* is playing on the stereo. It's the movie Dad and I would watch on Christmas Eve.

You get to see Marian in two days, I remind myself. *Hold out for two days. You can do that. Suck it up and get through today and tomorrow.*

"There she is!" Craig greets me, a Santa hat placed on his head. "Merry Christmas!"

"Merry Christmas," I try to say brightly. I sniff since all the sobbing did some major damage to my sinuses.

"Are you sick?" Paula comes up to me and places the back of her hand to my forehead. "You're really warm." She takes a step back and looks at my face. "And red."

I see my opportunity and take it. "I'm feeling a little under the weather. Do you think it would be okay if I stayed here today?"

The thought of having to spend the day with Paula's family is too draining. All they see in me is the kidnapped girl they don't know how to act around. And I have no clue how to behave around them.

She grimaces. "Well, let's see how you feel after presents."

"Paula," Craig says as he shakes his head. "Ally, if you're not feeling well, you should stay home. You've got your friend coming in a couple days. Got to be up for that!"

"Thanks." I sit down on the floor near their tree.

"Your pile is over there." Sarah points to a huge stack of presents near an armchair.

My eyes are wide. I've never seen so many presents in my life.

"We had a lot of Christmases to make up for," Paula states with that sad look on her face that appears whenever she looks at me.

"It's too much," I say, but she ignores me and starts unwrapping the gift I got her.

I'm relieved the presents I ordered online came in time since they each got me at least one present. I had to borrow Craig's credit card to make the purchases, and he's refused my repeated attempts to pay him back with the cash I have from my savings.

Paula rips open the present with the look of, well, a kid on Christmas morning. She holds up the Packers T-shirt. "Oh, what fun!"

I honestly had no idea what to get the people I didn't know existed a month ago. So I went with Packers paraphernalia. I figure since they know I'm going to be watching games here, they might want to start coming "to the dark side," as Craig once jokingly described it.

"You're next!" Paula says to me with a little clap.

I pick up a small silver-and-red-wrapped box from the top of my pile and run my finger along the seam. When I open it up, I find an assortment of earrings in all colors, shapes, and sizes.

"I thought you'd like some more jewelry to go with your new clothes," Paula says with a smile. She comes over to me and picks up the silver hoops on the top. "These are my favorite. You should put them on now!"

She reaches out the earrings to me, a hopeful smile on her face.

I take them from her. "Oh, thanks. They're gorgeous. It's just, um, I don't . . ."

Her face falls as she looks at my ears, which have never been pierced. "I didn't know . . ."

Why would she?

"It's okay!" I reply with a pat on her hand. I know Paula's repeated attempts to help me be more of a girly girl is her version of bonding. I appreciate it, but it's just not me. I'll let her dress me up and accessorize me, but there's no way I'm letting a needle go through my ears. Nope. Not happening.

"I'm sure Paula won't mind having to make a trip to the mall to exchange them for whatever you want," Craig says with a wink.

"Yeah!" I reply brightly, willing that sad look on Paula's face to vanish. "That sounds like fun."

She brushes my face with her hand. "Okay, sweetheart."

"Me next!" Sarah calls out as she picks up a large bag.

We go around one by one to open presents. Craig particularly likes the Cheesehead I got him, which he proudly puts on. My other gifts from Paula include sparkly shirts and short skirts I would never wear.

With every passing minute I fall into a deeper depression over how wrong this feels. They're doing their best to make me feel at home, but it's having the opposite effect. I feel terrible about it. Expensive presents aren't going to change how I feel. In fact, it's the opposite of how I'd spent the holidays. Dad and I would exchange one silly gift—last year he gave me this coin purse with a woman dressed up with a tiara that said, Dress for the Job You Want, while I got him a T-shirt that read, Totally Rad in big neon letters since he likes random weird sayings from the dark ages (aka the 1980s). The gifts weren't the point. It was spending time together. Like a real family.

That memory plunges me even further into my funk.

Sarah bolts up from the floor, which is littered with torn paper and boxes. "Can I FaceTime Stacey to show her what I got?"

Paula laughs. "Yes." Sarah takes an armful of her presents and goes into the kitchen. Paula's attention turns to me. "Feeling better?"

I shake my head. "Not really." I can tell that my face isn't as hot anymore, but that doesn't change that I want to simply hide under the covers for the rest of today. "Would it be okay if I went upstairs?"

Paula hesitates for a moment before telling me it's okay.

"Thanks." I start to gather up all my gifts. "And thanks for everything. It's really nice of you all."

I go upstairs and start putting my gifts into piles, so I can write thank-you notes. When I realize I left my glass of water downstairs, I head back out, but pause as I hear Craig and Paula's conversation drift upstairs. Even though their voices are hushed, I can hear what they're saying.

"She needs more time. This is all new to her, and today has to be really hard," Craig says.

My stomach churns, as it's fairly obvious who they're talking about.

"What about the past fifteen Christmases for me?" Paula says. "Those were painful. Now she's here and it's obvious she wants to be anywhere else. Is it too much to ask that I get to spend Christmas with my daughter?"

"I know, but, Paula, you need to stop getting mad at her—"

"I'm not mad!" Her voice rises.

"Yes, you are. This is a lot for her. I don't think you realize how you're punishing Ally for what her father did. You're still so angry about the past and what you lost that you are pushing her away. You're so focused on how *you* want her to behave you're missing out on the amazing girl who's upstairs. She's hurt. She's scared. This is all new to her; *we* are new to her."

"I don't think I'll ever get over it."

That makes two of us, Paula.

"Nobody would blame you for that, but let's think about Ally. Her feelings matter just as much, if not more than yours."

"It's like I've lost her twice. First it was because of Dan; now it's because she simply doesn't want to be here." Paula sighs. "I'm not angry, I'm frustrated. All I want is for her to be happy. Why can't she just be happy?"

I don't want to hear anymore. I go into the guest room and lock the door. I crawl under the covers of the bed and turn the TV on. Mindlessly flipping through the channels, I stop when I see *The Christmas Story*. It's at one of my favorite parts. When the bully pushes down the younger brother and because of his mega-snowsuit he can't get up.

My lip quivers as I ready for the line Dad and I used to say to each other when we'd get bundled up for winter in northern Wisconsin. We sometimes had on so many layers it was hard to move.

Then it came: "Randy lay there like a slug . . . It was his only defense."

A laugh quickly turns into a sob. I shut the TV off and throw the duvet over my head, burying myself away into a cocoon of sobs and misery.

Paula's right.

Why can't I just be happy?

Chapter

FORTY

Whenever there was a bad storm at home, my dad and I would walk outside after the clouds would clear and peer into the sky, looking for a rainbow.

"Just remember during a storm, Ally Bean, that light will always follow," he used to say.

The past few weeks have been a horrible storm for me, but today, today I get a taste of the light.

It's day fourteen. I get to see Marian and Baxter.

The last time I was at the Tampa airport, my nerves were swirling with panic and uncertainty. There was fear of the media that had swarmed the arrivals gate. There was the insecurity of what was waiting for me once I exited the airport.

Today is different. My stomach is jumpy, but it's for the excitement of seeing my two best friends.

Paula drove me to the airport. Things between us remain off.

Every time I look at her, I see only someone who wishes her daughter were someone else.

"The flight's landed," I remark to cut through the silence. Marian's flight from Chicago is here. I begin to scan the crowds of people coming out past security. It seems to take months before I finally see her dark hair bobbing up and down. I move to get a better look, but before I can wave to her, she sees me and breaks into a sprint.

"Ally!" she screams as she barrels into me. She's hugging me so tightly and turning me around and around I'm getting dizzy, but I don't care.

We stand there, hugging each other for what seems like an eternity.

"Good to see you again, Marian," Paula says. "How was the flight?"

"It got me here," Marian replies as she finally pulls away and gets a good look at me. "Look at you! So Florida with your open-toed sandals and tan."

I look down at my pale white arms. "I'm not tan."

"I know. You do realize that the sun is good for you, right? Vitamin D and all that." She peels off her bulky winter jacket. "Guess I don't need this anymore. It was so nice to carry on, since I don't need fourteen layers to step outside here."

Paula starts walking. "I checked with the airline, and we have to get Baxter at the special services desk in baggage claim."

Poor Baxter. Not only did he have to fly for the first time, but he's also too big to fit under the seat, so we had to put him in a crate. He's never really spent a lot of time in a crate before. Hopefully seeing me will make up for it. It would literally rip my heart out if he doesn't recognize me.

And then I'm making him stay in a weird place. I have to keep him in the backyard or Craig's man cave thanks to Paula's and Sarah's allergies. They're both taking an antihistamine, but I'm hoping if I keep everything really clean and they don't have any issues that I can keep him here.

"Oh, I also brought some Wisconsin cheese!" Marian holds up a plastic bag from Gleason's Grocer.

Score another point for why Wisconsin is better than Florida: the cheese.

"Yum! I can't wait to eat all of that." My stomach growls to prove my point.

We get to baggage claim, and I hear Baxter before I see him. He's straining his leash, barking at me, his tail wagging a thousand miles an hour.

I run to him. I fall to my knees, and Baxter starts licking my face. "Hey, boy." I try to hug him, but he's too excited to see me. I just pet him and let his kisses fall on me, finding comfort in another part of my home.

Marian's laugh cuts through all the slobbering.

"Ahem," comes from above. It's the person who has Baxter by the leash. It's then that I notice the shoes are familiar: green-and-white Vans.

I look up and there he is.

Christmas wishes do come true.

293

"Hey," Neil says with a wide grin on his face.

I stand up and nearly fall over. "What are you—You know what, it doesn't matter!" I throw my arms around him and breathe him in. He wraps his arms around me in a way that's gentle but firm. I bury my face in his jacket, not wanting anybody to see the tears that are starting to spill. Baxter is jumping on us and yapping happily.

Marian, Neil, and Baxter. Three huge pieces of myself have returned to me, and I don't want to let any of them go.

⟿

Marian turns her face up into the sun. "I have to admit, this is nice. But in a nice-place-to-visit-in-the-winter-and-during-spring-break way," she clarifies as she unfolds her legs out from under her to get some sun. "Not where-my-best-friend-should-live-permanently nice."

We're in the backyard watching Baxter run around sniffing every inch of the grass. He keeps coming back to me every few seconds to make sure I'm still here. He rests his head on my lap for a moment before a squirrel distracts him.

The sun is beginning to set. We've spent the past three hours talking a mile a minute as if we hadn't been speaking or texting every day.

"Okay, besides Disney World and the beach, we want to see your high school while we're here," Neil states. "You know, the Death Star."

"It's too big to be a school," I say with a laugh.

"I have a very bad feeling about this," Neil says, completing our new adapted Star Wars quote for the monstrosity known as my school building.

I still can't believe that he's here and that Paula and Craig kept it a secret because Marian wanted it to be a surprise. (Apparently Sarah wasn't informed, because they thought she'd spill.) Finally, a nice surprise.

"I also want us to take Sarah somewhere, just the four of us," I state.

"Cool," Marian says. "She seems really sweet."

"She is. We're growing on each other."

Neil leans into me, and goose bumps run up my body. "That's good."

"Oh, and I figure that I can let you two have some alone time," Marian says with a wiggle of her eyebrows.

Neil's face lights up. "That's really, really good."

Yes, it is.

⁓

Who knew being a tourist could be so exhausting?

Yesterday was spent at Disney World. Neil, Marian, and I ran around like little kids having a competition of who would get the most selfies with the costumed characters (Marian won since she spied both Minnie Mouse and Goofy when she went to the restroom). We ate cotton candy until our hands were sticky and rode rides until we felt sick. Neil got sunburn on his ears and neck because he forgot to slather them with sunscreen.

At the end of the day, we watched the fireworks overhead. Neil's fingers touched mine lightly before he entwined our hands. We stood there, our heads aimed at the sky, holding hands until it was time to go back to Tampa.

Now the three of us are sprawled out in Craig's man cave.

"Ouch," Marian says as she sits up. "My legs are sore. Am I so out of shape that simply walking around has made my legs burn? Actually, don't answer that question."

"Well, we did walk, what, like ten miles or something?"

Paula has a fancy watch that counts her steps, so she kept updating us as she hit different milestones. For the most part, Craig, Paula, and Sarah lagged behind us yesterday. A few times, Sarah was even able to pull them away to something she wanted to do, which left us alone.

"This couch is insanely comfortable," Marian remarks as she sinks farther down in the cushions.

"The pullout is even better," Neil replies. He's been sleeping here, while Marian's been crashing with me.

I stretch my legs out on the ottoman and fall a little to the right so I'm touching Neil. And, yes, I'm totally doing this on purpose.

Marian stands up with a few groans. "I'm going to go check in on Rob, make sure he hasn't burned down the town yet. That dude should not be left to his own devices. Yeah, anyway, I'll be a while. So . . ."

She lets that hang in the air as she goes downstairs.

Not going to lie, I've been waiting for this alone time with Neil.

I'd been comfortable lounging near him, feeling his heat radiate on my skin. Neil shifts a bit so he can see me better.

"Hey."

"Hey," I reply shyly.

Neil looks down at the floor. There's a beat of silence.

"I'm really glad you're here," I state for probably the hundredth time. It means everything to me that he made the trip.

"Like anything could've stopped me when you said you wished I was coming."

"Of course I wanted you here. I can't believe you thought I wouldn't."

Neil takes my hand. I like the sensation of being linked with him. I feel safe.

"I've really missed you," he says. "I can't even imagine how you're doing with your dad."

"It's really hard." My voice cracks slightly. The wall I've built with Paula with the "fines" and "okays" and just going along with everything has been shattered with the arrival of Marian and Neil. I don't have to hide how heartbroken I am about everything. "I feel so helpless about it because there's absolutely nothing I can do."

"It's not permanent," Neil reminds me. "This isn't for forever."

"This isn't for forever," I echo. "But then I get in this vicious cycle of thinking of how I could've stopped it from happening if I didn't apply to college."

"No, you can't do that to yourself. Your dad wouldn't have been okay with that. He wants a good future for you. None of this is your fault."

"I'm not completely innocent in all of this."

"Nobody's perfect, although you're pretty damn close." He gives my hand a squeeze.

There's a pause. I can talk to Neil about my dad anytime; that's always going to be hovering over me. Now that he and I are finally alone and don't have hundreds of miles between us, I finally do what I hadn't had the courage to do before.

"Do you want to know the truth?"

He smiles at me, and the butterflies in my stomach are flying a million miles an hour. "Always."

"I wish I didn't wait until I was leaving to do anything about us."

His eyebrows rise. "So there's an us?"

The old Ally would've been scared of her feelings. She liked her safe routines. She didn't want to make things complicated or messy.

Now, with everything so uncertain, it's nice to think about a future that isn't scary. A future that could be wonderful. A future with Neil.

"Yes," I say as I look him in the eyes so he knows I mean it. "Us."

We both move slowly toward each other. My skin tingles as he palms my face; our lips part and finally meet. This isn't our first kiss, but it's a new first. It's the first of us.

I sink into him as he continues to tenderly kiss me. My mind is only focused on one thing: Neil.

And my brain is alight with contentment.

Then Paula comes crashing in. "Are you going out for dinner?" her voice booms as she stomps up the stairs.

Neil and I part. I move to the other side of the couch and try to catch my breath. Neil, who's never been great about hiding his true feelings, looks both elated and busted.

"I wasn't sure—" Paula stops as she sees us: a teenage girl and boy alone in a room, both out of sorts. She knows exactly what's going on. "Well, I just wanted to know if you want me to order something or take you somewhere. Just, ah, just let me know." She goes to head back to the stairs, pauses before turning to us, opens her mouth to say something, but then changes her mind. "Um, I'll be in the kitchen, and, yes, ah, let me know. About the food. Yes, dinner."

Neil and I stay silent until we hear the door close, then we start laughing.

"I'm going to die from embarrassment," Neil says between his fingers, which are currently hiding his face. "But she means well, I guess." Neil moves his head around as if he's trying to place Paula. "She's a bit awkward."

"We just don't know what to do with each other," I admit. "But, you know," I say as I slide closer to him, "I don't want to talk about Paula anymore."

"But whatever should we do?" He taps his finger on his chin. "Hmmm."

"Just shut up and get over here."

I didn't need to tell him twice.

The days in Tampa pre–Neil and Marian dragged and dragged. With them, the time has flown by. The days of fun and feeling like myself are over.

I'd already cried saying goodbye to Baxter, tucking him into his crate for the flight back to Wisconsin. Paula was adamant that he couldn't stay. Now I can't even look at Marian and Neil as we stand outside the security checkpoint at the airport with Paula hovering in the background.

Marian's wearing her Mickey Mouse ears we got at Disney. Tears are running down her face, too. "I knew this was going to be hard. Maybe I can come for MLK weekend or something."

I hug her for the fortieth time in the past ten minutes. "Thank you for coming. I desperately needed this."

She steps away and Neil comes forward. He gives me a kiss on the cheek since Paula's watching. We had our proper goodbye before we got in the car, and there wasn't anything proper about it. "Hang in there," he says in a low voice. His hand is on my back, and my entire body burns from it. "It sucks to say goodbye, but remember, this isn't for forever."

That thought alone is what's going to keep me going until I can find myself in his arms again.

Chapter

FORTY-ONE

I had a moment of happiness. A glimmer into my old life.

Then everything came crashing back around me.

As the TV counted down to the new year, I felt dread, not hope. When I used to look to the year ahead, my mind would be filled with positive thoughts. Not anymore.

Craig got me a Green Bay Packers calendar when he saw me printing out the month of January before the new year. Every night as I give myself a star for surviving the day, I mentally prepare for the next one. I wake up and get ready. Breakfast is a flurry of everybody eating and making small talk. School is school. I keep my head down. I come home and do homework. Every night is different, but it's a rotating series of dinners with one or two family members or Sarah and me on our own. I prefer just the two of us. When Paula is at the dinner table, she asks me questions about my day and school. She told me she's sick of hearing me always respond with "fine" because that's what this life is. Fine.

A little over a week into the new year, on day twenty-seven of my sentence, Sheriff Gleason calls. I sit down as he delivers the news: the grand jury has issued their indictment against Dad. He's being charged with thirty-three counts. Thirty-three. There are two kidnapping charges, two for interference of custody, ten counts of forgery, and then I kind of blank out. It's too much to take.

But he has a suggestion for me, and I'm going to do everything I can to help Dad.

The biggest hurdle is that I need Paula's help.

I find her rushing around the kitchen, putting together her version of Taco Tuesday. I offer to help, but I still don't know where most of the items she needs are and I end up mostly being in the way.

I appreciate that they're doing this for me. I mentioned it one night when Craig asked me about the meals I used to have. Craig thought it sounded like a great idea and we should do it.

Since we had a tradition for almost each day of the week, I'm reminded every day about something we'd done. I get the saddest on Wednesday. That was when we'd watch a really bad movie. We would laugh so much at the horrible dialogue, bad special effects, and how on earth something like *Troll 2* could have been made. Like, the original *Troll* was such a hit, Hollywood thought the people needed more! Then we went through a phase where we'd only watch those movies where some species would be mega or combined with another species. I, of course, am talking about the cinematic masterpieces featuring Mega Python, Dinoshark, or Zombeavers, or something of the ilk. And I have zero shame in admitting that a new *Sharknado* was like Super Bowl Sunday to us.

Dad and I had started to come up with our own movie we were going to try to sell to the Syfy channel. It featured a starfish that has been exposed to nuclear waste and descends on a tiny beach town right before the one major event of the season when all the local businesses get all their money. An environmentalist tries to warn the sheriff (who, of course, is his ex-lover), but the shady town mayor looks the other way as people in the town start disappearing.

Seriously, this stuff writes itself.

Yeah, it was silly, but these were our traditions. They were what made me *me*. They gave me stability.

I push away these thoughts as I cut up the veggies for Paula.

"So," I begin, but she interrupts.

"Your birthday is coming up in two weeks," Paula says brightly. "Any idea what you want to do?"

No, because I already had my eighteenth birthday.

"Maybe we should have a big party. You can invite some friends. From school," she clarifies.

I don't reply. We both know it's been difficult for "Allison Johnson" to make any real friends.

"You need to make more of an effort at school. Join a club. And maybe if you didn't spend all your free time talking to your *other* friends, you would meet some new people."

"I've known Marian and Neil for a really long time. It makes me feel better to talk to them." I know I'm bringing up a touchy subject for her. She doesn't want to talk about anything in my past life. But it was *my life*. My real life.

"Well, you're here now." She wipes her hand on a towel, almost as if she's wiping away this conversation—and my old life—away. "So we are going to celebrate your birthday because it's the first I'm having with you since you were three. You can either tell me what you want or I'll do something."

"We can just go out to dinner, the four of us."

"We can do that anytime," she argues.

"Oh, well . . ." I don't know what to say. She asked me what I wanted; that's what I want. But, like with everything else since I got here, I try to guess what would make her happy. "Or we can have the whole family over. Might be fun. I would like to get to know the extended family more."

That's not entirely a lie. A few of my cousins are nice. Then there are others who treat me like I'm a freak. I think they expect some damaged person. The kidnapped girl.

Paula brightens up. "That sounds like a plan!" She claps her hands and starts making notes. I've never wanted a party where the focus is all on me.

Paula wouldn't know that. Besides, she has a vision of what she wants my party to be, what my life should be, where I should go to college . . .

What I want really seems irrelevant at this point. What kind of life is that?

So I'll go along. I'll have the party. I'll smile and eat cake.

"Sheriff Gleason called," I blurt out.

Paula freezes, her shoulders automatically tense.

"Yeah, he explained all the charges against my dad." I tear off the bandage. "I'd like to be there for sentencing. I want to give a statement."

"Absolutely not. Your father is finally going to do something right and plead guilty."

"I know, but my testimony may help reduce his sentence." What I don't tell her is that I really, really need to see him. If I'm in the courtroom, I can at least look at him with my own eyes. Although I realize I may not like what I see. Sheriff Gleason also mentioned that Dad's a little down and has lost some weight, but Dad's main concern is always how I'm doing.

"No," Paula states firmly as she grips the sides of the counter. "Your father committed a crime, and he should be punished."

"He is being punished. But I want the judge to see I'm fine. He took great care of me. He pushed me to be a good student. I wouldn't have gotten the grades I did if it wasn't for him."

"What a saint." The bitterness in her voice has reached a new level.

"I'm sorry that you don't want to hear that, but it's true. And since we're on the topic, I'd like to finally talk to his family. You can't keep me from my aunt and grandmother."

She turns around, and her face is filled with anger. "Yes, I can. You can talk to them when you finally start acting like a part of *this* family. Oh, believe me, you've been quite clear on how much your father means to you. Yes, you've made that obvious. I know he poisoned you against me."

Paranoid much, Paula?

She's been convinced this entire time that Dad bad-mouthed her. But he didn't because I had thought she was dead. All I do know of our relationship when I was little is that I didn't want to spend time with her when I was three years old.

So maybe I *am* the same person I was when I was taken.

"Dad never poisoned me—"

"I don't want to hear it!" She raises her voice at me. "I've tried to think about your feelings, but you really don't seem to be concerned about mine. I am your mother. You are *my* daughter. This is *my time* with you."

I decide to raise my voice as well. "Well, I'm here, aren't I?"

"*You* won't even call me *Mom*."

"And *you* don't call me *Ally*."

"ALLY IS NOT YOUR NAME!" she screams back. "You're just as stubborn as your father. Why can't you adjust?"

"And why can't you acknowledge how unfair this has been for me?" I scream back.

This actually feels good. Getting all of it out in the open. The Ally I've been burying to make Paula happy is starting to fight to come back to the surface.

And she's super pissed.

"WHAT ABOUT ME? All this time I've done everything you've asked. I've left my friends, my dog. I've worn the clothes *you* want me to. I've gone to every family function *you* want. I am here because this is what *you* want. *You* don't want to know anything about me. *You* have this idea of who you want me to be, and, guess what, I'm not her. I'm sorry I'm not this perfect daughter *you* have had in your head all this time, but I'm sick of pretending to be something I'm not." I'm shaking, I'm so mad. And I'm so tired of keeping everything bottled inside.

"You have put forth ZERO effort!" She points her finger at me.

"ARE YOU FUCKING KIDDING ME RIGHT NOW? Have you not listened to a word I just said?"

"Don't you dare talk to me like that!" She comes over and grabs me by my shoulders.

Craig runs into the kitchen. "What on earth is going on? I heard shouting all the way in the garage."

Paula ignores him. "I don't know what kind of vulgar child your father has raised you to be, but I don't want to hear his name ever again. Is that clear?"

Craig puts his arm around Paula to comfort her, but also to separate us. "Paula, please calm down."

"This is not my fault!"

"AND IT'S NOT MINE, EITHER!" Tears are streaming down my face. I let out a sob. I'm not going to hold it in anymore. It's been nothing but pure torture.

"JUST STOP IT!" She holds her hands in front of my face. "We are not talking about it anymore. PERIOD." She shoves Craig away as she runs out of the kitchen.

"Ally, are you okay?" Craig asks, but I run upstairs.

Of course I'm not okay.

I have tried. I've played along, but it will never be enough. And I am so done.

With shaking hands, I call Marian.

"Hey!" she answers cheerily.

I let out another agonizing sob.

"Oh my God, what's wrong? Are you hurt?"

I can't reply, because breathing is nearly impossible.

"Please, say something," Marian pleads.

"I—I—" I stutter out. "I need you to get everybody together."

"Of course. I'll send out the Ally signal. Whatever you need."

I don't want to be a burden. I don't. But I can't live this life anymore. It's too much.

I try to steady my breath. "I have to get out of here, and I'm going to need everybody's help."

There's a slight pause. "Oh, Ally, we thought you'd never ask."

Chapter
FORTY-TWO

Once Old Ally surfaced, she wasn't going to be buried again.

After Marian and Neil left, I didn't have anything to look forward to. My calendar was an endless sea of blank days I had to survive. But then I had a goal, a plan.

I had to get through fifteen days.

Day by day, I went through the motions.

Breakfast, school, homework, dinner.

Paula and I were polite to each other, but cool. Sarah and Craig tried to talk to me, to make things better, but I simply replied that everything was "fine" and "okay."

Breakfast, school, homework, dinner.

I sat at the dinner table and nodded along with everybody's stories. I'd answer questions about school when asked. But I wasn't really there anymore.

Breakfast, school, homework, dinner.

I had an end game. It made the charade that much easier.

Breakfast, school, homework, dinner.

And now the day I've been waiting for arrived.

This is my final performance as The Good Daughter. I'm going to smile, play along, and let Paula have her moment. This is for her. It's the last thing I'm doing for her.

Paula is fluttering around the room, chatting with people and laughing. She's the belle of the ball, while Sarah and I sit on a couch, both on our phones.

Sarah looks up at her mom. "Look at her! She can't concentrate on one person for too long. You'd think this was her birthday party."

Paula goes over to hug . . . I think it's my cousin Molly, but I'm not sure. I'm too embarrassed at this point to ask who people are again. I only remember Randy since he's the one who always comes up to me to talk about my "fame." He already cornered me earlier, telling me I need secure a book deal now because "interest is waning." Those three words were the best things I've heard come out of his mouth. Oh, he also offered to be my manager.

Yeah, I'm going to pass on that one.

"There you are." Grandma Amanda sits next to me on the couch and gives me a kiss on the forehead. "I know you said you didn't want any presents."

"Can you believe it?" Sarah says. "Everybody here owes her like years' and years' worth of presents."

That was my only request for today that was actually taken into consideration. At this point, Paula and Craig have given me too much.

Grandma Amanda hands me a tiny wrapped box.

"You shouldn't have," I reply.

"I'm your grandmother; I'm supposed to spoil you." She gives my leg a pat as I begin to delicately tear the wrapping paper. I open the box and find a silver pendant shaped like a sundial. "It was my mother's," she explains as she starts to put it around my neck. "She said that with this you always know *when* you are, not necessarily *where* you are, and, well, I think it suits you."

"I can't," I protest.

"Nonsense, every one of my grandchildren gets something from my mother when they turn eighteen. I'm happy that I am able to give it to you."

I touch the necklace as it lies on my chest. "Thank you."

"You're welcome." She takes my hand. "Listen, Ally, being an adult means you have to sometimes make tough decisions."

A lump gets caught in my throat. I have made a tough decision. And it's going to affect everybody in this room.

She cups my chin with her hand. "Even when you were gone, all I ever wanted was for you to be safe and happy."

"I was."

She smiles at me. "I know. And I want you to also be happy now."

That's all I want, too.

I open my mouth, but we're interrupted by Paula clinking her glass.

"Can I have your attention?" Paula says. "Just for a moment."

"That means shut up, Randy!" one of my older cousins, or maybe an uncle, shouts to the laughter of the group.

Paula smiles as she looks around the room and finally settles on me. "I can't tell you how thrilled I am that this day has finally come. My baby is back home for her birthday. And she's an adult! Eighteen." She shakes her head in disbelief. "I've had some dark times during most of those eighteen years, but our Amanda has come back to the light. I'm so proud of the woman you've become. My beautiful, smart daughter."

As much as we don't understand each other, Paula has loved me every day for the past eighteen years, even though she had no idea where I was or even if I was alive. I hope someday I can repay her with that kind of love. But love takes time. As does trust.

"Speech!" someone calls out.

See, this is how much my Florida family doesn't know me. There's no way anybody back home would ask me to make a speech. They would know how horrified I'd be. If I were ever in this position, someone would save me. Dad or Neil or any of the Gleasons.

Yet nobody is saying anything. They're waiting for me. And I do owe them something. There are going to be a lot of questions soon, so better let them know that it's not them, it's me.

I stand up and feel a bit wobbly on my feet. "Thank you."

"Speak up!" someone else shouts at me.

"Thank you," I say louder. "Ah, I'm not good with public speaking, but it means a lot to me that you are all here. I know many of you have memories about me from when I was little, and I'm sorry I don't remember them. I've missed a lot, but we have plenty of holidays and other occasions to make new ones. And I look forward to that."

It's true. There can be a future with my Florida family. I've got my whole entire life to make up for lost time. Thing is, it doesn't need to be right now. Family bonding can't be forced. It's something that will happen gradually.

There's some applause as Paula wraps her arms around me. "Oh, sweetie. That means so much to me."

I pull away so I can look her in the eye. "I mean what I said. It doesn't matter where I go to college or where I live, I'm still your daughter. We get to make new memories. And I never meant to hurt you."

She touches my cheek. "I know, baby. I only want what's best for you."

"Me too."

Chapter

FORTY-THREE

I look around the bedroom. It's surprising how little I feel about it, compared to my room back home. I place the note for Paula on the bed and touch it lightly before I put my backpack on and walk quietly to the door. Maybe I'm doing it the coward's way, but this will probably be best for everybody.

At least that's what I'm telling myself.

My cell phone chirps and I smile. I open the door and look around the quiet hallway. I tiptoe to the stairs and then hear a click behind me.

I turn around to find Sarah standing outside her room, rubbing her eyes. "What's going on?"

I freeze. "Nothing," I whisper. "Go back to sleep."

Sarah looks at me, fully dressed with a backpack on and carrying a suitcase, and realizes I'm full of it. She drops her hands and walks to me. "You're leaving?"

"Listen, I'm just going back home to testify for my dad and finish school. I know I promised that I'd stay until graduation, but I can't. I just can't do it. I will be back. And, well, I left a note to explain everything. I also said I'm going to call later this morning when she's had a chance to read everything I have to say. I'm going to talk to her every day. You too." I wrap Sarah in a hug. She hesitates before hugging me back. "I'm going to miss you, Sarah. But I have to do this."

She pushes me away. "No."

"Sarah," I plead quietly, not wanting to wake Paula and Craig.

"What are you going to do about the door alarm? There's no way to leave without waking the entire neighborhood."

Oh my God. I knew there was a security pad near the front door, but I'd never seen them activate it. "They do it at night," Sarah explains. "They probably didn't tell you because of this exact reason."

"I have to get back to my life."

She takes a second to think about it. "Not like this. You can't disappear on Mom again. Did you think what that would do to her, for her to wake up to see that you're gone? Don't make her go through all of that again."

"I'm coming back. I promise. I'll be here for spring break and summer and holidays. Honestly, you'll be so sick of me."

Sarah shakes her head. "That's not good enough. You owe it to Mom to tell her face-to-face."

"But she won't listen to me."

Sarah sprawls out sits on the floor, blocking me from going downstairs. "Then make her. You need to sit her down and tell her. I'll help you."

"You will?"

"Of course." Sadness takes over her delicate features. "I know how unhappy you are here. We all know. The only time you smile—a real smile—is when you're talking to Neil or Marian. I don't know what I would do if I were forced to live with someone else. So I get it. As long as you promise you're not leaving for good. A real promise this time." She holds out her pinkie.

"A real promise," I say as I link my pinkie with hers. "And you should come visit Valley Falls."

She grimaces. "You want me to freeze to death."

"It's not that bad in the summer."

"Uh-huh," she says as she gets up. "Let's go downstairs and get ready for the talk. I find it's best to bribe mom with food and coffee in the morning."

"Okay, okay," I relent.

Sarah's right. I wanted to sneak out in the middle of the night because it would be easier for me. But I'd essentially be doing the same thing Dad did to her. It wouldn't be fair. To either of us.

I pull out my phone and send a text.

"Who are you texting right now?"

"My ride."

Sarah goes into her bedroom and brings back her phone.

"Who are *you* texting?" I ask.

She raises her eyebrows. "Backup."

⁓

The kitchen smells of coffee and bacon. When in doubt, fry up some bacon.

Sarah and I have laid out breakfast on the kitchen counter for everybody. Sarah is eating a piece of bacon, but I can't touch anything. I feel nauseous.

What if Paula says no?

It doesn't matter what she says, because I'm an adult now, but I'd like her to be okay with it. Or at least not hate me for it. What I want, truly, is to have a relationship with her. To get to know her. But that can't happen when I'm forced to be here. It will happen, but only after I can finish high school and figure out my future.

There was a period of time when I didn't know where I came from, but I do know where I'm going, and I want Paula to be part of that.

I want my *mother* to be part of that.

"Smells delicious," Craig says as he comes downstairs, with Paula following him. When they see the spread of food before them, Craig shakes his head. "Okay, who's failing what?"

"Craig." Paula playfully taps him on the shoulder. "This is wonderful, girls." She picks up a plate and starts helping herself to the cheesy scrambled eggs I made.

"Good morning," a voice comes from the dining room.

Paula turns around. "Mom? What on earth are you doing here?"

Grandma Amanda takes a plate. "Why, I'm here to eat this delicious breakfast my granddaughters made."

With plates piled with food, the five of us sit down at the dining room table, which I made up like the first meal we had here.

"This is such a treat," Paula says.

I can't look at her. I know she's going to be devastated. Although she can't possibly be happy about our current living situation, either.

Silence falls over the table as everybody dives in, while I fidget with my napkin under the table.

"What's everybody got planned for this weekend?" Craig asks. "We've got a Lions game on Sunday, right? Think I might try to beer-boil some brats."

"Honey?" Paula asks me. "You're white as a ghost. What's going on?"

I try to talk, but my mouth feels like cotton. I take a sip of water. "I need to talk to you."

Paula and Craig exchange a look. "Is everything okay at school?"

"Yes. Actually, no."

"What's wrong? Should we talk to your guidance counselor? I'm sure we can look at your classes, or if you need a tutor, we can also do that. You're a very smart girl, it just takes time—"

"Mom," Sarah interrupts. "Please let Ally talk. And you need to listen to her."

"But I always listen when—"

"Mom," Sarah says firmly.

Paula closes her mouth and leans back in her chair.

This is it. There's no going back. As much as I want to walk out without an explanation, I need to do this. For both of us.

"I'm eighteen now."

"Yes, we—" Paula begins before Sarah cuts her off with a groan. "Sorry, continue."

"That means I'm an adult. I can start making decisions for myself. I want you to know that I have decided to move back to Wisconsin and finish school there. I also plan on going to college at UW–Green Bay."

"Absolutely not!" Paula gets up so fast her chair falls over, hitting a cabinet behind her and knocking over a glass vase. "I'm not going to stand here—"

"Paula!" Grandma Amanda's voice booms. "Sit down this instant."

Paula collapses into her chair.

Grandma Amanda gives me a nod. "Go ahead, Ally."

"You know about this, Mom?" Paula says. "And you come into my house and—"

"Paula." It's now Craig who scolds her with a raised voice. His demeanor is usually jovial. I've never heard him be so abrupt before. He reaches over the table to take her hand. "Your daughter has something to say, and you need to listen to her."

Tears have begun to stream down Paula's face.

"Yeah, Mom, hear her out," Sarah seconds.

This is the first time I've truly felt like a unit. Craig, Sarah, and even Grandma Amanda understand where I'm coming from. Now I just need to convince Paula.

"I am so happy to discover this other family I didn't know existed," I start. "To spend time with my mom. I have a sister now. And a stepdad. And a grandma and cousins. It's been great. But there's this whole life I left behind, one I really like. I don't want to abandon that life, but I can add to it. I want to add new memories of my family in Florida. I want to come down here as much as I can, but . . . if you demand that I stay here, you're asking me to give up myself. I didn't do anything wrong, just like none of you did anything wrong. You have to let me be me, let me make my own choices."

My mind flashes back to one of the essay topics I had to tackle.

"When I started my college applications, I had to answer this question about a significant event in my life, and I had trouble doing it. Turns out *this* is a pretty significant moment in my life, but I've realized that life isn't only about significant moments. It's lived and changed by the tiny moments we experience every day. The person I am right now is because of those moments. And I won't let one significant thing erase that.

"So please believe me that this isn't goodbye, it's see you later. You have to trust me. We can even get my tickets for spring break right now. I'll stay for the whole week."

A disgusted groan escapes Paula's throat. "A whole week? How lucky."

"Paula." Craig gives her a warning look.

"No, Craig!" she protests. "I'm allowed to be upset about this."

"You are," I admit. "You're allowed to be really upset with me. But don't you want me to *want* to be here? Wouldn't you prefer that when I come to see you and the rest of the family that I'm here by *choice*?"

"You don't like it here?" she asks in a small voice.

"Paula, you see how much she wants to go home." Craig rubs her back. "We owe it to Ally to let her live her life. The life she wants. Don't force the life you've built in your head on her. She'll come back."

"No. She won't."

"Yes. I will." I get up from my chair and kneel next to Paula. "I promise you, I'll come back. I want to get to know my family. But I need to go back to Wisconsin and finish school. To do all the things I had planned. We have the rest of our lives to make up for the past fifteen years."

I look at Paula, and my heart aches for her anguish. I've had this thought in the back of my head that I had to choose between her and Dad. But Craig and Sarah have made me realize that I have a greater capacity for love and family than I thought. Paula is family. She's my mom. And it's time that I start seeing her that way.

No competition with Dad. She and I can be something completely separate.

"*Mom*." I place my hand on her shoulder. "I'm sorry I've been closed off. This has been really hard on me. Really hard. I need time to adjust to this new life, which includes you. All of you. I want nothing more than to come back here in a few weeks and spend more time with my family. You're my family."

I wrap my arms around my mother and hold her close. Unshed tears start burning. I'm holding my mother. A mother had always been this concept—an enigma—to me for most of my life. Yet, here she is, living and breathing.

I'm not sure how long we embrace. I do know that there's a part of me that doesn't want to let go.

When Mom finally does speak, it's in a soft voice. "I only want you to be happy."

"That's all any mother should hope for," Grandma Amanda adds. "And oftentimes being a parent means putting your child's needs first."

Mom sniffles. "I know you're not happy here. As much as I want you to be, you aren't."

The room is quiet as we can all see the anguish in her face. She closes her eyes. "If going back to Wisconsin will make you happy, then . . . okay."

"Really?"

She nods as she wipes away her tears. "Really."

"Thank you." I wrap my arms around her again. "Thank you so much."

She pulls away from me and holds my face in her hands. "But would you be okay if we booked your next flight back right now?"

"Absolutely! Yes! Let's do that!"

Mom takes my hand as we walk into the living room. As mother and daughter.

⁓

"When's your graduation?" Mom has her calendar out. We already have three visits planned through the end of summer.

"More importantly, how cold is it going to be there in June?" Sarah asks.

"It's really not that bad."

"Uh-huh," both Mom and Sarah reply.

"Speaking of amazing weather, I'm thinking an excursion to Key West for spring break," Mom says. Seeing her plan all these trips is the happiest I've seen her since I arrived. Come to think of it, it's the happiest I've been, too.

"We should get a house for the week, invite the whole family," Grandma Amanda offers.

"Randy?" Craig asks with a laugh.

Grandma Amanda shakes her head. "Or better yet, let's have it just be us."

The doorbell rings, and butterflies start circling my stomach.

This is it. This is really happening.

"Oh, your ride is here! I'll get it!" Sarah says with an excited clap.

The door opens, and Baxter runs in and jumps on me. Mom backs away for a few seconds, before holding her hand out for Baxter to sniff.

"Ah, hey, Ally. Ally's mom," Neil says as he shoves his hands in his pocket.

"Neil." Mom gets up and gives him a hug. "Please promise me that you'll take good care of my girl."

"I will."

Neil approaches me cautiously, while an excited Baxter keeps running around the couch. "Everything okay here?"

"Everything's great." I give Mom's hand a squeeze.

"It really is." She brushes her hand on my cheek. "I wish you two didn't have to leave so soon. We could have a barbecue. But, I know, you need to get on the road to make it to Atlanta before dinner. Please send everybody my best."

In between booking flights and Mom discussing my new living arrangement with Marian's mom, I finally talked to my dad's mom and sister. For the first time since everything came crumbling around me, I'm not afraid of change. It can be a good thing. I'm still the same me, but now I have this web of people with whom I belong.

"Let me take a gander at the traffic," Craig says as he starts typing on his phone.

Grandma Amanda approaches Neil. "And I believe you're the young man my granddaughter's been talking about."

Neil's face lights up. "Oh, so she's been talking about me, huh? I hope only good things."

Grandma Amanda pats his shoulder. "Only the best things, which is exactly what she deserves."

"Yes, she does."

Grandma Amanda gives Neil a hug. I like seeing my two worlds collide, having the people who I care about know one another. Maybe Neil can join me on a few trips back here.

"Well, I guess this is it," Mom says as she hands Neil my suitcase. He takes it and Baxter to the car.

That's when I look out to see which car Neil drove over a thousand miles here. "Oh my God, Rob let you drive his Jeep?" Rob wouldn't even let Marian take it two towns over for McDonald's. We aren't allowed to eat or drink in his "baby."

Neil turns around. "Yeah. He insisted. I believe his exact words were 'bring our Ally back home' as he threw his keys down on the table."

I can't believe it. "Does this mean I have to be nice to him now?"

"Nah," Neil says with a wink. "It's the least he could do for the vast amount of emotional torture it is to be his friend."

I laugh until I turn around to see the family I'm leaving. I don't know where to start.

Craig gives me a hug. "Call if you need anything. Here." He tries to hand me some money.

"I can't," I reply.

"It's a stepdad's duty to spoil his stepdaughter by bribing her for affection."

"But I already like you."

"Well, then." He pretends to put the money back in his pocket before placing it firmly in my hand.

Grandma Amanda gives me a hug. "Neil seems like a nice boy."

"He really is. But I'm going back for much more than a boy."

"I know. And I am going to be so happy to meet the rest of the Gleasons at your graduation." She gives me a kiss on the cheek.

Sarah is next. She hugs me, and I don't want to let go. "It's see you later, right, Sis?"

"Yeah. See you soon, Sis." I'll be back here in less than two months. Seven weeks if you're counting, which Mom is. So am I.

"I'm going to miss you," she says softly.

"I already miss you," I admit. I like having a sister.

"FaceTime when you cross state lines."

"You can count on it." I give her forehead a kiss.

I've been able to hold it together so far, but I feel a heaviness build in my chest. Saying goodbye is way harder than I thought.

Mom takes both of my hands. "I'm so proud of who you've become, I would never want to get in the way of that."

That's it. The floodgates have opened. I cry as I hug my mom.

"Don't you start, or I won't be able to stop," she says through sobs.

"You two make quite the pair," Craig comments.

"Like mother, like daughter," Mom says between sobs.

We're both laughing through tears.

"You should know that I'm going to text you, a lot," Mom says as she wipes away my tears.

"Please do. Seriously."

"I mean a lot, a lot. Like really a lot."

We laugh as I give her another hug.

"Send pictures from the road and be careful. And be sure to

keep your phones charged, and if you run into any trouble, call Triple-A. You can use our account. And have plenty of water in the car in case—"

"Paula," Craig says gently.

"Sorry." She looks down at our locked hands. "It's really hard to let go."

"It is." I give her hands another squeeze before hugging her one last time. For now. "Thank you for understanding that I need to do this. I love you, Mom."

"Oh, Ally, I love you so much." She kisses me on the cheek before I head to the door. I hesitate for a moment. There's a pull to this house that didn't exist before. Maybe because I now have a choice. When I come back, it will be because I want to be here. I want to spend more time with Mom, Craig, Sarah, and the whole extended family.

With every second I stay, it's going to be harder to leave.

"See you soon," I say as I finally start down the walkway to Rob's car.

The four of them wait in the doorway, Craig's arms around both Mom and Sarah, Grandma Amanda holding Mom's hand.

I get in the passenger seat, and Baxter jumps in my lap. "Thank you for doing this."

"Hey, I got to take two days off school to rescue the girl of my dreams. I mean, come on. This is hero stuff."

I look out at my family and feel a tremble of my chin.

"Are you okay with all of this?" Neil asks. "Because you seem really sad."

"Yes. No. I—I . . ." I fumble for a minute to try to understand all my feelings. "I'm going to miss them, but that's a good thing. I need to go home."

I never would've thought this when everything tumbled apart, but I'm a lucky girl. I used to think only my dad is family. Then I had the Gleasons. Now I have Mom, Craig, Sarah, and the entire Cardiff and McMullen clan. Soon I get to go meet my Linsley family.

Pretty lucky, indeed.

Especially since I finally get to return home. Well, to one of my homes.

"Ready?" Neil asks as he starts the engine.

"Ready."

Acknowledgments

The idea for *Past Perfect Life* came from a segment I saw on the news a couple of years ago, about a teenage boy who had something similar happen to him. It caused me to think a lot about personal history, identity, and, above all, family. Writing this book reminded me how lucky I am to have been born to Dave and Judy Eulberg. And even though my siblings sometimes (wait, *oftentimes*) picked on their baby sister, I'm forever grateful to them: Eileen, Meg, and WJ. And then there are my nephews, aunts, uncles, and cousins, who always make me feel like I have someplace I belong.

I'm eternally thankful to my extended family at Bloomsbury, which keeps growing. Sarah Shumway not only came up with the perfect title, she also helped make this story stronger with her editorial insights. Huge thanks to the rest of the team: Diane Aronson, Erica Barmash, Hali Baumstein, Anna Bernard, Faye Bi, Frank Bumbalo, Liz Byer, Danielle Ceccolini, Phoebe Dyer,

Beth Eller, Courtney Griffin, Melissa Kavonic, Erica Loberg, Cindy Loh, Donna Mark, Patricia McHugh, Brittany Mitchell, Valentina Rice, and Claire Stetzer.

Friends are also family. Erin Malone, Tina McIntyre, and my sister Meg gave me invaluable insights when I needed fresh eyes. My other sister, Eileen, helped answer some questions about law enforcement. (Big families have their benefits!) Kirk Benshoff handles all the tech stuff so I can concentrate on writing. Alex London let me borrow his dog (good boy, Baxter). I owe so much to the countless number of friends I've talked about this book with over the years. So much gratitude to Rose Brock, Varian Johnson, Sarah Mlynowski, and Jennifer E. Smith, who have had to talk me down from the various ledges I stood on while writing this book.

Finally, a writer would be nowhere without her readers. Thanks to every person who has picked up one of my books. Thank you to every bookseller, librarian, and educator who has placed one in the hands of a reader. And of course, to all the bloggers and book lovers who give authors the best gift there is—telling people about a book they love. You're all family to me.